Connections

Drake Wilmore

ISBN: 0692296484
ISBN 13: 9780692296486
Library of Congress Control Number: 2014918186
De Stijl Entertainment, Waipahu, HI

"Who the fuck is he Rachel, and no more lies."

I could feel my blood boil, the heat rising from my chest as if my body had been set ablaze. My soul was on fire. At this very moment I knew there was a decision I would have to make, a path I would have to choose.

If only I had seen this coming, I thought to myself.

The truth of the matter was that I had seen this shit happening, a long time ago. Hell, the writing was on the wall the day I said, "I do" to Rachel Stanley. Once again I now faced her. Hoping she felt my hurt, my pain; hoping that she felt truly remorseful for her betrayal. Unlike before, I wanted her to feel my anger, my rage. Tonight our union hung in the balance of our emotions, and I was determined that it would be my anger that dominated this night. Every muscle in my body was flexed tightly, my heart pounding. With every breath I took, the air seemed to thicken. Unlike the night six years ago in New York, this time would be different. No longer would pride and love cloud my judgment. No longer would skeletons from the past rise to tempt my reason. Standing in front of me should have been the woman I had devoted my life to. The woman I would have killed for, and yes, if need be, the woman I'd die for as well. As I searched the vast emptiness of her eyes, I sadly realized that this was not that woman. Nor had she ever been that woman…

"You know Rachel on second thought; I already know who he is. Just tell me how the hell you could do this to me—to us—again."

"Why should I, Sean? I mean, why try to explain myself to you when you clearly think that you know the entire story? Why talk about this and rehash old arguments when all it's going to do is make you even angrier than you are now?"

"Because for once I would really like to hear the truth come from you, Rachel. For once I would like to hear the entire story from the one person who always told me that I had nothing to worry about— that I needed to let the past go and that you were all about me. From *you*, Rachel, not from some detective, not from a friend, and certainly not from some bum ass thug you fucked!"

Instantly her big brown eyes widened with a look of contempt. Her gaze, which had been solemn and soft, was now defiant. Her logic quickly returned, though, and her stare lessened almost as quickly. I knew those words would sting her ego, because even though she was guilty and at the mercy of my anger, she hated what that phrase implied…

"It was not like that at all. Jason and I shared a connection. You wouldn't under—"

"Connection!" I interrupted her. "What the fuck kind of connection is that? What about the connection to your husband, to your family, Rachel—what about that connection? How long did you know him?"

Her eyes went to the floor as if to search for the correct answer. Tears rolled gently down her face, plummeting into the darkness of her shirt. As angry as I was and as hard as I tried to ignore it, I couldn't help but marvel at her beauty. She was five feet eight and by every definition a ten. She was the immaculate conception of a father from Harlem and a mother from Thailand. Every inch of her was perfection, from her butterscotch skin to the silky, jet-black hair that flowed thickly to the top of her round bottom. It was the kind of beauty that intimidated common men. Wherever she went, she held audiences captive. I relished observing men check her out when we were together. It was always a blessing to have a woman with that kind of beauty. Only now it seemed like that blessing was my curse…

"How long, Rachel?" I repeated my question.

"A month," she quietly replied.

Her long black hair flowed around both sides of her face as if to shroud her from my look of disbelief.

"One month! Hold up: one damn month!" I exclaimed. "Wow, now that's a connection for your ass right there."

Rachel's eyes continued to stay glued to the floor. I couldn't believe my ears. One month, one damn month.

"Rachel, we've been married for six years, we have a handsome son that we created together, we have fought our way through some very trying issues, and now Dick Nasty comes on the scene for just one month and has a stronger connection with you than your bond with me?"

"This is why I didn't want to explain my actions to you, Sean. It was never just about the sex. It was something more than just dick. It was meaningful. I knew you wouldn't understand."

"Meaningful? What do you mean I don't understand, Rachel? I've been trying to understand for six and a half years now. You know, I guess

I didn't understand back then when I said 'I do' to you, knowing that you were carrying another man's child—a child you created while engaged to me. I guess I didn't understand when you begged me to give us another chance, and I guess I didn't understand when you lost the baby and I flew halfway around the world to be with you, even holding your hand as you called another man to tell him you had lost his child. You're right, Rachel. I guess I don't understand, and I guess I never will."

"I know what I said, Sean, but I've also told you more than once to just let me go, but you wouldn't." She said crying. "Now you're standing here blaming me for destroying something that I never truly wanted."

"If you didn't want this, then why did you marry me, Rachel? You know how I felt about you, and you know that I never wanted to end this."

After saying those words, I felt my heart swell with pain and the sudden weight of guilt pressing my lungs down, making it harder for me to breathe. I knew Rachel had asked out of our marriage, but I also knew—or at least thought I knew—that deep down she loved me and wanted this marriage. After all that I had sacrificed for her—my career, my family, my pride, even my feelings for Zara—was I being selfish for not wanting to let her go? How much of my hurt was really because of my love for her? Was my anger really about her exploits or my own? I could feel the burning of tears starting to glaze my vision, my throat turning as dry and barren as a desert, a lump in my throat growing to the point where it was hard to swallow. I closed my eyes and swallowed hard to regain my composure.

"I couldn't end this, because you had my heart, Rachel," I said, my voice beginning to tremble. "I only wanted you, and it was you who said you wanted this and wanted to change."

"I did want this and I did change, but you didn't notice it. You never would let me forget the past. You stopped spending quality time with me, and then you changed, Sean."

"I changed? How the hell did I change? It was always you, Rachel. You never did change, and that's our problem. The past never became the past, which is even more evident as we stand here yet again because of the same shit you did before. You never put a hundred percent of your heart into our marriage and making it work. You never became my wife."

"That's not true, Sean, and you know it. I did try to become your wife. I tried to give you a hundred percent. I tried to give you and our marriage a hundred percent of my life, but you fought me every step of the way. Nothing I did was ever good enough to please you. Every chance you got, you reminded me of just how much I had fucked up, every mistake I had made, and the hurt I caused you. The past never became the past because you wouldn't let it die. If I did something nice for you, it was never enough."

"That's my point, Rachel. I don't want or need to be treated nice by you. Treat me like you want to be with me, like you are proud to be with me. I want to be put on the pedestal you put those guys on. I wanted you to treat me like you treated your lovers and not like your damn best friend."

I could feel the turmoil being waged in my mind. The anger was strong, but I could not keep the hurt and pain from showing.

"Rachel, I've known and loved you for almost seven years," I said as I moved closer to her. "And yet you have always treated me more like your male BFF than your lover or your husband. You have always felt insecure about yourself around me, which for the life of me I still don't understand, and you shy away from me every time I see you naked, as if I were your worst critic. You have the most incredible body I have ever seen, and yet we can't make love in the daylight or any other light for that matter. I'm your husband, Rachel, the one man you are supposed to feel comfortable with, the one who accepts you uncondi-tionally. It should not be with someone you met off the Internet or at a

5

pizza parlor. How did you act around them? Did you make love in the light with them? Why give them the special, intimate parts of you that should have been mine?"

"Sean, you are making things worse in your mind than how they actually were. Before I met Jason I didn't care what any of those guys thought of me. For the most part, I only needed or wanted to hear them feed my ego. That's all it was—just two people sharing drinks and letting our inhibitions down, being able to say what we normally wouldn't have the courage to say otherwise. I felt less about them than I did about you. I care what you think about me."

"You are doing a terrible job at making me believe things are worse in my mind than reality. Do you hear how that sounds? You care about how I view you, so with me, you're like Snow White, and when you are with them, you turn into some porno star—a drunken porno star, I might add—for those other punks and you lose all your inhibitions? How the hell do you even know everything that you did? I know you're sugarcoating shit, Rachel, but that's cool. So if it isn't that bad and you are not sincere about them, then what kind of connection can you call this latest tryst with Jason?"

"I was not some drunken chick just going to bed with any- and everyone," Rachel said sternly. "Like I said, most of the time it was just flirtatious conversation. I know it may not sound right, but it's the truth. I don't have to sugarcoat anything, and before you interrupted me, I was going to say that I was this way before I met Jason. After Jason and I met, his first concern was for me and my marriage to you. He didn't want to disrespect you or come between us. I chose to go to him. He was different from Tony."

"Oh my God, so that's your connection?" I yelled in disbelief. "You got played, Rachel. Jason doesn't give a fuck about me, you, or us. He just wanted to fuck you, that's all. He just didn't come at you like a thug like Tony did. This guy lives in another state,

Rachel, and when he found out you were married with a family, did he stop calling you? Did his conscience and concern for me stop him from begging you to leave your family and fly out to meet him? Why couldn't he find someone in his own city—hell, his own state—to share a connection with? I'll tell you why. It's because he knew he could fuck someone from out of town who didn't know he was a bum. Someone he didn't have to make a commitment to, someone who would be his personal freak for the weekend. Oh, he connected with your ass real good."

"Fuck you, Sean!" Rachel screamed as she shoved me, tears running down her face. "I'm not a freak, unlike what you think. You may not believe this, but I am sorry. I never wanted to hurt you, but I never wanted this marriage either," she sobbed.

Seeing her cry made me regret mocking her. As much pain and hurt as I felt because of this woman, I never wanted to see her hurt. At that moment I wanted to believe her about everything. I couldn't think about her pain or her hurt, though. If tonight was the night we were going to end this marriage, then I had to let her know how I truly felt.

"I'm sorry for saying that, Rachel, but look at it from my side."

"That's my point, Sean: it's always your side, and your side is right all the damn time."

"Have I cheated on you, Rachel? My side is not always right."

"I don't have people watching your every move, Sean. I don't have any spies, no detectives to observe your every business trip. All I have is your word."

"That's not just my word, Rachel. It's called trust. I've never given you a reason to doubt my love or devotion to you or this marriage."

"Well, you haven't given me any reason to let me know you still wanted this marriage, either."

"See, that's the other problem I have with you, Rachel. Why can't you just admit you wanted this marriage and that you love me? If this is something you didn't want, why do you expect me to show you that *I* still wanted it? That is, unless of course, this marriage was in fact something that you also wanted. The problem is you were too afraid to let go of your past. You just didn't want to buckle down and work at it. You wanted it to be given to you. You are the one who screwed up, not me. So it is up to you to either end it or, like you said to me, change and work at making our marriage stronger. You knew I wasn't leaving or going to let you go."

"But why keep me if you were not going to help me change, Sean? I needed your help, but I felt like you abandoned me and stopped loving me."

"Rachel, how many times do I have to say I love you before you believe me? How many nights must I give you to show you that I want my marriage, my wife? What else could I have said or done to show you I wanted to be with you? I can give you compliments all day, tell you that you are the most beautiful woman in the world, buy you whatever you want, spend time with you, and help—or at least think that I am helping—you and your insecurities. I can do it all, Rachel, but it doesn't mean shit to you. But then let some broke-ass-stay-at-home-with-his-mom thug from Minnesota start instant messaging you sweet nothings, and now you have a damn connection!"

I could feel the anger in me intensifying. My hurt was feeding the rage. I had suppressed my feelings for a long time, trying to be the cement that held a doomed building together. Tonight that battle was lost, and my building was crumbling all around me.

"Not just words, but your actions—sincere actions as well, Sean. We don't go places anymore. You won't take me out. You are always working, and when you're not, you show no effort toward making us work. I would love to go out with you and have fun, just us two, but when I suggest going someplace, you turn into a smart-ass and throw my past up in my face, asking if I found this spot with someone else. What was I supposed to do?"

"I'm not trying to throw anything up in your face, Rachel, but for the record, if you hadn't cheated on me, we wouldn't have a past to throw up, now, would we? Can you not blame me for being a little apprehensive when I see your enthusiasm about a certain place? Need I remind you of Nick's? Again, why wait for me to make plans for us to go out? You can plan a trip to Minnesota to meet some guy off the Internet, but you can't make us dinner reservations down the street! Like I said, show me you want this, and show me that I should treat you like my wife again."

Rachel stood in silence, facing me, trying to read my stance. She shook her head and once again looked down at the ground. I moved toward her and raised her face. Our eyes met.

"Your past was not the issue for me, Rachel; it was your lack of initiative for this marriage. If you didn't want this, why lead me on by saying you wanted to change, and if you did want this, why not change and work for it? I thought since we moved out of New York, we could leave those skeletons behind and start over. I sacrificed for you and this relationship. I started my career over for us, remember? So why couldn't you just be my wife and tell me exactly how you really felt about me—about us?"

"Would it have mattered, Sean? I mean, really, would you have listened or would you have thrown Tony and my past into my face again?"

"Baby, give me a chance to make that choice. Don't make it for me."

9

"But you would always make the wrong choice. You, my family, your mother—everyone else always pointed out my flaws."

"No, no, baby girl, don't try to flip the script and start blaming everyone else for your actions, especially my mother. What she may have felt for you a long time ago is gone, and you know it. This is about you and your lack of commitment to anything in your life, especially this marriage."

"I have to, Sean. You don't understand how much shit I got about my looks from my brothers when I was growing up, or what it was like being talked down to and overprotected by my dad, and my mom always telling me to know my place rather than listening to me tell her how I felt. I didn't know who I was or what I wanted to be. Then I met you and I really wanted to be with you, but your mom made me feel like I didn't measure up to her standards as a professor or to her precious, darling Zara."

"Why is it that every time we have a disagreement or we're discussing what you've done to us, you always reach back to Zara? You know the real problem is you blaming everyone for the way you act. Grow up and acknowledge your faults, and stop blaming others—and certainly, stop bringing up ancient history."

"Ancient history, my ass," Rachel hissed. "Do you know how much it hurts every time we go and visit your mother and I have to see a picture of that bitch in her living room? With that fake-ass smile as if she's looking at me. It's as if she's trying to tell me that I don't belong there with you."

"Now look who's making things worse in their mind than what they actually are. We've been through this before so many times, I'm sick of it. I've told you—hell, even my mother has told you—that the picture and her feelings for Zara are not meant to disrespect you. My mother has strong feelings for Zara, as if Zara were her daughter—and she respects you as my wife. Besides, you are married to me and not my mother. Zara was there before you and she was there at a time when my mom needed someone when my dad died. You know that, Rachel. Shit, she practically buried my father."

"I know the story, Sean. I also know she is rich and in the position she is in because she stole your ideas and made a fortune and a company for herself. Yet here you are, defending her as if she were a saint. Tell me, why didn't you tell your mom the truth about what really happened between you two? Was it because of your stupid male pride or was it because you still loved her?"

Suddenly the table I had had an ironclad grip on had been overturned. This was no longer a woman taking her punishment, facing the consequences of her actions. No longer was it about being remorseful. Rachel also seemed to be bent on letting me know how she felt. She was looking for answers—answers to questions I thought I had been fortunate enough to suppress.

"What happened in my life with Zara was over before I met you. When I told you about my life and the emotions I felt in the past, I had no idea that one day they would be thrown back into my face. My past does not even contain you, but the part of your past I'm speaking about is all about you and us. It contains me, it involves me, and it affects me!"

"But Sean, you won't let the past go. I've tried to be a better person, but you won't allow yourself to see it, and your past has affected us."

"How is running off to Minnesota to meet a man you met over the Internet while your husband and son are at home make you a better person? How has the past been erased in your mind? And again, my past is not the issue."

Rachel stood motionless, her eyes staring out into the darkness of the night. Wow—the night. All this time I had forgotten we were standing outside. The night could not have been more perfect. It was so incredibly beautiful, so calm. It was a warm night in Potomac, Maryland, one of the most affluent areas in America. Not bad for a brother who had had to start his entire career over. I had left a lucrative position at LAN MAR Productions in New York to move here—a move I had hoped would save my marriage, to keep the woman I had married mine. I knew she was standing there thinking the same thing. I would have done anything for her. I don't know of any other man who would have dealt with the shit I had had to endure. We had left New York and left behind not only her demons and tormentors but the skeletons hiding in my closet as well.

Now I was the president of my own firm. We had had a very difficult time at first, but thanks to hard work, patience, and God, I had built De Stijl Marketing into one of the most reputable creative marketing firms on the east coast. With all the things going wrong in my personal life, such as Zara running off with my ideas, my father dying, and Rachel's infidelity, succeeding at my professional life seemed like a piece of cake. At work I was viewed as a successful trendsetter, a talented, bold, strong black man who was successful in every aspect of his life. If only my friends and colleagues knew the true demons that lay in my closet…

"I guess you are going to ignore me now, huh?" Rachel said, interrupting my thoughts.

"I'm sorry. What did you say?"

"I asked, 'Are you sure the past is the past, Sean?'"

"What kind of question is that, Rachel? I devoted my life to you and this marriage. If I didn't want this, I wouldn't have married you to begin with."

"But why me, Sean? I've done so much to hurt this marriage and you. Why stay married to me? You don't trust me, you say I haven't done anything to help this marriage, so why not let me go? Let's stop living a lie."

"Oh, so now we've been living a lie! I didn't say you don't contribute anything to this marriage. I just know you are not giving it your all, and you know it as well. This may seem like a lie to you, but it's my life, damn it. And I've spent seven years of it loving you and putting up with your betrayals—your shit, Rachel. I'm not going to allow you to once again walk away from a relationship this important having given only something as small as an apology."

"So are you punishing me because of my past before you? Who's bringing up past relationships now? Has it occurred to you even once that maybe I don't feel it, Sean? Maybe I don't feel the way about this marriage that you do. I am sorry for hurting you, but this marriage isn't the same for me."

"What do you feel then? Do I mean that little to you? Does your family mean so little that you don't even want to work to save us?"

"Don't you see, Sean? You and Devin mean the world to me. That's why we have to end this. I am trying to save us from destroying any more of our lives. You know I could never regain your trust, nor could I ever love you the way you want to be loved—the way you deserve to be loved, Sean. I am not that one, and I don't think I ever will be."

"I thought you were, Rachel. Don't throw this away for Jason."

"Oh please, I'm not throwing this away because of Jason, but being with Jason did show me just how insecure I am. I can't be with anyone right now. I need to get myself together."

"So six years into marriage and now you need to get your life together, alone. Rachel, I couldn't let you go because I loved you and wanted to make this marriage work, but if you don't feel the same, why didn't you leave me like you did in your past relationships? Why allow us to go on for six years like this in the first place? Why put me through all of this if you really didn't care?"

"I don't know, Sean," Rachel said softly. She was unable to make her eyes look into mine. "In the beginning, I did love you. I don't know what happened. We had so many things against us. I never wanted to be hurt, so I figured I'd keep my heart out of it. When I realized you did love me, it was too late. I had done too much damage. I guess maybe I was selfish, because you did put up with a lot: Tony, the baby, my insecurities, everything. I had never had anyone accept me and forgive me the way you did. I got comfortable with you, knowing you'd always be in my corner."

"What about now?"

"Now everything has changed. I didn't think I'd ever cheat on you again after Tony and the baby. Yet I have allowed my insecurities to once again cloud my judgment. I needed to feel desirable, Sean. I know you are still upset and hurt about what happened in the past, but when you kept giving me the cold shoulder, I needed to feel wanted. Jason made me feel like I was the most important woman in the world. Not his job, family, or even his pride came before me."

I could not contain the contempt I felt after those words left Rachel's mouth. Had I been that oblivious to her needs? Had I mistreated her to the point that I had driven her into another man's arms? No way.

"You know the one thing that hurts the most about this?" I asked. "It's your selfish 'all about me' attitude. Look at what I went through. My wife was carrying another man's child, but not once did I think about finding love or desire elsewhere. I could never give myself to someone else, even if it was just meaningless sex. I love you too much. Do you have any idea how much it hurts knowing that another man made love to my wife? Yet I'm supposed to block that out of my mind every time I touch you, every time I make love to you—wondering if he squeezed your ass like I do, if you moaned his name the way you do mine. I'm supposed to block all that out and go on and make you feel like you're the best wife in the world while you 'keep your heart out of it,' as you said. Don't you dare talk to me about not feeling desirable or not feeling important. You have no fucking clue of what hurt and pain feel like."

"Then let me go, Sean," she pleaded. "I can feel your anger and pain. For once, swallow your pride and let me go, please."

"It's not about pride anymore, Rachel," I said as my voice began to tremble again. "My pride, my manhood, was destroyed a long time ago, thanks to you. I guess I should have seen this coming."

I could feel the lump in my throat swell, blocking my airway off. My eyes again, started to burn with the pressure of tears ready to escape. As much as I tried to hold them back, I couldn't. Gently they made streaks down my face, hanging on my chin only to drop to the ground in front of my wife. Until this point, I had cried in front of her only once. All night I had fought them back, and now, knowing that our marriage was finally over, they flowed like a spring shower on the Potomac.

Rachel moved into me, the softness of her body so close that I could feel it. She raised my face and gazed into my eyes. I could see her tear-stained face, her hair sticking to her forehead from the heat of our emotions. With a soft hand she wiped my cheek. "Sean," she whispered. "I'm sorry. I know this is not what you want. You are a wonderful man, a terrific father, and you deserve so much more than this—someone whom you can trust and someone who's as devoted to you as you are to them. I wish it were me, but it's not, Sean. We both know that."

"I thought you were, or at least I thought that you could be if you tried, Rachel. I truly believed in us and I truly wanted you to be my wife, but I guess there is no going forward now, is there?"

"Even if we wanted to, Sean, it would only prolong the inevitable. I know this will help both of us in the long run. No more lying to each other."

"What have I lied to you about, I've always told you I loved you, and I've always meant it."

"This has nothing to do with your feelings about me, Sean. Rather, it's about unresolved feelings I think that you hide even from yourself."

"I still don't understand."

"I've never mentioned this to you before, Sean, but you've called her name out in your sleep."

I could feel the hurt as Rachel turned her back to me. She took a couple of steps away and stopped by the edge of the pool. I walked up behind her and stood motionless. She stared out into the darkness...

"I know you and Zara shared something special. She was your first true love, and hearing you call out her name made me realize that you were not truly over her. I know she hurt you, maybe even in ways worse than I have, but I know you still hold her in a light different from me. You know, sometimes I'd be so scared that you would come home one day and tell me that you were leaving me to go and win her back. I still wonder why you didn't, given all that I put you through."

Rachel's words hit me like a bolt of lightning. True, I had dreams about Zara. Some of them were fond dreams, but mostly they were hurtful, angry dreams of Zara's betrayal of me and our relationship. Zara Rivers had indeed been my first true love, my first soul mate. She was also my first heartbreak and my first true enemy. I met her my senior year of college. I was at Morehouse and she was attending Spellman. We were both marketing majors...

Zara Rivers

"You and Dad enjoy Belize and take plenty of pictures for me, okay?"

"We will, Zara, and we hope to see you when we return. No cancellations next time."

"I promise, Mom, but you know I had no choice but to cancel. The firm really needs to score the Littman account, and I didn't want to see all my efforts end up for naught."

I closed my eyes as I always do when I hold the entire truth from my mother. Never mind the fact that we were more than 4,500 miles apart. Atlanta, Georgia, and Patricia Rivers's house always seemed closer to Frankfurt when I talked to her.

"Well, I still think you should let more people help you out now, Zara. You are no longer building a company, you know. I think they could handle one crisis without you."

"They can handle things without me, Mom, but you know something of this magnitude requires me to be there as well."

"You know you can't pull the wool over my eyes, Zara."

"Mom," I pleaded. "Please. I promise I will definitely make it back home for Christmas. I'll even bring some of the ice wine Dad loves."

"Well, right now you just make sure you make it over, but trust me, your father does not need any ice wine. The doctor is still on him for not taking his blood pressure medicine as he should."

"How's Dad's health?" I asked, sitting down on the sofa. My upbeat vibe dulled with concern for the only male rock who had never left my side.

"Oh, don't you worry about your father," she said reassuringly. "He's your typical Rivers man, you know: spoiled rotten and as hard-headed as ever."

"That sounds like Dad." I laughed a sigh of relief.

"Well, he's sounding more and more like he's ready to be a grandfather."

My laughter subsided as soon as I heard the *grandfather* word. Now Frankfurt felt just a little farther away. "Oh really." I struggled to get the words out. "Can he sound like something else? Like maybe just a proud father?"

"Well, Zara, you know that clock is ticking away and, well...you know."

"I know that I don't want to rush and have a child just because my biological clock is ticking or because my parents want to be grandparents," I responded with a little scowl in my voice.

"Zara, you have been in Germany for the past ten years, and I can count on one hand how many boyfriends you have talked about."

"Mom, that's really none of your bus—"

"You know I spoke with Sean's mother last week," she interrupted.

I felt the knot tighten inside my stomach just as it did every time I heard Sean's name. Even though I hadn't spoken to him for almost nine years, just hearing his name made me nervous.

"I know you are not bothering Sean's mother about him for me. He's a happily married man now, Mother."

"Well, from what Joyce has told me, that marriage won't last another year."

I didn't want to feed into her insinuations, but hearing that Sean Winslow might be available sent a sudden rush of excitement down my spine. So much time had passed, and I knew he was a family man, but still…*No, I can't do it. You reached out once already, Zara, remember?*

"I can't believe I'm having this conversation with you. Mom, did you hear Sean say his marriage was over? No, and besides, Sean and I were so long ago, and we have both moved on."

"You can try to hide your feelings from yourself, Zara, but your actions all these years can't hide them from me, and I believe Joyce when she says that marriage is over, because we both know the same thing."

"What's that? That the two of you are psychics?" I joked.

"No, that we are both parents and we both know our kids and the connection they will always share. That carries more weight than any psychic prediction."

"Look, Mom, I appreciate your concern for me, but really, I'm fine. I enjoy my freedom and I enjoy my life just the way it is. Trust me, when the time is right, I am positive I will find the man who is right for me and we will have a family."

"The right one for you has and always will be Sean Winslow, and the way you two allowed your own individual pride to ruin a great relationship is way beyond me."

"Well, then I guess it wasn't meant to be that special a relationship!" I shot back angrily.

There was dead silence on the other end of the phone. I knew I shouldn't have snapped like that, but Sean Winslow was still a touchy issue with me. I closed my eyes and let out a deep breath. "I'm sorry for that, Mom. It's just that I know how special Sean was to me and how much it hurt when we broke up. I also know how close our families still are, but we can't just pick up where we left off nearly ten years ago. He's changed, as have I."

"Zara, I'm sorry as well. I would never try to push you into the arms of a man just to see you with one or to give your father and me a grandchild, but deep down if I know that you are unhappy without him, and that he is a good man, I would do or say anything to help you find that happiness again."

"I will find that happiness, Mom, and it will be true and just as real, just not with Sean Winslow. Thanks for caring about me so much. I better let you go. I have another brief to prepare. Enjoy your trip, and tell Dad I said hello and that I love him."

"I will tell him and we will, sweetheart. Good luck on your proposal. I know you will get the account."

We said good-bye, and soon I was headed down the autobahn on my way to the office to finish the Littman brief. I couldn't stop thinking about Sean and me. We had met at a job fair for companies in the Atlanta area looking to hire college interns for the summer. Sean was the image and soul of what you call a "strong, handsome black man." He was in the top 10 percent of his class, educated, smart, funny, and definitely bent on being successful. If his personality and intelligence didn't woo you, then the strong, masculine bodily features this Egyptian king possessed would. He had the smoothest caramel-coated skin, beautiful, soft brown eyes, broad shoulders and chest, abs you could grate cheese on, and strong arms that could hold a sista up in the air and make love to her for hours. Needless to say I was hooked. He found my aspirations and intelligence equally attractive, not to mention my five-foot-five frame and all the assets a Nubian goddess can possess. I put the apple in bottom, and was proud of it. I could work a pair of jeans or fit a dress like a model.

His dad was a judge in Atlanta, and his mother was a professor at Clark University. My mom and dad had been successful entrepreneurs, owning several McDonald's franchises as well as a movie theater in southern Georgia. Sean too was an only child. I was hired by Turner Broadcasting, and Sean took an internship at Coca-Cola. Outside of classes and work, every minute I had was spent with him. Our chemistry was contagious. He was my first intimate lover. Our families became close, and though marriage was never mentioned, it seemed inevitable. We talked about starting our own marketing firm and how we would one day ring the bell at the New York Stock Exchange. The sky was the limit.

Coca-Cola asked Sean to stay on after graduation and join their marketing team. Likewise, I was asked to stay at Turner Broadcasting. Within a short time after school I had a great job and a handsome, successful man to share my life with. Nothing could bring me down from my high. Unfortunately, though, that wasn't the case. As I found out, fate can play cruel tricks on your mortal happiness.

Sean would always discuss business ideas with me and I with him. He even confided in me about a plan he was working on to submit to

Coca-Cola about a new line of products to market in the global theater. The European market was rich with youth thirsting for American culture, wanting everything from soft drinks and music to shoes and clothing. He even told me about other potential prospects who had offered him large sums of money to purchase possible plans. Some even offered him a partnership in their firm.

One of those firms belonged to a gentleman I had worked with on a Turner Broadcasting deal. His name was Karl Schumacher. Though at first I'm sure he was more attracted to my ass than to my business savvy, the latter won out, and soon Karl respected me for my professionalism as well as my expertise. He even offered me a position in his firm whenever I wanted to leave Turner and strike out on my own.

I had already begun contemplating such a move, and Sean himself had mentioned the idea of possibly living abroad. So one day I called Mr. Schumacher and made a proposal I knew he couldn't resist. It was the chance to start a new firm and grow it into an international name—as long as it was run by Sean Winslow. He read a copy of Sean's resume that I provided, and agreed. His only stipulation was that the entire process be kept secret for fear of another firm, namely Coke, catching wind of it and beating us to market. I agreed and left for Germany as soon as my resignation paper hit my boss's desk. I couldn't tell Sean where I was going because I knew he would be more skeptical than approving. This was going to be my big surprise. I called him a couple of days after I left and told him Turner Broadcasting had sent me overseas on a business trip to help them tap further into the telecommunications market abroad. I tried to reassure him that there wasn't a problem with us and that I would be home in a week or so.

Well, that week or so turned into several months, and part of me felt Sean slipping away. I wanted to call, but my gut was telling me that the only thing that would make it up to him would be his stepping into his new office for the first time. Then one day I called my mom, who informed me that Sean had called and asked her about my whereabouts. She had told him the same thing I had, but something told me he wasn't buying it anymore and time was no longer on my side.

I accelerated to a modest 110 mph, and the cars began to blur as I began to vividly recall the day Sean burst into the conference room in Frankfurt. I could still remember the anger in his eyes as he looked at me, as if I had driven a knife into his back. I wanted to speak, but I froze. He just turned and walked out. By the time I was able to move, he was gone. He wouldn't take my calls. He never spoke to my parents again, and I never told them what had happened between us.

Sean left Coca-Cola shortly afterward and moved to New York. An old college sorority sister of mine told me he had gone to work for a friend. I was planning to go and see him in New York, but then his father suffered a major stroke. When I got the news from my mom, I immediately flew home to Atlanta to be by his side as well as his mother's. She had become like a second mother to me. I remember feeling a little guilty because I also saw it as an opportunity to finally see Sean and explain my actions.

Sean called when he made it to Georgia, but when his mother told him that I was there, he for whatever reason decided not to stop by. He checked in on his dad in the hospital in the middle of the night while we were not there and flew back to New York that same night. Saddened, I broke down and told his mother the truth behind our breakup and made her swear not to tell my parents or Sean. I returned to Germany, only to fly back a month later when his dad went into a coma. The doctor said there was nothing else they could do and suggested he be removed from life support. Reluctantly his mother agreed. She knew Mr. Winslow wouldn't want to live like that.

Sean and I finally met face to face, but under the circumstances I couldn't bring myself to ask him for a moment alone. I was there for him and his mother, and his dying father. As we said good-bye to his dad, the one thing that stood out for me even more than his father's death was the way Sean looked at me as I wept with his mother. I remember the feeling of anger and contempt he felt for me. He left his mother in charge of making funeral arrangements, and I felt compelled to assist her. Our bond only strengthened, and everyday Sean saw us together, he would abruptly have something that would take him away from us. After the funeral he flew back to New York, barely saying good-bye. His mother figured that was his way of dealing with his father's death, but I knew a bigger piece of him was still angry with me. I stayed behind and helped his mother finish settling his father's estate.

I called him a few times to ask his advice and approval on certain matters, but again he ignored my calls. So then I got a "fuck-it" attitude and stopped trying to reach out to him. I tried to move on with my life and date again, but it just hurt too much, not to mention there were not too many American black men to choose from in Germany. Maybe it was also my own insecurities about trusting again, or the guilt I still carried, knowing what I had taken from Sean, even if I had initially done it for him.

The absence of closure for our relationship tore my heart apart. I ended up putting my personal life on hold. My job became my love, and success became my children. I helped build the Rivers-Schumacher Corporation into a powerhouse firm, and I was enjoying the fruits of my labor. A multi-million dollar home right outside Frankfurt, expensive cars, jewelry, clothes, and most importantly a very handsome retirement nest egg, everything had come to fruition, but not even the biggest house or fastest Mercedes could make me feel whole. I made an oath that I would never let another man make me feel guilty for trying to do something for him or hurt me or cloud my judgment. I dated a few times, but nothing came close to the relationship I'd had with Sean. No one seemed to be able to break the spell he had woven around my heart or erase the guilt sealing my soul.

This should have been both of us together, driving to seal this deal. I guess he didn't need or want my love or the decency to give closure to our relationship. A couple of years passed by, and then Sean's mother told me that she believed he was going to marry his new love, Rachel, and that if I truly wanted him back, the time to act was now. Too afraid to see him in person, I wrote him a message in a card and enclosed a sample of what my hard work had generated for us. Anxiously I awaited his response, hoping for the best, but soon I just wanted to hear a no.

After several weeks of waiting I gave up and finally let go or thought that I was letting go of any hopes that Sean and I would rekindle our relationship. I told his mother that Sean had made his choice and it was Rachel. Again I made her promise to never tell him the truth and said I would stay out of his life. Our connection was lost from that moment on. I guessed Sean's love for me was not as strong as I thought. Hell, he never cashed the check I sent him, so I guessed his anger was stronger than his love. However, I was proud of the company I built, and though it had initially been for Sean, it turned out to be for me as well. Still, the thought of how different things could have been had continued to haunt me. If he were by himself now, the least he could do was tell me how he truly felt and give our relationship the closure it deserved, or better yet a rekindled start. Maybe it was time to say hello to Momma Winslow and get some more updated information.

Rachel

I remember how hard it was to say "I do" to Sean. He had a way of not seeing past his own wants for this relationship, to the point where he even masked his unresolved feelings for Zara. True, there were times when I actually felt like I could love him and be the wife he wanted and deserved. I even went back to school to finish my teaching degree. I wanted to prove to him that I didn't need his money, that I also had goals, but I also wanted to show his overprotective mother that I had my own career—a career I later put on hold to give him a son All of that changed though, after I saw Zara's picture in his mother's living room, deep down I knew I could never be that wife. I had my own issues, and playing second fiddle to Zara Rivers was not going to be one of them.

After that trip to his mother's house, I had more questions about his past with Zara than I had answers. My insecurities were always my Achilles heel, and having my new mother-in-law covet an ex who Sean had made out to be the worst woman created, wreaked havoc on my emotions. When I was ready to walk away the first time, Sean finally told me everything. I remember him breaking down and crying in front of me. I had never had a man cry like that in front of me. Feeling his weakness made me feel sorry for the things I had done that Sean didn't know about. He knew about Tony and now Jason, but there was also Justin and Trey and Khalid—not to mention the fact that I never fully broke it off with Tony.

All of that was water under the bridge now. My main issue at hand was I had to figure out a way to end this night and end this marriage as quickly and painlessly as possible. I just hoped that I was making the right decision now with Tony. Yes, there had been others, and although Sean was head and shoulders above them all, he still could not make me forget about Tony. Something about Tony kept me coming back for more. Maybe it was the fact that I had lost the first child I conceived and that Tony was the father. Whatever it was, Tony always had me in a vulnerable position—Tony Anderson, a.k.a. Tony True.

Tony was the next self-proclaimed big rapper from the Bronx. He had checked me out one day in my parents' store and had just kept coming around, laying down his game. He promised to put me in his first video —that I'd be on his arm at all the best parties. Everything a woman with insecurities needs and wants to hear. He showed up when I was unsure about Sean's sincerity about our commitment. His approach was more provocative and bolder than the way Sean courted me. I guess it's true what they say about women loving bad boys, and Tony had that persona. It wasn't the bad boy I was afraid would leave me, but rather a man like Sean who was already successful and could seemingly find someone from his own class. It wasn't until Sean proposed with a perfect five carat princess cut platinum engagement ring that I finally got it. By then I was two months pregnant, and I knew the baby wasn't Sean's. My parents were proud of me and glad that Sean was successful and could give me the life they had wanted for me. There was no way I could tell them I had made yet another mistake. So I did what any scared woman would do. I decided to take the logical choice and not the one I really wanted. I didn't think Sean would even take me back after I told him, yet there he was, telling me how he was glad that I had told him and hadn't just run away like Zara.

I asked for his forgiveness, and Sean forgave me and said he believed that if we could make it through this then nothing could tear us apart. He told me he'd stand by my side, not as my fiancé but rather as my husband. How could I say no to someone so willing to forgive me? Next thing I knew, we had made a hasty trip out to Las Vegas, where we were married. I remember how hard it was to make love to Sean that night. He was a terrific lover, but carrying Tony's baby inside of me dulled my senses. When we arrived back in New York, we broke the news to our parents. My parents were sad they had not been able to attend but were very happy that we had wed. I could tell from Sean's conversation with his mother that she was not happy at all.

Two long months passed—months filled with both arguments and breakups. I wanted to leave, but Sean wouldn't let me. I knew a big part of him wanted to break up, but I don't think his pride would let him throw the towel in. He thrived on challenges, and I sensed this was just another business venture for him. A part of me began to wish Tony would try to contact me, but he didn't. No phone calls, no letters, nothing. Instead I was left with this mess of a marriage. I was relieved when Sean was asked to attend a business seminar in Paris. Maybe some distance would help our relationship, I thought. Three days into the conference, I felt a sharp pain in my abdomen and knew something was wrong. The next thing I remember was waking up in an ICU bed and Sean holding my hand. The doctor told me I had lost the baby and almost my life.

It felt weird being in the hospital with Sean, with all the doctors and nurses offering their condolences and Sean's coworkers, and my parents sending sympathy cards. Everyone offered hugs and prayers as if it had actually been his flesh and blood that had died. As far as they knew, it had been his child. I was torn between sorrow and guilt. I tried to put myself in his shoes. Regardless of how it had happened, whether right or wrong, Sean had sacrificed his own manhood in accepting my affair and the consequences of it. He was prepared to raise a child that was not his without bias or malice. That's when I really felt like I loved him. We named my child Derrick and had a small ceremony in the hospital chapel. After the ceremony Sean told me everything happens for a reason and that maybe this was God's way of allowing us a chance to start our own family the right way.

"Rachel, let me take you away from all this hurt, all this pain," he would say. "Let's start over someplace new, and if you come with me, I promise I will give you another son."

I was emotionally drained from the ordeal, and hearing Sean's vow to me gave me encouragement that maybe this was where I was supposed to be. So I agreed. When we got home from the hospital, I felt compelled to tell Tony what had happened. He was the father, and I understood his right to know. He took it like the thug Sean had figured him to be. After a quick apology and heartfelt "I'm sorry for your loss," his next sentence was about how much he had been thinking about me. Sean snatched the phone and told him to stay the hell away from me or else, then hung up.

As we were packing our things up a couple of months later in preparation for our move to Maryland, I stumbled across an unopened letter from Zara. I guess it had been overlooked as just another "congratulations on your marriage"card. I didn't open it, but I couldn't throw it away either. I wanted to see what Sean would do when he found it. Would he share the contents of the card with me or would he hide it? He ended up hiding it, even from himself. I remember finding it in a briefcase unopened years later. I wanted to take it, but figured if he hadn't opened it by then, he never would. So I left it. Now standing here with him on the verge of ending our union together, I needed to know what his true feelings were for Zara.

"After everything that happened with me, Tony, and the baby; why didn't you go after Zara? Why didn't you tell your folks what really happened between the two of you?"

Moving closer to me, Sean placed his hands on my shoulders. It seemed as if we both were seeking answers to questions that had plagued us for years. He gently rubbed my shoulders. His actions gave me a little solace, and I placed my hand gently on his and moved my cheek to it.

"I told you, Rachel, all the hurt, all the anger I felt for Zara was just too strong. I just wanted her out of my life. If I had told my folks, there would have been too many questions to answer, too many people trying to help out, and then my father fell ill and passed away. I didn't want to drop that on my mother. I just wanted to pick my life up and move on."

I turned to face him. My eyes looked into his as I tried to gauge his answers for truthfulness or lies. He sensed that I wanted more.

"Look, before you there was Zara, and before my world revolved around you, yes, she was my life. What she did to me, though, I will never forgive her for, and though she is still in my life through my mother I can assure you that is as far as I will ever go toward acknowledging her existence. Yes, she meant a lot to me, but it wasn't until I found you that I found true love. I never proposed to Zara, Rachel. I proposed to and married only one woman: you."

"Okay, so why didn't you tell your mother about Tony and me, about the baby? Why paint a perfect picture for everyone when you were dealing with so much?"

"I knew that deep down, my mother still maybe held a candle for Zara and me getting back together. I knew that if she had known about Tony and the baby, she would have gone ballistic and done everything in her power to split us up."

"So you did it to protect my feelings, or were you doing it to protect yours?"

"Both, I guess. I knew I loved you, and that was all that mattered to me. Besides, my life was so screwed up, I didn't see a need to have someone else pass judgment on you or me."

"Maybe she wouldn't have passed judgment but she could've given you advice, Sean."

"Advice? I've never gotten any good advice about my personal life especially from my mother, and I certainly wasn't looking for it when I was going through the second-worst pain of my life."

It was Sean who tried to turn away this time, but I wouldn't allow it. I grabbed his shirt. "No, please don't turn away now, Sean," I begged. "I need to know why you have to hold so much inside. People love you; your parents love you, your friends, me. Why won't you let anyone in?"

"That's just it Rachel, I did let people in. I let Zara in, my father...you. I let you in, and every time I did, I was hurt. I may be a man, but I hurt too, you know. I feel pain, and I feel rejection just like you."

"Why hold it in and let it eat away at you? At least talk to someone about—"

"Talk to whom?" Sean interrupted, laughing. "I can see that conversation now: 'Hey, everyone, did you know my first love is a millionaire because she stole my ideas and left me high and dry, or better yet that on my wedding day my wife was pregnant with another man's child? But this is the kicker: she is still banging some guy off the Internet.' That would be the talk of the town. Do you know of any guys who would open up and talk about this shit? Do you know how less of a man I would be in those people's eyes?"

Hearing Sean rehash my indiscretions renewed the guilt I had been feeling earlier. I loosened my grip on his shirt, and he pulled away from me. I could sense his anger, but I could also feel his pain. To my knowledge he had never cheated on me despite all I had put him through, all that I had hidden from him. I wrapped my arms around him. I could feel the muscles in his back tighten against my breasts as I felt his skin. He was so strong and so damn fine. Any woman would kill to have him, but why couldn't I see that?

31

"It doesn't make you any less of a man, dealing with what you've been through, Sean. You are all man in my book."

"Hmm, not man enough to keep my woman satisfied at home."

His statement caught me off guard. While arguing about his past and Tony, I had never even thought about it from that angle. "What did you say?" I dropped my embrace and moved in front of Sean. I know he could see the look of astonishment in my eyes. Even though I had stepped outside of our marriage, the one thing I knew for certain was that it hadn't been because of bad sex at home. "Do you think that's what it was about? That you are not satisfying me? Oh God, no, Sean, that wasn't it at all."

"Well, what am I supposed to think it was, Rachel? My wife cheats on me twice—with different men, I might add. Hey, I know how the story goes. I wasn't handling my business as well as I thought I was."

For a minute Sean and I held a gaze, as if we were each searching for the person we had married long ago. Once again I moved into him, placing my hands on his chest. "All this time, Sean, and I never thought about it like that. I mean, here I am arguing about how it is always about your side, and I never bothered to think about how you really felt. Besides the anger of knowing I had hurt you, I never knew what you went through. I guess I was only concerned with my own needs."

My hands caressed his chest, and then I rubbed his shoulders before gently sliding my hands down to hold his. "I want to tell you something right now," I said, my voice choking with tears. "You may not believe this, but it's the truth. You are the best lover I have ever had. You made me feel special, and I was not with either of those guys because they were better than you. They stroked my ego and that's what I needed, or I guess I should say what I wanted. Sex was not the issue."

"So why couldn't I be the one to stroke your ego?"

"I guess I needed to feel it from someone else. I knew I had you, but I needed to know if you were just saying it because I was your wife."

"I was not saying it because I was your husband. I said it because I meant it, and unlike others, I didn't expect you to do anything in return."

"Sean, please no more. I'm tired; I don't want to fight anymore."

"I don't want to fight with you anymore, Rachel. It's hard for me to let you go, but I know that it is something that is inevitable. I guess I have to be happy knowing we will always be together through Devin. We both know what we have to do, so where do we go from here?"

"I'm moving back to New York, to the Bronx; time to put all those years of school to use, and not just be a teacher at home. A friend told me about a Lectureship position at Columbia opening up and offered to assist me in getting accepted. If all goes well I can start this fall."

"What about Devin? He is going to want his mother."

"If it's okay with you, I want to take Devin with me."

"Are you sure about that? I mean, you did say you wanted to get your life together. Plus if you're going to start teaching, I don't want Devin to overwhelm you and become too much of a burden."

"Sean, my son will not be a burden," I snapped. "My family is still living there, and you know my mom misses spoiling him. Besides, I need to refocus my attention on him and be a better mother, and with your job, you may have to go out of town on business unexpectedly. I just prefer that he be with family and not a nanny."

"Okay, we can try that, and I'm sorry. I didn't mean he'd be a burden to you. I apologize. I just wanted to help in any way I could and give you some space to sort things out."

"I'm sorry for snapping at you."

"No apology needed."

"Wow, that was weird," I exclaimed. "We had a conversation where we actually agree and disagree, and yet apologies are everywhere."

"Yeah, I know." He chuckled. "Too bad we have to split up before we respect each other."

A silence fell over us. It was an unsettling silence, for neither of us knew what to say after that. That comment had summed up our entire lives, at least until this point. I knew how he and Zara had ended, and I knew his mother didn't hold me in that same light. How would he portray me to her?

"Are you going to tell your mother?"

"Not right now. My father's birthday is coming up, and she is in one of her moods. I don't want to lay all of this on her yet."

"I guess you're right. Are you going to be okay—I mean, your company and all?"

"You know me, Rachel: nothing like a little misfortune to get those creative juices flowing. I need to get my life in order, too, I guess. I mean, I'm a thirty-four-year-old man who's had only two serious relationships in his life. I need Oprah."

We both laughed.

"Will you think about me, Sean? Will you think of me in a good way?"

"That's all I try to do, Rachel. You and Devin are my world; not everything between us was bad. I will always cherish our good memories"

"You're right, Sean. I know I only have positive thoughts about you. Plus, you know, we still make pretty good parents."

"Very true: not bad for a country boy from Georgia and a city girl from the Bronx."

"My big-booty country boy," I joked.

"Whatever. You wish you had my country ass." He laughed.

Our laughter drew our eyes into each other, and once more we were swept into that eerie silence.

"I will always love you, Rachel. Never forget that."

"I won't forget, Sean. Know that I love you." Tears were now running down my face. I did love Sean, I really felt it, but the guilt of the betrayal he didn't know about fueled my tears. "Know that I'm sorry for not giving you what you deserve, and thank you for loving me."

Sean placed a hand on my face and cupped my cheek. I placed my hand on his and closed my eyes. He moved his hand to my chin and lifted my face toward his. I opened my eyes and we gazed at each other, hoping to sear each other's image into our minds for eternity. As my lips touched his, I tasted the saltiness of his emotions. Tonight a new path had been chosen for me, and for once I was happy and sad that it had been chosen. I felt guilty still holding on to the lie of a friend in New York and the teaching job. I didn't know what tomorrow would bring. All I knew was that tonight a part of me had died with Sean's love for me. Just like Zara's betrayal and his father's death, I too was guilty of breaking Sean Winslow's heart.

Alanya

Suddenly I felt like I was in the wrong place. I didn't want to mingle anymore. I saw the bar and decided to take refuge near the bartender. I sat down and ordered a Crown and Coke. Tasting the liquor reminded me of the night I had found out about Corey and ended up drunk and sleeping with Kevin, so I pushed the drink away. I was about to leave when a very attractive sista stepped up to the bar beside me.

"Excuse me, but is this seat taken?"

"No, it's not."

"May I join you?"

"Actually I was just about to leave," I said, standing.

"Not quite your atmosphere huh?" she said, smiling.

"You could say that."

"I felt like that the first time I came to one of these parties."

"Do you come to them often?"

"Hardly. They have good intentions, but some of the women in here are just like men—like vultures looking for their next meal."

We laughed. She extended her hand. "Hi. My name is Ava. Nice to meet you."

"Alanya. It's nice to meet you, Ava," I said, shaking her hand.

"Alanya. Wow. I visited a place in Turkey named after you."

"That's where I'm from." I blushed. "Well, actually where my folks met."

"Well, it's nice to meet someone from such a beautiful place. Please, can I offer you a drink?"

I almost forgot I was standing, getting ready to leave. Ava's warm and inviting personality was intriguing. She was about my height, light skinned, and very pretty, with a short Halle Berry hairstyle and light hazel eyes. Her red twist-back dress accentuated her curves. She would easily have been my competition if we were at a straight club, and yet she wasn't coming across as stuck on herself. Not to mention the fact that she had visited my homeland fed my curiosity enough to at least get to know her.

"Sure," I said.

"Great." She motioned for the bartender.

"I'll have a glass of Chardonnay, and she'll have…"

"I'll have the same."

Ava had a smile on her face after I ordered. "Are you a wine drinker?" she said, pointing to my glass of Crown.

"Actually I am." I smiled. "I just wanted something stronger but then realized this was not what I needed tonight."

"I see, so you are from Turkey?"

"Yes. My name is from where my parents met in Alanya but I grew up in Antalya."

"What brings you over to our nation's capital?"

"Well, I actually live in New York. I'm here with a girlfriend."

"I see. A girl *friend* or a girlfriend?"

I laughed. "We're just friends. She thought it would be a good idea for me to get out and broaden my world."

"Is your friend a lesbian?"

"Yes, she is." I smiled. "I never knew I would be in a club having this conversation."

"Well, you know what they say: life is full of surprises."

"That it is. So why were you in Turkey?"

"It was business. I work for an investment firm that specializes in international resort properties."

"Oh, that sounds interesting. What did you think of Alanya?"

"I absolutely fell in love with it." She smiled. "The people, the culture, everything was amazing. Oh, and the beachfront views were breathtaking. It is truly a piece of paradise."

"It is very beautiful," I said, thinking about my homeland. "I really miss it sometimes."

"How long have you lived here in the States?"

"Since I was seventeen; I came here with my mother, stepfather, and stepbrothers. We settled down in Connecticut."

"And how long have you lived in New York?"

"I've been in New York for about five years now. I moved there after I was accepted to NYU."

"NYU—that's a good school; what's your major?"

"Journalism."

"Interesting choice, so do you want to be a writer who stays behind the scenes or do you see yourself in front of the camera?"

"Hmm. A little of both, I guess. I mean, my ultimate goal is to land a lead anchor position for CNN."

"That's very ambitious. I like that. Well, Alanya, I wish you much luck and success on your journey."

"Thank you, Ava."

"CNN would be very lucky to have you," she said, smiling seductively at me.

I returned her smile. Her gaze clearly showed not only her sincerity but her admiration and her interest in me. I suddenly felt awkward, knowing that a woman was attempting to feed my ego, but the more I looked at Ava and how beautiful she was, the more head blown I became. I had always felt confident in my ability to attract fine-ass men, but knowing I could also attract beautiful fine-ass women really stroked my ego. The bartender slid our glasses of wine in front of us. Ava raised hers in toast.

"To paradise." She smiled.

"Paradise."

As the sweetness of the wine descended my throat, sending a warm wave of calmness throughout my body, I began to feel that familiar sensation I used to get when I desired the company of a male suitor for the night. It felt weird and right all at the same time. Never mind that this suitor was just as soft and feminine as I was. As with most men who would try to pick me up, I knew I could have her whenever I wanted. I felt confident in knowing that I could have Ava eating out of my hand by the end of the night. I felt like flirting and elevating our game of cat and mouse.

"So how long will you be in town, Alanya?"

"I'll be here until Sunday."

"Aww, leaving so soon? What are your plans for the rest of the night?"

"I don't know, really. It depends on what my girl friend has planned."

"Okay, so who's this girl friend?"

"She's out there dancing. The light-skinned sista in the little black dress."

I pointed toward the dance floor and Mia. She was dancing with Jasmine, and they were definitely enjoying each other's company. The way they danced it was as if they were joined at the hip. As usual they had gathered a crowd of onlookers who seemed equally impressed by their chemistry.

"Not Mia Nicholson," Ava gasped.

"Yes. Why? Do you know her?" I questioned curiously.

"Yes, I do know her—well, sort of." She returned her gaze to Mia.

"How do you know her?"

"Well, I don't know her; I know her girlfriend, Jasmine."

"Oh, so do you know Jasmine or do you *know* Jasmine?"

"Oh no, I mean, not like that." She laughed. "I'm a regular in the core class Jazz teaches at her health club."

"Oh, okay." I sighed, relieved. "I didn't know if there was about to be some drama I didn't want to hear."

"No drama. Jazz is a very nice and caring person. I just remember Mia coming to the club on several occasions to pick her up. Jazz and I are cool because we met a while back at one of these parties, so she introduced us. After seeing them together, I knew that nothing could or would come between those two. They are perfect for each other."

"That they are," I said as I too returned my gaze to Jazz and Mia.

It's funny how you can look at someone else's happiness and realize just how much your own life is missing. Jazz and Mia were indeed happy and totally in love with each other. I remembered how shocked I had been when Mia finally came out the closet followed by her telling me she was leaving New York to follow Jazz here. The more I hung out with the two of them, though, the more I could see the bond between them grow. They had the kind of love I thought could exist only between a woman and a man, and yet there they were, happy and in love, and I was here alone without that love and a man.

"Well, from here I'd say your friend will be tied up for a while." Ava smirked.

"It certainly appears that way." I laughed. "So what did you have in mind for us?"

"I live nearby, and the views of the Potomac from my terrace are breathtaking."

"Why, Ava, you haven't turned into a vulture, now, have you?"

"No, I haven't." She laughed. "I figured we could grab a bite to eat and continue this conversation in a more relaxed atmosphere."

"Good, because I'd hate to think you were targeting me for your next meal."

"Well, I didn't say I wasn't hungry." She smiled seductively.

"Really? Well, I would have to see the view first," I teased back.

"You just let me know when you're ready."

I drank the rest of my wine in one large gulp and looked at Ava. "Lead the way."

We left the bar and made our way toward the dance floor. Ava and Jazz exchanged hugs and kisses. Mia pulled me aside and gave me a hug. "Girl, I didn't know you knew Ava. She's beautiful and very successful' the last I heard, she was definitely available. Where did you two meet?"

"Calm down girl, don't hitch me up just yet." I laughed "We just met at the bar and started to talk. She seems very nice, and we're going to go grab a bite to eat and talk."

"She is. Jazz introduced us a while back, and I can tell you, girl-friend has her shit in order. Damn, Alanya, you sure can pick 'em. Don't turn her out too bad."

"Whatever, girl; it's not like that."

"Hey, whatever, girl." She smiled. "Just have fun and enjoy yourself."

"I plan to," I said, smiling as Ava took me by the hand and led me off the floor.

We left Acropolis and the valet brought Ava's emerald-green Jaguar convertible around. She let the top down as we made our way up Connecticut Avenue to Giorgio's Italian Pizzeria, where we picked up some calzones. Soon after, we were pulling into an under-ground garage at Ava's place. The building itself let me know that this was a ritzy residence. She led me to the elevator, and we got off on the twelfth floor. Ava unlocked her door and ushered me into her penthouse. I knew from her ride she was classy, but upon entering her home, I was impressed by her expensive taste. It was as if I had entered an exclusive art museum exhibition. The clean white marble floors made our heels echo deeply. Her worldly travels were showcased throughout the living areas. The walls were adorned with fantastic art and exotic paintings, all accentuated by track and recessed lighting. Her taste varied from Egyptian to Byzantine. There were sculptures on tables and pedestals throughout the foyer and living room. I walked into the living room, where my eyes were immediately drawn to an abstract painting representing Turkish life. I read the artist's name: Mehmed Melih Devrim Nejad. Ava walked up behind me. "You like it? I actually picked this one up while I was in Antalya."

"It's beautiful," I whispered. "The most beautiful thing I've ever seen."

"Strange. I used those exact words tonight when I saw you at Acropolis."

I turned and faced Ava. "You have a way with words. You know, I'd swear you were a guy."

"I don't know if I should take that as a compliment or an insult."

"Let's just say I'm enjoying your company and your compliments."

"In that case, you are really going to love my next treat."

"Is that right?"

"Definitely. Come here. Let me show you something."

Ava led me through the living room and to a wall covered by floor-to-ceiling blinds. With one touch of a button the blinds began to retract, and my mouth opened in awe as the views of the Potomac came into full display. Ava slid open the glass door and I stepped outside and stood for a moment to soak it all in. The lights of the city were in the distance. The air felt warm, and yet a soft, cool breeze gently kissed my skin. Ava slipped back inside as I walked out onto the terrace. I was marveling at a boat making its way up the river when I felt a soft hand on my shoulder. I turned and Ava offered me a glass of wine. I took a sip and returned my gaze to the river.

"It's beautiful, isn't it? So quiet and so peaceful; this is where I unwind."

"You have a very beautiful home, Ava."

"Thank you, Alanya."

"So what's the deal with you?"

"What do you mean?" she asked, puzzled.

"I mean, no disrespect to you or to your orientation, but you are very beautiful and obviously very successful. Why hasn't a man tried to sway you back to the other side?"

Ava let out a heartfelt laugh. "You assume I was even on that other side to begin with."

"Well, you were, weren't you?"

Ava looked out at the water once more. "Ever since I was a freshman in high school, I knew I was different from the other girls, you know? I mean, I would sneak into my brother's secret stash of *Playboys* and look at all the beautiful women. I'd imagine what it would be like to kiss them, to have them hold me, love me. My mom sort of figured I was not quote/unquote 'normal,' so she would try to set me up with every one of her friends' sons that she deemed worthy."

"That must have been awkward."

"It was tough dealing with my folks at home and then peer pressure at school. You know, no one wants to be considered weird or an outcast. So I would go out with these guys, and just like men, they would do something stupid that would give me a reason to break up with them. Pretty soon I just got the label of being a stuck-up materialistic girl who only dated older guys for their money."

"That's crazy, Ava. I mean, I know people can be cruel, but I guess I never felt like that growing up."

"Yeah, well, it happens, but hey, it saved me from having to go to the prom with a boy I didn't like," she said, laughing.

"How are you and your parents now?"

"Well, I haven't spoken to my father since I was a freshman in college, and my mother and I started talking again two years ago."

"At least that's a start."

"I guess so. My mother finally took steps toward modernization, and my dad is still holding a candle, hoping that one day I'll come to what he thinks are my senses."

"Well, I think your senses are just fine." I smiled.

"Do you? And what, pray tell, are your senses saying?" Ava asked as she turned and faced me. "Is that Alanya speaking or is it the wine?"

"I don't need an excuse to say what I feel," I said as Ava moved closer to me—so close I could feel her body heat.

"Have you ever been with a woman before?"

"Not all the way, but far enough."

"Really." Ava smiled, looking straight into my eyes. "Far enough that it made you stop with fear?"

"No. Far enough that it made me realize that I wanted more."

I leaned forward, and without even thinking about what was happening, I let my lips touch Ava's mouth. Our tongues met with enough electricity to light up Washington, D.C. Her taste was as sweet as I had imagined mine was to the men I made love to. Ava moved closer into my body, and I felt her breasts press firmly against mine. The feeling turned me on, and I could feel myself opening up. She ran her hand through my hair, twirling it as she went. Her steady movements turned me on, and I let out a soft moan of approval. Ava traced her tongue on my lips, and with a final gentle kiss, she pulled back and looked at me. "You are very beautiful, Alanya."

"You are very beautiful yourself, Ava. Why did you stop?"

"I'm not looking for a one-night stand or a fling. Nor do I want to be someone's one-time fantasy fulfiller."

"Ava, I'm not looking for any of that either, but I can't lie to you and say I'm looking for something serious. A couple of weeks ago I was a full-bodied heterosexual woman, and now I have all these feelings for you that my body is trying to process. It feels so right, but I don't know if it's all lust, experimentation, or where I truly want to be."

I turned and went once more to the railing, peering out toward the river. Ava stood beside me and looked out as well.

"Look, Alanya, I don't want you to rush into anything, and I definitely don't want to take advantage of you, but I would be lying if I said I wasn't attracted to you. Tell you what—why don't we just enjoy this night out and take it from there?"

"I would really like that as well." I smiled.

"Would you like to see some more art?"

"I would love to."

Ava led me back into her penthouse and showed me the complete layout. After an impromptu art lesson, we relaxed on the couch. She dug out her CD collection, and we were going through some old-school R&B. I had to kick off the Manolo Blahnik heels and dance when Bobby Brown's "My Prerogative" came on. I was definitely enjoying my time with Ava. The more I looked at her, the more beautiful and flawless she seemed. Never in a million years could I have envisioned a woman of her pedigree solely dedicated to another woman. For the first time in my life I truly saw a woman's body as a man did. I wanted to feel her soft skin. I wanted to hold her. I laughed when I saw her excitement at finding her Salt-N-Pepa CD. She was clearly having fun as well. I had to join her on the dance floor when "Push It" came on. Though our chemistry paled next to Jazz and Mia's, we did have a good body vibe. As the song finished, we collapsed on the couch, laughing like two schoolgirls.

"I haven't had this much fun in a long time," Ava said, trying to catch her breath.

"Me either. I haven't done that since I was in high school, when I thought I was Salt."

"Hey, I was Pepa."

We laughed, and then a silence fell over us as we lay on the couch looking at each other.

"Well, it's getting late," Ava said. "I better get you back before your friends start worrying."

"I believe we finished that entire bottle of wine. I don't think you should be on the road, and besides," I said, turning on my side to face her, "I'm not ready to leave."

Ava turned on her side to face me as well. She smiled as she ran her hand down my shoulder. "I'm not ready for you to leave, either; I just didn't want you to think I was trying to hold you hostage."

"Hmm. Being held by you right now doesn't sound bad at all."

Ava stopped rubbing my shoulder and ran her hand down my cheek. I closed my eyes, taking in the softness of her touch. Once again she stroked my hair, pausing right behind my ear. She smiled and brought my head closer to her face. Once again our tongues touched and I began to feel the heat rise from my midsection, spreading like a wildfire throughout my body. Ava's touch was not tough or butch-y, but just as feminine as mine. Having another lover whose touch was just as soft, just as delicate, created an even more heightened sense of arousal like I'd never felt.

Normally I was the passive one in the bedroom, but now I became a sex-starved explorer. I rolled over until I was on top of her. Ava slid a hand down to my ass and squeezed it gently and lovingly before running her hands back up to my back. I ran my hands across her breasts, feeling the curvature of her body. Soon I felt her hands on my sides slowly pulling up my dress to my waist. Feeling my bottom in the cool air sent goose bumps down my arms. I felt her hands once again on my ass, tracing the outline of my thong. Her touch, ever so gentle and so sensual, kept pushing me closer and closer to being all out of control. Then without any warning her hand was on my breast, sliding down my stomach and resting right on my womanhood. The feeling of another woman's hands right there made me stop kissing her. I paused and opened my eyes. Ava was staring right at me.

"Hmm. Let's see if Alanya's nectar is as sweet as her tongue."

With that she pulled my ass forward until her head was positioned right between my thighs. I could feel her breath rustle gently across the satin crease of my thong. My curiosity mixed with lust took over. I slid my thong to one side, exposing myself to her. She smiled as she gazed at my swollen, pierced clit.

"Oh, that's beautiful, Alanya."

"Would you like to kiss it?" I teased.

"I want to do more than just kiss it," she replied with a seductive smile. "I want to make it mine."

The way she gently parted my lips with her tongue sent a shiver down my back, and for a moment my knees buckled from the sheer excitement my body felt. My mind was running in many directions as her tongue delivered wave after wave of sensations throughout my body. My abs twitched and tightened. I reached down and ran my hands through her soft hair. Ava was a seasoned pro. She stopped squeezing my ass, and her hands made their way back to my breasts. My breathing got heavier as Ava's hands gently pulled down the top of my dress. She let out a soft moan as she gazed upon my blue lace bra. My 32D breasts always drew praise from the men lucky enough to see them. Now I had a woman equally appreciative of my assets.

Suddenly I felt a strong rush of warmth rushing throughout my body, followed by chills as I felt myself coming closer to an orgasm. I had never had one strictly from oral sex, much less as quickly as it was happening. My hips rocked back and forth as Ava held on to my thighs, holding me in place. I couldn't hold it in much longer. My back arched upward and I let out a scream of ecstasy as Ava took me to my climax. My legs completely numb, I fell forward over Ava's head where she rolled me over onto my back. Sliding up to my neck she gently kissed my lips.

"You taste so good—just as exotic as your birthplace."

"You have a magical tongue," I gasped, trying to catch my breath. "I've never cum from oral sex."

"Really?" she asked, somewhat amused at the thought of being another first for me. "You have missed out on a lot, haven't you?"

"I guess so." I smiled. "So will you bring me up to speed?"

"As a matter of fact, your next lesson is about to start," she whispered.

Ava slid back down, kissing my navel piercing and my thighs, sliding my dress completely off. A look of hunger in her eyes let me know she was going to enjoy every part of this night and every part of my body.

Sean

Seven long months had passed since I had said good-bye to Rachel. She was back in the Bronx, getting her life in order. My son, Devin, was adjusting like a three-year-old would. He had plenty of questions and wasn't really buying the answers he was given by both Rachel and me. Rachel's mother was doing what any good grandmother would do: spoiling him rotten. He must have felt like he had won the Toys"R"Us lottery.

When they came to visit me at my mother's home in Georgia for Christmas, Rachel and I barely had any time alone. We both had fun with Devin opening presents and playing with his new toys. She didn't give any details about her social life, such as whether she was dating or seeing anyone. She did have a couple of cell phone calls, which she took in another room. I assumed she was indeed too busy with her new career and raising Devin to add anything to her plate. Plus, with my mom hovering over both of us and quizzing me about why I had let Rachel move back to New York with Devin, I didn't bother asking Rachel any personal questions.

Rachel was still the bombshell she always had been, and although we didn't talk about our marriage, there were numerous times we caught ourselves looking at each other or holding each other just a little longer than a casual embrace. Her smiles and demeanor were warm and even seemed to suggest that maybe we had made a mistake.

Because we had gotten married in Vegas, it didn't take too long to terminate our union. Our divorce was finalized December 16. At Rachel's request, we had decided to move ahead as quickly as possible. We operated under the belief that since she was in New York, we could move on with our lives and minimize the hurt and pain on both sides as well as help Devin adjust more quickly. The funny thing about the whole process was the fact that you can spend years getting to know and love someone, and even raise a family together—years that can be declared null and void by the signature of someone you don't even know, someone who's never seen the hurt, the pain, the joy, and the happiness of that union.

Again, Rachel was right about my work schedule and taking Devin with her. The business side of my life was going fabulously well. I was expanding my company on two new fronts. I had made several trips out to the west coast. De Stijl Marketing had expanded to offices in California as well as my hometown of Atlanta. We were on the verge of increasing our presence in New York to give my old colleagues at LAN MAR a run for their money. I had managed to recruit a group of exceptional, highly talented marketing consultants. We were in the business of making other businesses look appealing to the consumer. Producing everything from commercials to new designs for product packaging, we were solidifying our name in the industry.

Focusing on the business side of my life kept my mind occupied. I had not been out on a date since Rachel and I split. I saw no need to move on, because deep down she was the one I still wanted. With the additional success of the company and my exceptional staff, I could easily see myself moving more away from day to day operations and winning her back. I wanted to concentrate on spending quality time with her. It took seven months for me to see the error of my ways, and I was ready to change and let the past go. I was ready to move on. This time it would be me asking Rachel to give us a second chance. I knew the decision I had been pondering all morning was the correct one. I just needed to lock in the final piece of my management team.

"Carol, could you send Robert in, please?"

"Right away, Mr. Winslow."

There was a knock and then the door opened. Robert walked in, a handsome brother standing about six foot four with an athletic build. He had come to me right out of Howard University. He was young, educated, and thirsty for success. He was also a bona fide player from what I gathered from Carol. She would always keep me posted with the juicy gossip from the water hole. I didn't bring him in to discuss "How to be a Playa," rather, I needed him for another important job—one that I knew he had earned.

"You wanted to see me, Mr. Winslow?"

"Yes, Robert, come in and have a seat. And please call me Sean."

"Thank you, sir…Sean."

"How long have you been here at De Stijl, Robert? Four years now?"

"Four years and two months. Thank you again for giving me an opportunity," he said uneasily.

"You've handled some pretty big clients for this company, most notably your ad campaign for the Nationals—very impressive."

"Thanks, Sean. I studied your work, and I learn from the best."

"I see you know how to bullshit with the boss too." I chuckled.

"Yes sir, I do." He laughed.

"Well, now that we've gotten the formalities out of the way, there's something else I need you to do for me."

"Anything, Sean."

"As you know, we've expanded our offices to include California and Georgia."

"Yes sir, I'm very aware of that."

"You also know we are on the verge of taking on our most serious competition in New York."

"Again, sir, I am very aware."

"Good. Then you must also know not only the importance of these new ventures, but the importance of reassuring and maintaining our current clients' businesses as our top priority."

"Oh absolutely Sean, we must assure our current clients that while we are expanding our products and services; their needs will still be met with the highest level of expertise they've come to expect from De Stijl."

"That's why I'm promoting you to senior marketing director for the East Coast region."

"You're doing what?" Robert asked in disbelief.

"I said congratulations, Robert; you are the new senior marketing director for the East Coast region."

"That's incredible!" Robert exclaimed. "Thank you, Sean...uh, I mean, Mr. Winslow, thank you."

"It's Sean, and you've done an outstanding job, you know this region better than anyone else. You've earned it. Besides, I have to keep the good ones on board. Well done, Robert."

"I won't let you down, Sean."

Robert stood and extended his hand to shake mine. I took his hand, but instead of the professional office handshake, I felt compelled to give him a real brother-to-brother hood embrace. The move surprised Robert, and he stepped back a bit.

"I didn't know you had that in you, Sean."

"I'm sorry if I offended you. To be honest I don't know what came over me. It was like you are one of my boys from college."

"No apologies needed. It's actually good to know you remember who you are and what you represent. I've met so many cats from hoods worse than mine, and now they act as if they were born on Rodeo Drive or some shit."

"I know what you mean, Robert."

"Rob, call me Rob," he said.

"Rob. I will never forget where I'm from, the sacrifices my mother and father made to give me the best chance to excel, and the friends I met along the way who sold themselves out to get ahead. I always keep it real—professional but real."

"True, Sean, that's very true. Judging from how far you've come, you've got that down pat."

"Well, judging from your work and our conversation right now, I'd say the same about you as well, Rob. You remind me of myself, and I recognize your drive, it will carry you to success."

"I told you, I've been learning from the best." He smiled.

"Whatever, man." I laughed. "Did I say senior marketing director or was that junior intern?"

"You have to keep it real now." Rob laughed. "I have your word and word is bond."

We both laughed.

"So how do you do it?" Rob asked.

"Do what?"

"You know, balance your business, your wife and kid, and do it all at the top of your game."

"I wouldn't say that," I said, sitting back down. "Rachel and I have been divorced for almost a year now."

"I'm sorry. I didn't know."

"Don't be. I haven't broadcast it in the office yet. I guess it's about time I let people know."

"That's your business, Sean. That's your personal life, and whenever you're ready, you call the shots. Not rumors or snoopy-ass people."

"Thanks, Rob. Hey, can I get you a glass of Scotch? Sit down and tell me about yourself outside of this dynamic work façade."

We sat in my office and shared a few glasses of Scotch. In between we talked some more about business and the transition phase for him. Then we switched to family. He was homegrown from Baltimore, one of five children and the first to complete college. He had a sister who was a stripper in a Washington, D.C., club and also went to Howard.

His younger brother was in jail for selling drugs, and his oldest brother had been killed several years earlier in a car accident on I-495. He was raising his youngest sister, who was a junior in high school with dreams of being a doctor. He had seen a lot.

Then our conversation switched to my upbringing in the South. I told him about being the only child of a judge in Atlanta and a professor at Clark University. How failure was not an option for me, but how I strove to make it on my own without their help. How I met Zara, and how my life had nearly been destroyed at twenty-five when she ran off. Then I talked about the loss of my father, and my subsequent marriage and divorce from Rachel. We talked as if we were long-lost friends catching up on our lives after being reunited. The two of us clicked well. We were about the same age, he being four years my junior. He could relate to me, and it felt good to at least scratch the surface of everything I had been holding inside.

"Damn, Sean," Rob said, still trying to soak it all in. "I have got to hand it to you, man. I couldn't have done it."

"Love is love, man," I said, sitting back in my chair. I interlocked my hands behind my head. "I never thought I would do some of the stuff I did, but I guess it's true. You'll do strange and crazy things when you love someone."

"I guess it is. So you never called Zara out or at least sued her ass for some of the royalties she made off you?"

"No, I didn't. I was so mad; I didn't want a damn thing from her. The way she did it was like wow, I never imagined she would let money come in between us. Even though those were my ideas, she still had to make them work, you know. Besides, revenge for me is the fact that I have my own company that I built from the ground up."

"I guess you're right, but I still would have made her ass sweat a little."

"I wanted to, but she was there for my mother when my dad died, so she's family, in a way."

"Yeah, that's the least she could've done. She must have been a dyme piece, because you know you were supposed to check that."

"Oh, she was a dyme piece," I said, remembering Zara's image. "That was history, though. When I met Rachel, my past ceased to exist."

"So how do you feel about that?"

"I miss her, you know. I mean, we were a family with a son, and for the past seven years I've known only her love. It's hard to let that connection go."

"Yep, you got it bad," Rob replied. "I bet you still carry your wedding ring in your pants pocket don't you?"

"How the hell did you know that?" I exclaimed, feeling the ring in my pocket.

"Sean, I said I couldn't have done what you did, but I didn't say I haven't tried," Rob said, smiling. He stood up and prepared to leave my office.

"Hey man, we haven't finished this conversation."

"I have to pick my sister up, and it's almost four thirty."

"Damn. I didn't realize we'd been in here that long," I said, looking at my watch.

"Dinner tonight at Chadwick's , my treat."

"Don't start big spending already." I laughed. "I'll be there at eight."

"Eight o'clock it is."

He left the office, and I sat back, pondering our conversation and his last statement. I took out my ring and put in on my finger, staring at it for a minute. I took it off, and then I remembered my last confrontation with Rachel and how I had mentioned not knowing of anyone who had been through what I had been through. I thought about how much I missed her, how lonely my bed was, how lonely the house was without her. Then I thought about the last time we made love. I remembered how my anger would not allow me to chase after Zara.

I won't allow my sadness or anger to prevent me from fighting for you, Rachel, if it's not too late, I will get you back.

I closed my schedule and left the office to go home and freshen up before going to meet Rob.

Alanya

It had been a whirlwind romance for seven months between Ava and me. After we had met in D.C., she transferred to her firm's Manhattan office to be closer to me. At first I felt Mia had been right, that maybe my destiny, my love, was with another woman. Our chemistry in the bedroom was great. I had never imagined I could be satisfied without the touch of a man, but I was happy.

We would go out, and guys would try to pick us up. It was a turn-on to see their mouths drop to the floor when Ava would push me against a wall and slide her tongue inside my mouth. Every man's fantasy of having two girls was within their grasp, and yet we took not one of them home. Just hard dicks left to wonder what we were doing to each other behind closed doors. I felt like I was finally giving the male species a little payback for all the lies and betrayals that had been bestowed upon me.

It was too early in our relationship for me to bring her with me to my parents' house in Connecticut for this year's family reunion. Instead I made the trip up by myself, and soon I was in the midst of my family and missing Ava terribly. I stared out at my stepbrother Christian and his wife Bridgette playing with their son. A sudden feeling of emptiness started creeping into my stomach. I remembered the time Corey and I had had a serious talk about getting married and having kids. Christian loved his family and had always been devoted to Bridgette, even when they were just dating. Somehow I knew I would never find that love, but here I was, standing there, wondering how I would have been as a mother, a wife.

Christian saw me standing by the door and ran over to me. "Hey, Lani, are you okay, you seem like you are a million miles away?"

"Oh yeah. I'm fine, Christian. You know, you're very lucky there, big brother," I said, looking at Bridgette.

"Indeed I am," Christian replied with a smile as his glance turned to his wife. "I'm the luckiest man in the world."

"Why aren't there more guys like you out there in this world?"

"There are plenty of good men out there. You just can't get wrapped up in looking for them, sis."

"I think I am done with even looking for them."

"Uh oh." Christian turned and faced me. "I take it things are not working out with you and Corey?"

"There is no me and Corey, that is, unless I want to play the third wheel."

"I'm sorry to hear that, Lani, but don't let a guy like that get you down on the rest of us. To be honest he didn't seem to be on your level at all. He wasn't a real man, and he lost out on the best woman he could ever wish for."

"Thanks, Christian. I really needed a little cheering up."

"Trust me, Lani, the right man for you is out there waiting for the right moment."

"Hmm...I don't know. Maybe I wasn't meant to be with a man."

"Wow, Lani, that's a little extreme, don't you think?"

"No, not really. I mean, look at my friend Mia. She's totally happy with Jasmine, and they have this connection that I thought could only exist between a man and a woman. Maybe I have been looking at the wrong side."

"Hey, I'm not knocking your friend or her girlfriend and being lesbian, but come on, Lani: surely you can't see yourself going that route...You haven't gone there, have you?" he asked nervously.

I gave Christian a look that told him the story behind my statement.

"Oh no, Lani...Why? How?"

"How is not important, but why not?"

"Lani, you can't let one bad apple take you out of the orchard."

"It's not just one bad apple, Christian; it's the whole damn tree. I want to feel loved and cherished. I want a family. After my father died, I saw how it crushed my mother. Then she met your father and I saw that love can be reborn. I want that type of love in my life, and I don't think I will ever find a man who can be that for me."

"Lani, for God's sake, you're only twenty-four years old. You have your entire life ahead of you. You know what, this is merely a phase. Right now most guys your age are not looking for that type of long term love. A mature man is ready for a commitment, but then again, I'm not telling you to rush to the local old folks home, either." He smiled, and I laughed. "Bridgette wasn't the only woman I dated, you know. I mean, I had my share of heartbreaks too. You just gotta dust yourself off and get back on that horse."

"That horse is gone for me, and besides, I am very happy right now."

"Lani, you are not happy; you're content."

"How do you know?"

"I've known you since you were a self-confident sixteen-year-old brat. You always made the best out of any situation, but you always kept your eyes open for an opportunity to excel. You can't stand here and tell me through all of this that you are now a hundred percent satisfied."

"No one is a hundred percent satisfied."

"I am."

"Well, then you are the exception. You know what? Let's just drop this subject."

"Lani, I'm sorry, I'm not trying to rain on your parade or pass judgment, but you are my sister, and deep down I know you want more than what she can give you."

"Her name is Ava, and right now she is giving me everything she can and more."

I showed Christian pictures of Ava on my phone. The look on his face showed the conflict in his mind as he viewed Ava's beauty and the happiness on our faces. He shook his head in disbelief. "I don't know what to say, Lani. She's beautiful, very beautiful, and there's no man in her life?"

"She's never been with one."

"Wow. Never?"

"Never."

"Well, I must admit you two look very happy together. I never saw you going this way, though." He laughed. "I always had you pegged to marry some Hollywood actor you would interview, or an up and coming politician."

"Boring!" I laughed.

"So when are you going to tell Mom and Dad?"

"I don't know. I thought it was too early to bring her with me."

"Good choice." He smirked.

"Yeah, well, after seeing my brothers' crash and burn a few times before, I knew I'd better play it safe."

"Told you; you always looked to excel."

"Christian, there is one thing I did think about," I confided.

"What's that?"

"Do you think I would have made a good wife—a good mother?"

"Of course, Lani, and I'm not just saying that you would have in the past. You are very caring, very loving, and I still think you will make an excellent wife and mother."

"Holding that candle, huh?"

"I am, and something tells me deep down you are too. Mr. Right will rescue you, Alanya. I know it."

"I guess we will just have to wait and see, won't we?"

Christian gave me a wink, and we hugged. "Got time for one more snowball fight before you leave?"

"I think I am deserving of a little payback." I smiled.

Soon we were swept into a snowball fight with Bridgette and their son, Peyton. Driving back down to New York, I couldn't help but think about Christian's last statement to me. *Should I feel guilty for having doubts or even wishing that somehow he was right?*

Zara

"Zara. Hey, lady, what's going through that beautiful mind of yours?"

"I'm sorry, Mikel. Repeat the question?"

"You're a million miles away." Mikel grinned. "Do I even have to ask his name?"

I laughed. "And how do you know I was thinking about a man?"

"You only have that stare when you are thinking about home and him."

"Well, I was thinking about being back home in Atlanta with my folks."

"And him?"

"Are you trying to read my mind?"

"Am I right?"

All I could do was smile and shake my head. "Just order me another glass of Riesling, Mr. Mind Reader."

"I knew it." Mikel laughed. "Man, I wish Lauren thought about me as much as you think about Sean, and we're still together."

"You know, it's not always a good thing to miss or think about someone so much, especially when you won't see that person again."

"It doesn't have to end like that, though, Zara. Why not just call the man?"

"It's not that simple, Mikel."

"Yes it is. We both have global iPhones."

I laughed. "No, stupid. It's not that simple. I mean, I'm not a home wrecker."

"Forgive me for being so damn nosy, but were you not the one several months ago who told me that a certain person was having problems in his marriage?"

"I did, but I…"

"And isn't it true that we have confirmed reports from this past Christmas that said a certain Suzy wannabe homemaker is actually living back in New York— alone?"

"Yes." I nodded.

"C'mon, Zara, just a simple phone call to say hello, you know that was your home first."

"Times have changed, Mikel. Sean has a family even without her being around. Maybe if it was just Sean and Rachel—but they have a son together. She will always be in his life."

"I understand, Zara, but that shouldn't stop you from doing the right thing. Sean will always be there for his son, but when will you see that he can and should be there with you? You can't keep all that sexiness on lockdown forever."

"You are crazy." I laughed.

"No, I'm not. I mean, you won't take any offers from any of my friends, no one has ever seen you kiss a man, and the Christmas party with Karl's drunken ass doesn't count. You won't reach out to Sean. What gives? You are beautiful, smart, and did I mention rich? You are a bona fide treasure."

"Mikel, you always know how to make me feel good about myself. Now I remember why I hired you." I smiled.

"That's right. You also have great taste." Mikel smiled back. "Seriously, what harm could come from just a phone call? Are you still visiting your folks when they return from Jamaica next week?"

"I am."

"Well, maybe a side trip to Maryland can be added to your itinerary."

I laughed. "Mikel, I'm not desperate. Besides, Sean may have other options he's exploring—that is, if he and Rachel are already not reconciling."

"Zara, how many excuses are you going to come up with? It's been almost ten years now. Hell, even LeBron James and Cleveland have forgiven each other." He laughed. "This is Sean Winslow we're talking about: your knight in shining armor. All he needs is your handkerchief."

"Aww, so sweet, but so wrong. Look, I will make a deal with you. If we can change the subject about Sean and me, I'll tell Lauren that you are always thinking about her and she should buy you that snowmobile you want for your birthday."

"Damn, you drive a hard bargain." Mikel squirmed. "Okay we can change the subject Zara, but at least promise me that you will consider it. I want to see you complete your circle of success and get the man you want and deserve."

"Deal," I replied.

We toasted and went on with the rest of our conversation about Mikel and Lauren's upcoming ski trip, but in the back of my mind I was thinking about maybe just taking Mikel's advice and visiting Maryland and Sean. Ever since my conversation with my mom months earlier, my thoughts for Sean had intensified. I knew his ears had to be burning as well. I needed to know why he hadn't responded to my letter, even if only a negative response. Besides, I needed this to either be the closure my life needed or the beginning my heart desired.

Rachel

Driving over to my parents' house to pick up the rest of my belongings reminded me just how much my life had changed. It was harder than I had imagined, leaving Sean and the life I had spent the last six years helping make miserable. Looking back, I realized my newfound independence came with a steep price. Although I loved lecturing at Columbia and being independent, the relationship that I had envisioned with Tony was anything but heaven. At times I found myself missing the love Sean gave me, and the attention he showed during our good times made me smile. I knew it was too soon to have Tony move into the apartment, not to mention I was afraid that Sean may plan a surprise trip to see Devin.

Tony and I shared wonderful chemistry in bed, but he still held on to some of his playa ways—ways he had professed he would give up for me. To his credit he had put aside his ambition of being the next big hip-hop star and was focusing on the talents he had. He dedicated himself to his job as a strength and conditioning coach at Columbia as well as, of all things, his work as a guidance counselor. Having his own boyish aspirations brought him closer to the younger generation. Tony relished how a lot of the students looked up to him.

Still his eyes wandered, and too many times I'd had the pleasure of walking into his office while he was giving a young naïve woman some private conversation time. You could tell from their looks what the

71

women were after. Away from home for the first time, they were eager to be seduced by an older, handsome, real man.

All of that was the least of my concerns, though. Devin was having a tougher time adjusting without his father near him. When Sean and I were together, Devin rarely raised a whimper when Sean was away on a business trip, but now, knowing his father was no longer readily available or coming home in a couple of days, he made his unhappiness known.

We had spent Christmas in Georgia with Sean and his mother. Seeing Sean's mother and having to deal with her constant less-than-covert attempts to find out why we had split—or, even more, what I had done wrong—left me feeling bitter. It was still nice to feel Sean's arms around me. He still had a look in his eyes that let me know he missed me and he cared. A part of me wondered if he had moved on and better yet, whether he had told Zara.

It's too late to cry over spilled milk now, I thought to myself as I pulled over and made my way up to my parents' house. I wanted to just grab my things and run, but my mom was in, and that meant we needed to talk.

"So how's the apartment?" she asked.

"It's fine, Mom."

"How's Devin doing?"

"Devin is adjusting rather well."

"I know he must still miss his father."

"He does, but it's an adjustment phase, Mom, and it's not like his father has abandoned him."

"I know, Rachel, but you know how life is today for kids in single-parent homes. You must see kids like that every day, struggling to make something of themselves."

"As a matter of fact, I do," I replied, rather annoyed. "And for the most part they do exceptionally well—sometimes better than the ones from traditional stable family homes. They know what real life and real struggles are about, and they want to succeed."

"Well, it still must be hard."

"What are you saying, Mom?"

"I am saying I know it's hard to raise a child with two parents, let alone one."

"Well, I am not alone, and whenever Sean wants to see his son, he can and does."

"That's good to hear."

"What's wrong with you?"

"What do you mean?"

"I just feel like there's more to your questions, that's all."

"I'm not trying to imply anything or probe you, Rachel. I'm just concerned about you and Devin."

"Well, we're fine. It's not the end of the world, you know. Sean and I agreed that it was better this way for both of us."

"Something tells me this was more about your wishes than Sean's."

"I expected something like that from Sean's mother, but not from you."

"Tell me I'm wrong then, Rachel. Tell me Sean no longer wanted you and that he was in no way swayed by your actions."

"My actions!" I shouted. "Sean made his choice, and my actions had nothing to do with it."

"You can't believe that."

"I can and I do."

"Rachel, you were married for six years, and you did everything to end it. I still wonder why you got married in the first place."

"I was pregnant, remember?" I shot back.

"Yes you were, and I remember how happy Sean was with you and the love we could see in his eyes for you. Losing the baby really devastated him."

"I was hurt and devastated too, or do my feelings not count?"

"Of course your feelings matter, Rachel. Your father and I love you so much, and we wept for you when you wept. We will always love you, and we will always be concerned about your welfare. As much as we've been through as a family, you know we will always be there for you."

I was once again reminded of all the times my mother and father had indeed been there for me. Even with all the disappointments, all the embarrassment that had happened as a result of my indiscretions, they had been there. I did hate that I had put them through so much. I hated to think that it was all my fault.

"Are you still seeing Tony?"

"Yes I am. Why?"

"Is he treating you okay, and has Devin seen him yet?"

"He's treating me fine, and I have had Tony over only a few times around Devin. I am taking it slow."

"That's good to hear."

"You know, I didn't come over here to have judgment passed on me. I just came to pick up the rest of my things and say hello." I got up to leave, and my mom grabbed my arm.

"Rachel, wait. I'm not passing judgment. Please don't go like this. I just want you to be happy and well."

"I am trying to be happy, Mom, I found my love for teaching again, I am trying to be a better more attentive mother to my son. Trust me, I am finding my happiness."

"Were you not happy with Sean?"

"I loved Sean, but I think I was more content than happy."

"And Tony?"

"I don't want to discuss this anymore," I said, turning for the door.

"Okay...okay. Rachel, wait. I met this wonderful lady at church a couple of weeks ago, and she's a doctor."

"A doctor? Please tell me you didn't talk to a shrink about me again."

"She's not a psychiatrist, she's a specialist."

"A specialist in what?"

"Sexual well-being."

"What? Okay, Mom, conversation over. Gotta go."

"Rachel, please," she said, grabbing my arm more sternly. "As much as I love you and have gone through with you, please, it wouldn't hurt to just talk to her. Something about her and the way she talked made me believe she could truly understand you and help you." She handed me a business card. "Please—for your father and me."

I stared at the card. Dr. Jackie Solomon, PhD. I wanted to rip the card up and storm out the door, but when I looked back up at my mom and saw tears in her eyes, guilt suddenly filled my heart. I clutched the card tightly in my fist.

"I'll think about it, Mom," I said, holding back tears of my own. "Listen, tell Dad I said hello, okay?"

"Okay, Rachel. I love you."

"I love you too, Mom."

I made it back to my car and started it. I looked at the card one more time, and then I glanced up at the house. Deep down I had always wanted to talk to someone who would understand or help me understand why I felt the way I did, but I had always been afraid of the stigma. I mean I had degrees as well. I knew I was smart and intelligent, I was a book worm, but growing up I had not been a social butterfly. I used to think that my father was embarrassed by my looks, but I was always told that I was beautiful. *Why did I need to feel like I was the center of every man's affection?* Now I was lecturing at an ivy-league school, my own penthouse apartment in New York, more importantly I'm a mother now. Things have got to change. Maybe this Dr. Solomon could help.

Sean

"A severe winter storm advisory is in effect for much of the Eastern Seaboard throughout next week. Look for at least six to eight inches of fun powder for the D.C./northern Virginia area as well as at least ten inches for New Jersey and New York," the radio weatherman said.

"Just my luck," I said aloud as I drove to Chadwick's.

I had a meeting in New York on Monday, and I had decided to surprise Rachel afterward. I wanted to take her out and tell her how I felt. I wanted to see where things stood from her side and, ideally, fly back home later in the week with my wife and son with me.

Wisconsin Avenue and K street in D.C. were their ever-bustling selves, a favorite junction on which to shop and eat for locals and tourists alike. I arrived with twenty minutes to spare. Robert was already there, sipping on a drink at the bar and flirting with the bartender. She was an attractive white girl with a nice tan, sandy-blond hair, and busty. Rob saw me approaching and stood to greet me. "Sean, glad to see you could make it."

"I can never turn down a free meal." I grinned.

"Well, don't go overboard on the crab cakes. I haven't seen my new salary yet."

Chadwick's was a cozy little spot on K Street that was one of my favorites. It was a nice place to relax and talk business or to meet that someone special for a nice meal. They had the best crab cakes on the East Coast—not to mention their signature mud pie, which had caused me to retire from playing basketball. Our table had a window view of the street. It was always interesting to stare at the many pass-ersby. Some were deep in thought as they walked to their destinations, whereas others seemed confused and downright lost.

"Hello, I'm Tracy. Can I get you guys an appetizer or drinks?"

"Yes, you may, and I also know what I want for my main dish. May I order that now too, Tracy?"

"You sure can, sir."

"Perfect. I'll have the shrimp martini for my appetizer, and for my main course I'll have the crab cake platter."

"And for your drink?"

"I'll have one of your best bottles of Chardonnay."

"An excellent choice, sir," she said, smiling.

"Damn, Sean, I hope you're going to make me partner after this meal. I guess I'll have a salad."

We both laughed. Tracy didn't get it but smiled politely. "Just a salad, sir?"

"No, I was only kidding. My appetizer will be the hummus plate, and for the main course I'll take the New York steak-house platter, medium well, please."

"And your drink?"

"A bottle of your best Merlot."

"Also an excellent choice. Are you guys famous? You look familiar."

"Shh!" Rob exclaimed. "We're movie producers, and we're thinking about filming in D.C. Can you act?"

"No, but I can sing."

"Who do you compare your vocal talents to?"

"Well, I've been told I sound like Joss Stone."

"Oh really," Rob said in amusement.

"That's right. I have my demo in my bag. Would you like to hear it?"

"This is Sean Winslow, and he's the president and owner of De Stijl Marketing. If you sound good, he could hook you up with a label."

"Really!" Tracy blushed.

I had sat back and watched in amusement as Rob got Tracy worked up. I had thought he was trying to score for himself, but now I suddenly got the feeling he was trying to hook me up.

"Well, Rob, I don't think that that's a good—"

"Oh, don't worry, Sean. We'll screen it, and if it's good, you can give her a call," Rob interrupted, winking at me.

"This is so cool. I'll go put your orders in and I'll bring my demo back."

Tracy skipped off as if she had just won *American Idol*. I just looked at Rob and laughed. "Okay, pimp, how am I going to get out of this?"

"Relax, Sean. Hey, you never know—she may have talent. I know you have some contacts, and besides, I figure you needed to start exploring your options."

"My options?"

"You said you've been divorced for almost a year, right?"

"Yes."

"You were married for six years, right?"

"Yeah. So?"

"You'll never get back into the life of the living unless you take that first step."

"Is that so? So taking this girl who looks like she's barely old enough to order alcohol is my first step to living again?"

"You've got to start somewhere, Sean. A pretty young thing is what you need to get those creative juices flowing. Besides, I know you and I know what you've been through."

"Before I even tell you I'm not a cradle robber, I need to ask you about that."

"About what?"

"Earlier today in my office you knew I still had my wedding ring on me, and now you say you understand me. So what's your story? And don't front."

"After hearing your story about Zara, and then Rachel, I knew I had a bond with you. I didn't think any guys like me existed."

"Come on, man, spill it out."

"Okay, okay." Rob sighed. "I got married to my high school sweetheart Kim when I was nineteen. She was twenty and in the Air Force. We moved over to Germany and lived there for two years."

"Wow, Germany. I bet that was an experience."

"Yeah, it was at first, but after a couple of months, it changed, you know. I started missing things back in the States."

"I got you: culture shock."

"To the heart. No real friends, no family, hell no good radio stations—I mean, I even missed commercials. It was boring. Kim was always working, so that was a strain as well. Then one day we had a big argument and I decided to come back to the States."

"Did you guys try to work it out?"

"Not exactly," he said, his eyes looking as though he were now miles away in thought. "She came back long enough to tell me she had met some military cat over there and that she wanted to know where our marriage stood. I told her I still loved her, but the ball was basically in her court. The next morning her wedding ring was on the coffee table."

"Damn, man, did you go after her?"

"I wanted to, but my pride wouldn't let me you know. I packed up all her shit and sent it back to her. By the time my heart wanted to reach out to her, she was already three months pregnant."

"Damn!"

"You know what was ironic about the whole thing, though?"

"What?" I asked eagerly.

"The ironic part was that the son of a bitch she got pregnant by had a wife back in Arizona. When Kim found out, she got his ass in trouble, his wife divorced him, and he got booted out of the military."

"So did you and Kim try to work it out after that?"

"It was three years later when she got back to the States. She got stationed at Andrews Air Force Base in Camp Springs, and she had a two-and-a-half-year-old son named Jaden."

"Then what?"

"I don't know. We went out on a few dates, but we lost that connection we once had."

"Oh, so your feelings did change?"

"Yeah, I guess that was it. I mean, I still cared for her, but I just couldn't see myself taking her back, especially after she had had a child with someone else. Someone she had chosen over me"

"Yeah, that's a tough one to swallow, especially given the circumstances."

"For real. So like, up until that point I had carried around my ring in my pocket, hoping to one day put it back on."

"So how were you able to finally put it away and move on?"

"I met someone who I thought was my real true love. Her name was Toya, and she was everything to me that Kim wasn't."

"Well she sounds like a winner. What happened?"

"For two years she helped me get my life together. Helped me get my grades up in college, helped me with my drive. She made me realize I needed to make something of myself. She was young and successful, and I wanted to be that way also."

"Okay, so what happened?"

"She had an affair with her boss, got him to leave his wife, and he married her."

"What the fuck!" I exclaimed. "I don't believe it."

"Believe it, brother, I just didn't realize that her ambitions ultimately were about the dollar sign which is why when you told me about Zara's betrayal it kinda reminded me of Toya's."

Tracy brought us our appetizers and drinks. She then slid her CD to me and gave me a wink. Rob laughed.

"Okay, Casanova," I said. "Now I have to ask you, how do you do it."

"Do what?"

"You know: go through two heartbreaks and then come out on top as a bona fide playa."

"A playa?" Rob said, laughing. "You've been talking to Carol, huh?"

"Well, I must admit your reputation is well noted by some of the ladies at the office." I chuckled.

"The thing that I learned from my relationships is that once I felt comfortable knowing that I had done everything I could to sustain and nurture them, it was their loss. Before, I used to look only at myself like what was I doing wrong and what, if anything, was I lacking."

"Exactly. You felt like you weren't handling your business."

"Right, right. Then one night it just happened, you know. I went out without trying to hook up with anyone, but I met this girl at the gym and we hit it off."

"I'm listening, playa."

"We hit it off so well that we 'hit it' that night. It was incredible. Everything about her was fabulous. I straight turned her ass out, but she also fed my ego, which was more important than anything else."

"Man. So why didn't you guys hook up?"

"It's all about the timing. I knew I wasn't ready to share my heart with someone, and I didn't want to do to her what had been done to me, so I told her everything that I had ever held in."

"How did she take it?"

"She took it well—so well that we still occasionally hook up for some late-night aerobics."

"No way."

"She's really cool. She ultimately is the reason why I am what I am. I learned the game of love and intimacy from her."

"I'm impressed; you give props to the lady."

"There is no game without the lady. As much as I hate to admit it, think about it. If our ladies didn't want to cheat on us, they wouldn't. No matter what game cats were spitting, if she'd said no, then that would have been that. Once she says yes or gives us the sign that she's interested it's up to us to keep that attention spark"

"I see," I said, sitting back in my chair.

Rob saw my stare and realized where my mind was. "I know you still love her, Sean, but surely you have to see what I'm saying."

"I do. It's just hard to swallow, you know."

"Are you planning on seeing her when you go to New York?"

"I thought about it. You know, see where things stand."

"That's your heart talking, Sean, not your mind. You know where things stand. Do you know if she's seeing other people?"

"I don't know. I mean, it's a possibility," I said uneasily.

"Sean, you know I'm not trying to pry, but I've been down that same road you're contemplating now. Rachel is a very beautiful woman, who is back in New York in a new career where she is bound to meet a man who she may be attracted to. I'm not going to tell you not to follow your heart, but I am going to tell you to guard it, because only you can protect it."

"I understand, and thanks for looking out. You know, I've never talked to anyone about this before, much less gotten any advice."

"You're good people, Sean, and I can see that. You are successful and handsome, and a lot of women out here would die to have you."

"Well, if you wouldn't hog them all, maybe I could see that," I joked.

Our main course arrived, and the crab cakes were on point as usual. I was almost too stuffed for dessert. I said *almost*. As I was enjoying my mud pie, Rob just stared at me with a grin.

"What, man? Do I have chocolate on my face? What?"

"You know Carol's been checking you out."

"She has not."

"You know some of the ladies at work have expressed a keen desire to see what Mr. Sean Winslow is like outside the board-room."

"Whatever, man. Carol is married."

"That doesn't mean you can't look at the menu—and don't act like you didn't check out the menu when you and Rachel were married."

"That was different. I don't look at employees."

"You don't know what you're missing."

"Yes, I do: a lawsuit." I grinned.

"Point taken."

"Look, I know what you're saying, but to be honest I can't think about any other woman but Rachel. She's the woman I want. I did learn something from how I handled my relationship with Zara, and that's I didn't fight for what I wanted. I know that now."

"I hear you. If you don't mind my saying so again, Rachel is a very beautiful woman, and when I saw you guys together, you looked very happy. I hope things work out for you two."

"Thanks, Rob. I appreciate that. You know, you're all right, man."

"You're not too bad yourself, Sean. You're a cool boss to have."

"Not just a boss," I said, raising my glass.

"A friend," Rob said, raising his glass as well.

We finished our meal and said our good-byes. I took Tracy's CD and promised to check it out. I went home and relaxed in the Jacuzzi, thinking about my upcoming trip.

Zara

I was awakened from my sleep by the sound of my iPhone going off. I managed to glance over at the clock...3:00 a.m. This couldn't be good. Preparing to hear either Mikel's or Karl's voice on the phone, my heart stopped when I heard sobbing on the other end.

"Mom? What's wrong?"

"Zara." She struggled to get my name out. "It's your father. I'm at Jackson Memorial hospital in Miami, and he's...Kevin's dead..."

I couldn't move. I just held the phone, squeezing it tighter and tighter.

"Zara, I need you to come home. I need you to meet me in Miami. Zara, did you hear me?"

"Momma," I said, tears now flowing from my eyes. "Momma, did you just say Dad is dead?"

"Zara, I am so sorry, baby. I can't explain it now. It's all happening so fast. Please, baby, I need you to come home," she pleaded.

Before I could even collapse into a heap of emotions, I heard the devastation in my mother's voice and realized she was in even worse straits than I was. She was in Miami and didn't have anyone there for her. I took the information and hung up. After I called Karl, he sent a driver over to take me to the company jet. It probably took less than an hour to become airborne, but everything seemed to be going in slow motion.

It seemed like days before the plane touched down at Miami International. I made it to the hospital chapel where my mom had told me she would be. I opened the door and saw her sitting in the front pew. Every step I took seemed to take a super human effort. *What would I say to her?* I knew I would have to be strong. She needed me. All the while I couldn't help but remember the way Sean's mother had been affected by the passing of Mr. Winslow. I stood beside her and gazed at a woman who looked as if she hadn't slept in days. Her boarding pass was still clipped to her jacket. I knelt in front of her. "I'm here, Momma. I'm here."

She opened her eyes and looked at me. All she could do was shake her head. Tears began to run down her face as she reached out to me. We hugged, and I held my mom as she cried on my shoulder. I tried to hold back my tears, but I couldn't control my emotions. I began to cry too.

"What happened, Mom? Why did he die?"

She shook her head and pulled away from me. She stood and walked to the front of the altar. "They think it was a heart attack. We had just gotten back from parasailing. We had always talked about doing it but never had. It was breathtaking. Kevin looked fine. He was laughing and whooping up a storm. When we got back to the ship, he said he felt dizzy and wanted to lie down for a minute. When I went in to check up on him, I couldn't stir him." She began to cry. "I couldn't wake him."

I wrapped my arm around her shoulder, and once more her emotions overflowed.

"Zara, I felt so helpless. All I could do was call out for help."

"It's nothing you did, Mom," I said reassuringly. "There was nothing you could've done."

"We should never have done that damn trip. Gallivanting all over the place, we had no business parasailing like some young, energetic kids."

"Mom, you can't blame yourself for this. You and Dad were doing what you loved. You worked hard all of your lives and this was your time to enjoy each other, and even if he did die after parasailing, at least he died doing something fun and died with the one he loved. Not at some job, not alone and unloved."

She looked at me and rubbed my tear-stained face. "You are so beautiful; you have so much of your father in you. You always know how to take charge of a situation," she said with a weary smile.

"Hey I got that from you as well," I said, smiling back. "I'm proud to be your daughter, and we will get through this together. Where is he?"

"He's down in the morgue."

"Can I see him?"

She nodded. She led me out of the chapel and down to the morgue.

When they pulled back the sheet, I was struck with how at peace my dad looked. He looked as if he had just slipped into a gentle sleep. I touched his forehead. He was so cold. My mother held my hand and began to cry. I said the Lord's Prayer and kissed him on the forehead. We went back upstairs, and I was fortunate to meet one of the attending doctors who had worked on my father. He was almost certain my father had suffered a major heart attack. They were able to get a pulse back on the ship and had even kept him alive on the helicopter ride back to Miami. He had died in the emergency room, though. I thanked the doctor and made arrangements to have my father's body flown to his hometown of Macon, Georgia.

My mother and I flew back to Atlanta together. Arriving at my parents' house seemed surreal. Everything was quiet. The house seemed empty and cold already. I put my things on the coffee table in the living room. My mother quietly slipped into her bedroom. I went into the kitchen to get a drink of water. I stared at the picture magnet on the refrigerator of us together at Christmas. I closed my eyes and sobbed. Gaining my composure I poured my mom a glass of water and went toward her bedroom. She was lying on the bed, clutching a wedding album. She had cried herself to sleep. I placed the water on the bedside table and slid her shoes off. Feeling helpless, I crawled into bed behind her, wrapped my arm around her, and fell asleep.

Alanya

"Lani! Hey, wait up."

I turned and saw Mia running up the street toward me. "Hey, Mia, I thought you were leaving today."

"No. I still have some unfinished business to deal with for Jazz."

"I see. So how are things going for you two?"

"Wonderful, as always," she gushed. "How are things going between you and Ava?"

"Things are going okay." I sighed as I turned and continued to walk down the sidewalk.

"Well, that didn't sound like the usual 'We are so happy!' reaction I normally get."

"It's not that I'm not happy, but after visiting my family last week, I was reminded of how much I want a traditional family."

"Lani, what's a traditional family?"

"You know: a husband and wife, two kids—a boy and a girl—house with a white picket fence, and a dog."

Mia laughed. "Other than the husband, why can't you have a traditional family?"

"Well, I need the husband."

"Says who?'

"Says tradition."

"You know there are some traditions that have been outdated for far too long. You can be happy if you want to. It's funny, because Jazz and I have openly discussed becoming a family."

"I know, and I look at you for inspiration. I mean, how do you do it even when a lot of mainstream society is still reluctant to recognize your union?"

"We believe in perseverance. Our love will not diminish because of people's perception of tradition."

I didn't know how to take her comment. Maybe I had offended her with my comment on tradition.

She saw my look of uncertainty. "Lani, I didn't mean that for you, but I'm really sensing that you are rethinking your identity and orientation."

"I love Ava, I really do. She has been nothing but wonderful, but part of me feels as if I have to stay with her. She moved up here to be with me, and she's been supportive of both my schoolwork and my life,

I don't want to seem like a hypocrite now, but why am I feeling like there is still something missing?"

"I told you before, Lani, it's not easy to change the only way of life you have ever known. I wanted you to experience life and see the joys and pains we all go through, and in the process you met Ava, and she was someone you needed at the time. Now I think you are ready to love that special man who will capture your heart."

"Mia, what are you saying?"

"I am saying you need to have a talk with Ava and tell her exactly how you feel."

"I don't really know how I feel."

"Yes you do, Lani. You and Ava have great chemistry and you care for each other, but you don't share that connection that will keep you, nourish you, and enable you two to grow your union and bond."

"Are you my counselor as well as my best friend?" I asked, laughing.

"Hey, I remember how you felt last year when you caught man-child cheating on you, I know how hurt feels, and I know you deserve to be happy, even if it's with a man." She laughed.

I laughed too, but I began to have thoughts of seeing Corey in bed with his little freak. I remembered her smile.

"Hey, don't go back to that time now," Mia said, grabbing my arm. "Remember, that's behind you, right?"

"It is, but do you really think I could ever find that love with a man? I can't see myself trusting a man again."

"That's still the hurt in your heart talking, Lani. It would be the same if Ava were to hurt you."

"I don't know, Mia," I said, stopping once more. "Would you give Jazz another chance if she betrayed you?"

"It depends on the betrayal and if she was sincere in feeling remorse for her actions and willing to work at repairing our trust. I've loved Jazz for five years now, and I really can't see myself with anyone but her."

"I was beginning to feel that way about Corey, and look at what happened to us."

"Key point Lani, you were on that level, and he wasn't. Besides, you were more mature than Corey. Lani, you were going to school and Corey's immature ass was still working a dead-end job. He was content to stay in the position he was in, and play video games all day. I think you would have realized that and ended the relationship yourself."

"You think so? I mean, I don't know."

"I know, and I know the desire you have to succeed. How many times did I have to drag you out with us, just to take a break from your books? It was always school, and then you got sidetracked with him, and the rest is, like I said, in the past."

"I'm glad it is."

"Listen, just take your time and really talk with Ava. The sooner you do, the sooner she will be able to understand and accept your feelings. If she really cares for you, she will see your honesty and respect your decision."

"She returns from Barbados next Friday. I'll let her get settled and maybe we'll talk sometime next weekend."

"That sounds good. I am so glad you two decided to keep separate apartments. In the meantime, how about we do a little shopping at Brioni?"

How could I say no to that? I laughed. "To midtown!"

Rachel

My Bluetooth went off in my car. I looked at the caller ID and let out a sigh. *Let me hear the excuse this time.*

"Hello?"

"Hey, sexy, where are you?"

"On my way home...Where are you?"

"Here in Queens with some of my boys. Listen, about tonight..."

"Save it, Tony. I already know you're not coming."

"Come on, Shorty, you know I want to see you tonight."

"So what's stopping you this time...your boys?"

"No, it's not like that. Carter's little cousin is here visiting and he's debating what school to attend next fall. His stock went up after this AAU summer camp, and I am trying to persuade him to come to Syracuse."

"I thought you were going to say Columbia." I laughed.

"No, I'm not trying to take Coach's job," he said, laughing, "but my boy David is one of the assistants at Syracuse, and I know they will give Marcus playing time his freshman year."

"I guess I can understand that." I sighed.

"Hey, how about we meet tomorrow at Nick's for dinner?"

"Nick's? Wow. I haven't been there in a while."

"I know." He laughed. "I think it would be cool, you know—kinda rekindle those good memories."

"I don't think all of those memories were good," I reminded him.

"That's right. I forgot about Mr. Straight and Narrow."

"Tony, please don't."

"Okay, okay, I won't talk about baby daddy like that, but hey, for me Nick's will always be our place. So what do you say—unless you're afraid of ghosts."

"I'm not afraid of ghosts," I said, laughing. "I just want to know if you'll really show up."

"Of course I'm going to show. We work tomorrow, remember? My niece is taking Devin to the mall so we can meet up with them afterwards."

"What, no personal counseling sessions tomorrow with your little admirers?"

"Are you jealous?" He laughed.

"Jealous of whom—some young-ass, immature girls away from home for the first time? Hell, no."

"Trust me, those girls can't do half the shit you do."

"Okay, so now you're making me sound like a ho."

"No, Shorty, not like that."

"Please stop calling me Shorty."

"Damn, Rachel, what's wrong with you?"

"Nothing. I just don't want to be called by the same pet name you use for everyone else."

"Rachel, I was just…"

"Listen, my mom's on the other line," I lied. "I'll see you at work tomorrow." We hung up the phone and I pondered my decision to leave Sean for this again. I thought about Nick's and how it had hurt Sean when he had found out about Tony the first time. I just happened to look down and saw the card my mom gave me the other day sitting in the ashtray. *Maybe now isn't the right time after all, Dr. Solomon.*

Sean

Okay, so now I remember why I didn't miss the commute out of New York when I moved to D.C., especially in bad weather. Traffic was horrible trying to make it into the Bronx. My business meeting had wrapped up rather quickly, as I had anticipated. As long as you're keeping rich people rich and have ways of making them richer, they pretty much agree with everything you have to say and let you keep steering the ship. I had tried to call Rachel on her cell phone, but apparently she had turned it off. Her home phone proved to be useless as well, since the machine picked up both times I tried. I figured she probably had Devin over at her parents' house or just hadn't made it home yet.

I had not seen her parents in almost two years, and I didn't even know how they had taken the news of our divorce. Still feeling nervous about how I would approach Rachel, I figured I should at least drop by to say hi to her folks. They lived in Williams Bridge, and it wasn't long before I started thinking about the times I would drive up with Rachel. Then I remembered the first time they saw Devin. How proud they were of her and how Rachel seemed so happy to be with me.

As I pulled into the driveway, my stomach was suddenly full of butterflies. It was still a cozy house. Mrs. Stanley was looking out the window, and when she saw me approach, she disappeared, only to reappear at the door moments later. She seemed both startled and happy to see me. "Well, isn't this a surprise."

"How are you doing, Mrs. Stanley?" I said as I gave her a hug.

"I'm doing good, Sean. You are still tall as a tree, I see."

"A tree that has bad roots for knees," I joked.

She laughed and invited me into the house, which was filled with the heat and aroma of another wonderful meal in the kitchen. I could smell the chicken, onions, garlic, and rice. Suddenly I felt hunger pains in my stomach. It had been a long time since I had enjoyed a traditional Thai meal.

"Is that my favorite Khao man gai? I see you still throw down in the kitchen, Mrs. Stanley."

"I see your pronunciation is still very good as well Sean. Yes it is and you are welcome to stay for dinner. The boys are away. It's just me and Gerald."

"I may just have to move back up here so I can help Mr. Stanley out."

"You are still the charmer, I see." Mrs. Stanley grinned.

"And you're still the greatest cook in the world; just don't let my mom know."

"It'll be our secret. So what brings you up to New York in this weather?"

"Well, I actually came up on a business trip. It wrapped up early, so I was hoping to catch Rachel."

"Oh, I see. Does Rachel know you're here?"

"No ma'am, she doesn't."

All of a sudden I felt a nervous, uneasy feeling creeping inside my gut, as though I had committed a crime and was waiting to be caught. Mrs. Stanley stood up and paced the floor. She was rubbing her hands. She stopped in front of me. I looked up at her and she smiled. "It's been a while since I've seen you, Sean."

"Yes, ma'am, it has been a while. I didn't know how you felt about me after Rachel moved back to New York."

"Oh, don't be silly. You'll always be welcome here."

"Thank you, Mrs. Stanley. It's nice to know you feel that way."

"So how are things between you and Rachel?"

"They are okay," I said, shifting positions on the sofa.

"When was the last time you saw her?"

"Actually I haven't seen her since Christmas."

"And things are okay?"

"Okay for now. Rachel told me she enjoys teaching and spending time with Devin. We haven't really had a chance to discuss anything else."

"I see," Mrs. Stanley said, nodding. "So are you okay with this situation and all?"

"To be honest, Mrs. Stanley, no, I'm not. I never should have let Rachel leave Maryland. I miss her, and I want her back."

"You still love Rachel, don't you?"

"With all my heart. I haven't been on a date since we divorced, and I think of her constantly. I even still carry my ring on me. I know I can be the man for her, because she is the woman for me."

"Are you sure she's the one for you? I mean, what makes you so sure she's the one?"

The question stumped me. Coming from Rachel's mother of all people, it took me by surprise. I knew my mother had had her reservations about our relationship. I even knew and had faced Rachel's own doubts about her devotion to me. I had at least assumed her mother was in our corner.

"I'm not sure if I understand, Mrs. Stanley."

"I know that startled you, Sean. You are a very smart, kind, and loving man. I knew that when I first met you."

"Thank you, Mrs. Stanley, but I—"

"You are so different from any of the men Rachel ever allowed us to meet," she said, interrupting me. "The men before you were selfish, rude, and up to no good. None of them had real goals to make something of themselves, but you, you were different."

"Mrs. Stanley, I still don't understand…Rachel's past—"

"Rachel's past always seems to be her future," she interrupted again.

She walked over to the living room window and stared out at the snow. "We tried hard to give our kids what they needed and wanted: a good home, safe neighborhood, good values."

"You did, Mrs. Stanley. Rachel has always spoken fondly of everything you and Mr. Stanley did for her. She loves you."

"Somewhere along the way something happened; I guess we went wrong somewhere with ensuring she didn't just depend on her beauty to get anywhere, teaching Rachel confidence in herself, pride in being a woman, and decent morals."

"She has those attributes," I said reassuringly. "She is smart I mean she's even teaching again. Rachel is a terrific mother and she was a good wife."

"Sean, you don't have to defend her. We had hoped when you two were married that the madness would be over, and when she had Devin, we thought she was finally over her sickness, but when you guys divorced, we knew it wasn't over."

"Madness, what sickness are you talking about Mrs. Stanley?"

"Rachel has a narcissistic personality disorder."

"Rachel has narcissistic personality disorder?"

"Yes, you see Rachel craves constant attention from men, and it doesn't matter if these men mean her well or not. All she knows is that she wants to feel desirable and constantly admired."

"Wow," I said, rehashing the past seven years of my life.

Her mother sat down beside me on the sofa once more and took my hand. "I don't know everything that happened in your marriage, but what broke up your marriage is something Gerald and I thought she was over. I'm sorry, Sean."

"How do you know she's still dealing with this? How do you even know it is a narcissistic personality?"

"Before you, Gerald and I used to get phone calls from boyfriends or men who were upset that Rachel had cheated on them. We had no idea how promiscuous she was. She was quiet, shy, and reserved around us."

"I thought that was her personality. She was always very timid around me as well."

"Well, after we had had enough phone calls, Gerald talked to a therapist about her problems and brought back all this information on narcissistic personality disorder, and it fit her personality to a T."

"Did you talk to Rachel?"

"We tried, but Rachel just dispelled it as nonsense. She always blamed the guy."

"I don't know what to say."

"I'm sorry you had to hear this, Sean, much less live through it, but I think Rachel is no closer to being over this now than she was ten years ago."

"So what am I supposed to do Mrs. Stanley? Do I turn my heart away from her or should I try to help her through it?"

"I can't tell you that, Sean. We love Rachel, and we have tried to get her help. She is a grown highly educated woman, and you can't force her. You have to do what's best for your life. We won't resent you either way. I know you've tried to give Rachel a good life, and it is more evident with you being here today. For that I will always be thankful to you."

"Mrs. Stanley, where is Rachel now?"

She sighed and stood once more. She walked to the window. I stood up and put my coat on, waiting for the information.

"Rachel is at Nick's Pizza in Queens. You remember that place, right?"

Hearing her say Nick's in Queens sent my blood pressure up. I would never forget that place. Since Mrs. Stanley said it, I knew Rachel had told her what had happened there years ago.

"I remember. It was nice seeing you again, Mrs. Stanley, and thanks…thanks for everything."

"Promise me you won't make any trouble," she demanded. "You are a businessman, and you've got too much going for you to throw it away on some punk."

"I promise, no trouble," I said, kissing her on the cheek.

I hurried out of the house and to my car. As I sped off, my mind was working at a hundred miles an hour. I thought about Rachel and our marriage, all the arguments, the deception, and now this. I made it to Queens and parked on Ascan Avenue. As I walked toward Nick's, I began praying that I wouldn't find what I knew I would. I hoped it was just a coincidence, but Mrs. Stanley's words burned in my brain like hot coals. *Rachel's past always seems to be her future.* It felt like déjà vu as I approached the restaurant. The snow had begun to fall once more, and there was little activity on the streets. Nick's was not very busy either. There were only a few people inside.

As I looked into the window, I stopped dead in my tracks. Seated in a booth facing the street, sharing a slice of pizza, was the woman I wanted back and the man who had destroyed us in the beginning. Rachel looked happy with him. I wanted to go inside but couldn't bring myself to move. She was so sexy, and she was smiling as if he were promising her the world. I felt stupid about the whole idea of our getting back together. As the snow fell, so did my emotions for Rachel, and then I guess she felt someone looking at her. She turned and looked out at me. Our eyes met, and Rachel sat frozen as if she had just seen a ghost. Tony looked at her and then looked at me. I stopped glaring at Rachel and glared at Tony instead. He looked down at his tray and then back to Rachel. I turned and started back to my car.

Rachel hastily got out of her seat and made her way outside. "Sean, wait!" she shouted.

I wanted to stop, but again something inside me controlled my actions, and I continued walking. Rachel caught up to me and grabbed my arm. "Sean, please don't do this."

"*Me* do this?" I shouted. "You've got a lot of nerve."

"Sean, let me explain, please."

"What the hell is there to explain, Rachel? We're divorced and you're sharing pizza in the same fucking spot with the same fucking guy who helped destroy us in the first place."

"What are you doing here anyway? Are you spying on me again?"

"Please don't try to turn this around. Actually, I came up here to make what would have been the third-biggest mistake of my life."

"What mistake are you making, Sean?"

"I came back to ask you to be my wife again."

Rachel's expression turned from shock and fear to soft and surprised. She let go of my arm. "Are you serious, Sean? Why?"

"Because I'm an idiot who thinks with his heart," I blasted. "Because I love you and I thought that you still loved me and that maybe, just maybe, we could work things out."

"I don't know what to say, Sean."

"Oh, don't worry: you've said it loud and clear. It took me almost seven years to hear it, but it's crystal clear now."

"For seven months, Sean, I—"

"For seven months, Rachel, I never stopped thinking about you," I interrupted. "Seven months and no other women have been on my mind because of my love for you. Seven months and I've never touched, kissed, or made love to any other woman because of you."

"You've felt like that for all this time?"

"I told you it never left my heart. I told you the night you left that I will always love you, and for the past seven months I've still carried this shit around, hoping to one day wear it again. Well, I guess that won't happen now, will it?" I pulled the ring out of my pocket and tossed it to her. It fell at her feet. Rachel knelt and picked it up. She stared at the ring and then looked at me. "I didn't mean shit to you, huh?"

"No, Sean, you do mean a lot to me—more than I can say," she said, tears swelling in her eyes.

"Bullshit!" I yelled. "I guess I'm not one of the lucky ones who can cater to your narcissistic cravings."

"That's not fair, Sean."

"Whatever. Your mother is right, you need help."

"You talked to my mother?" she said, surprised. "I know you didn't bring her into this."

"Please, Rachel; your mother is the one who shed light on this for me. She said your past is your future, and damned if she wasn't right. So don't let me stop you."

As I said that, Tony came up. He was about five foot eleven with a medium build. He had on a big winter jacket, dark jeans, and Timberlands. He studied my eyes, trying to feel the situation and whether he should prepare to defend himself. He was carrying Rachel's jacket.

"Is everything okay, Rachel?" he asked, looking at me.

"Rachel's fine. Take your ass back inside and finish your pizza."

"I'm not talking to you, Sean."

"It's nice that you remember my name. I see you still remember my wife as well."

"Ex-wife, brother."

"You little punk mutha—"

"Sean, no!" Rachel said, stepping between us.

"Rachel, move," Tony said. "Obviously Mr. Winslow here wants to settle some things."

"In the worst way," I said, trying to push Rachel aside.

"Sean, Tony, please don't do this," Rachel pleaded.

As we stood in a face-off, seeing Rachel between Tony and me felt like a knife slowly inching its way through my heart. Then I remembered what Rob had said in the restaurant. *Only you can protect your heart.*

"You know, this shit isn't worth it," I said, looking at Rachel. Then I looked at Tony. "Who knows, maybe I'll see both of you on an album cover one day."

"Oh, I put that on the shelf for now, it's not about street dreams anymore."

"Really, so tell me what are you doing with yourself these days, Tony?"

"Actually, I went back to school and got my degree in physical training."

"Physical training, I'm impressed," I said, amused. "So do you use what you've learned or do you just walk around juiced on creatine all day?"

"Oh trust me, I use it every day and night," he said, smiling as he took a gaze at Rachel. "I teach physical education and I'm an assistant coach for the men's basketball team."

"Tony, don't do this now, please," Rachel begged.

Hearing Rachel's pleas sent goose bumps down my arm. "So where do you coach, Tony?" I asked, looking at Rachel.

"Columbia. Oh, I thought you knew," Tony said, smiling.

"Knew what?"

"Tony," Rachel pleaded.

"I've been at Columbia for two years now. Hell, I even persuaded Rachel to leave your punk ass and resume her career and teach there."

Rachel slowly managed to look me in the eye. What strong resolve I had to win this battle had just been blown up. I was now defeated and embarrassed in the face of my enemy. Everything fell into place now: her decision to return to New York, her decision to teach again, but more important, her connection for a job had been revealed to me.

"All the time we were married, supposedly trying to let the past go. Something you professed that I didn't do, and you still were in contact with him? All this shit I went through for you because of him. Is this the so called friend willing to help get you on at Columbia?"

Once again Rachel's face went to the ground, unable to admit her guilt. Unlike before, I now knew what the true answer was. Tony put her coat over her shoulders and moved beside her. He placed his arm around her and looked at me in triumph.

"You know what? Don't answer, Rachel. I told you, I hear you loud and clear now." I turned and began to walk towards my car. Rachel made a noise as if to speak out but then became silent. I knew Tony had pulled her arm to hold her in place. I waited until Nick's was long gone in my rearview mirror before I let out my anger and hurt on the steering wheel. *How could I have been such a fool?*

My cell phone rang a short time later. The caller ID read Rachel's cell. I let voice mail pick up. Rob had been so right to not let his heart go back. From that moment until I arrived back at the hotel, every song on the radio was a slow, depressing love song. I didn't want to stay in New York for another minute. I packed my bags and headed to the airport. The snow had stopped falling, and I was hoping I could get a flight back to D.C.

Rachel

"C'mon, Rachel, what's your problem?" Tony quizzed. "You haven't said two words since Mr. High and Mighty left."

"Not now, Tony."

"Look, you tried calling the man twice and he didn't pick up. Don't tell me you're still catching feelings for him."

"It's not like that, but I wasn't trying to hurt him again either. You didn't have to gloat."

"You should have told his ass the truth from the jump, you know. You are a grown-ass woman, and if he can't accept the fact that you don't want him, then that's his own fault."

"It's not that simple. I was married to him for six years; we have a son together."

"Well, if it weren't for him stressing you out, you would have my son, too, you know."

"That's not fair, Tony."

"Isn't it? How many times did you guys argue over me and you, he was always stressing you out."

"How would you know? You never called me. You never gave me a clue that you really wanted to be with me. At least Sean showed me he cared about me."

"Okay, so now you're defending him? Look at what he just did. He tossed you his ring just like he tossed away your marriage."

"I'm not defending him, but I was wrong too, and you're right: I should have told him the truth."

"Well, why didn't you?"

"I don't know."

"You gotta know something."

"Damn it, Tony, let's just drop it."

"Hell no!" His tone was getting louder. "I'm not going to drop it. You belong to me now, and seeing you stand between us and you now standing here defending him is totally disrespecting me."

"I belong to you?" I asked in disbelief. I could feel my anger rising. "I am not your property, so let's get that straight. I did not want either of you getting hurt over some nonsense, that's all. I was not trying to disrespect anyone."

"Rachel, I'm not the enemy here. Lover boy started it by showing up in the first place. I was standing up for my woman. That's what I meant."

"So I'm your woman? Why not show that same conviction when you have your little throng of groupies hanging around?"

"What the hell is wrong with you? Why are you trying to turn shit around on me now?"

"I'm not trying to turn anything around, but maybe I finally see that I have held too much inside—things I should have said before."

"Wow. So now you want to get a conscience."

"What's that supposed to mean?" I asked.

"Nothing," Tony said, trying to backtrack. "Yeah, you're right. Let's drop it."

"No, let's not," I said, stepping in front of him. "What the fuck do you mean?"

"Hey, don't try to loud talk me out here," Tony said, looking around at the few people still walking in the snow.

"Tell me what you mean. You don't think I had a conscience before?"

"Those are your words, not mine."

"Well since you now want to be a punk about it and not say what you mean, I guess so."

"Oh, so I'm a punk now, huh?" he said, nodding. I could see his contempt growing by the second. "Okay, well, since you want to hear it...you didn't seem to have a conscience when you were fucking me while you were still married to him."

Never had I really felt physical abuse at the hands of a man, but Tony's words felt like a slap in my face. Suddenly I felt dirty and scandalous. "So what are you saying, Tony?"

"I'm saying that when you were telling me you were leaving Sean and contemplating coming back to New York, we were sleeping together—and going raw, I might add. But not once did you seem to care about him or his feelings; look at us, we are even working at the same school. Now big man finally grows some balls and turns the table on you and walks off, and you decide to get a conscience."

I couldn't hold back my anger. I reached out and slapped him. Tony's look scared me as I braced myself for his retaliation. He stepped toward me and stopped; the look of rage on his face dissipated, and he flashed an evil smile.

"You know when people react like that, it usually means that what you said to them is true and they can't stand to hear it."

I couldn't move. I just stared at him. His look of triumph over being able to bring me down another notch spoke to just how much I didn't know about him or myself.

"I'm right, aren't I? Even back when you were engaged to the man, you never thought about all the dirt you were doing. 'Cause you knew he was pussy whipped, and you didn't care about his feelings."

"I can't even begin to tell you how much I am regretting you right now."

"It's okay, Shorty," he said, smiling. "When you need some more good dick, you'll forgive me."

Almost as soon as he said those words, I felt like I was standing naked in front of him. I suddenly saw myself through Tony's eyes and the property that he actually saw as his.

"You think I'm with you for the sex?"

"Well, you surely left Moneybags because of it." He laughed.

"Not to burst your bubble, but our sex was not the reason why I left Sean. I didn't feel the same way about him as he did me, and I was tired of living a lie."

"Yeah, you keep telling yourself that, but your actions showed me different."

"Wow, those little girls have really gassed your ego up." I laughed, trying to regain some ground.

"Hey, they never left a husband for me."

"Fuck you, Tony," I said, feeling that ground give away underneath my feet.

"Oh, you have, and well," he heckled me.

"Just leave me alone." I turned and began to walk in the opposite direction, hiding the tears that had begun streaming down my face.

"I will, Shorty!" he shouted. "Tell Sean I'm done with it. He can have my leftovers!"

I turned the corner and tried to run, but lost my balance on the ice and slipped and fell. The only thing I could do was lie there and cry at the fool I had made of myself. All I could think about was Sean. How I wanted to tell him I was sorry. How I wanted to tell my parents they were right.

"Ma'am, are you okay?" a police officer asked as he helped me to my feet.

"I'm fine," I said, trying to hide my hurt and my tears.

"Are you sure?" he said, looking at my tear-stained face. "I can call for some help."

"No thanks," I said. "I need to call for my own help."

He looked at me puzzled as I walked off. I pulled my cell phone out once more and dialed Sean's number. I stopped short of placing the call. What did I want? What was I going to say to him? Did I want my marriage back? I reached in my purse once more and took out my old house key. If Sean didn't take or return my calls, maybe it was time for me to make a trip back to Maryland and my home.

Alanya

Was I crazy to think Mia was right about Ava and me? I had briefly let Ava know that we needed to talk, and I knew she had sensed my distance. As luck would have it, another business trip came up and she had to leave abruptly giving me only more time to ponder my situation. I mean, could I really find real love again with a man? It couldn't be that hard, but hell, let's face it: the pickings weren't as abundant as I had first thought. Surely there had to be a man out there with his shit together and who turned me on in every way. Would I be willing to take that chance again? And would I even know when to…

"Hey, Alanya…hot caramel is coming your way."

I looked up to see what had caught Gail's eye, and that's when my heart stopped. I had to give Gail credit on this one. This man was fine: not screaming thug passion fine like Gail normally likes. This brotha was a gentleman, a refined, well-groomed cultured appeal fine. Dressed in a long dark grey cashmere coat his caramel complexion seemed to illuminate the terminal. He was tall and bald with a thin, sexy goatee that had me glued to the sexy full lips it encased. I had just been thinking about it, and now this. Talk about divine intervention. I figured Gail would have moved a mountain to get him through her line, but before she could even make a move, he was in front of me.

"May I help you, sir?"

"One way to Washington, D.C., first class, please."

He placed his Maryland driver's license and platinum business card on the counter. I noted the Patek Philippe on his wrist. I read the card: De Stijl Marketing, Sean Winslow, President. Then I looked at his driver's license. Sean Winslow. Okay, so he's the president of his own company? Oh yeah, he's definitely spoken for. *Sean Winslow, who are you going home to?* He seemed a million miles away as I studied the nice silk tie underneath his coat.

"All right, let's see. Oh yes. You are in luck, sir; we have a flight leaving in two hours. I can still get you on that one if you like."

"Please. The sooner the better."

I could hear the hurt in his tone. It was like he had just lost the love of his life. I could relate to that tone. "Did you enjoy your stay in New York?"

"About as much as I enjoy the dentist," he said sarcastically.

He was definitely feeling hurt about something, but I also heard a little anger in his sarcasm. I glanced over and saw Gail looking at him with a stare that let you know she was in an erotic moment with Sean in her mind. I looked back at him, and for a split moment my mind was blocked by my desires.

"Well, we'll get you home, and hopefully that special someone will cheer you up," I said, smiling.

"That someone special is a bottle of Pyrat XO rum and a couple of Cohibas."

The comment caught me off guard. Could it be? No man goes home to enjoy a Cohiba and rum alone. Maybe this wasn't a business trip. There was only one way to find out. "Cohibas, now that's an excellent way to relax. A shame you have to enjoy them alone, Mr. Winslow," I said in my best sexy, make-love-to-me voice.

Then it happened. He caught on to my tone and looked up out of his thoughts. His dark brown eyes filled with intrigue and admiration, as if he were looking at a fantasy. I had gotten his attention, but even more, he had mine.

"Shall I cancel your flight for Wednesday, Mr. Winslow?"

"My what?" he stammered, distracted from staring at me.

"You have an original return flight for Wednesday; shall I cancel it for you now?"

"Yes, that's fine, you can cancel it, Alanya," he said, looking at my name tag. "You have a very beautiful name."

"Thank you," I said, smiling shyly. "No one has complimented me on my name before."

"Well, I guess your beauty takes all the compliments. By the time a man sees your name, it's irrelevant."

Okay, so either he's a playa or a dog. Which one is it? "That was pretty smooth, playa. Are you sure you're smoking those Cohibas alone?"

"I'm as serious as your beauty."

"Do you fly to New York often?"

"I will in the future, and I hope with better results," he said, smiling at me.

He had gotten my attention, and my curiosity was at a high I hadn't felt in a long time. Still, he was obviously in Maryland and probably had his hands full with women there. A little flirtation had helped stroke my ego, though, and at the least, maybe we would see each other again. I looked at his birth date on the screen. *Thirty-four.* Well, if his business was successful, maybe there was a chance I'd see him again. I wrote my cell number down on a yellow sticky note and put it on top of his boarding pass as it printed off.

"I think you will. When you come back and decide to share some Cohibas, give me a call."

With that I slid him his ticket. He took it and glanced at the sticky. He then looked at me with delight. I looked back at him and returned his smile. I had one more gesture for him before I finished his transaction—something I knew he didn't need me to do but just to let him know that I could. "There will be no charge for your first-class seat, Mr. Winslow. Terminal D, gate seven. Enjoy your flight."

"Thank you, Alanya," he said, surprised. "That was nice of you."

"Just promise you will keep me in mind for a Cohiba."

"Oh, most definitely." He winked. "It's a shame you are in New York and not Maryland."

Hearing him express such an interest in me made me feel warm inside. He was stroking my ego, and I suddenly felt warmth exuding somewhere else in my body. "Don't be surprised. I have friends who live in D.C."

"In that case, this phone call may come sooner than you think."

"I'd like that very much," I said, biting my bottom lip seductively.

"Well, I better get to my gate; it was nice meeting you, Alanya," he replied in a deep sexy voice.

"Likewise, Mr. Winslow."

I watched him walk down the terminal. He turned back a couple of times to look back at me. I couldn't help but fantasize about feeling his hands on my body and holding me. My dream was quickly interrupted when Gail gave me a nudge in the ribs. "Now, that brotha was fine," she chimed.

"Yeah, he was," I said, still staring in his direction.

"Think he's gonna call you?"

"Excuse me?" I stuttered.

"I saw you slip the yellow sticky on his boarding pass, Alanya. Hell, I would have done the same thing. He seemed to be very interested in you."

"I don't think so," I said to prepare myself in the event of disappointment. "He probably has women in every city he goes to."

"Well, sister, as fine as he was, I bet he's got the dick to keep 'em all satisfied," she moaned.

She skipped back over to her terminal, and for the next few minutes I thought about Sean Winslow. I finished work and stopped by the store to pick up a bottle of wine. I made it home and checked my messages. Ava had left me another message saying she was sorry she had to leave and that when she returned we would talk. She told me she loved me, and wanted me to give her a call. I deleted the message and stared at my cell phone. No messages or calls from Sean. Oh well. I guessed he had found someone to share those Cohibas with.

I drank half the bottle of wine and listened to my favorite Raheem Devaughn songs I decided that when Ava returned from her trip we would sit down and have the conversation that would officially close that chapter of my life. I knew it was going to be difficult, but after seeing Sean Winslow and experiencing those feelings again, I knew I needed more, and I knew that I was still feeling empty. Ava was great, but our chemistry was good for the moment, and at this point in my life, that just wasn't enough to sustain what I needed forever. I fell asleep imagining it was Sean Winslow singing to me instead of Raheem.

Sean

I spent all of Tuesday morning cleaning up the house. I removed all the pictures of Rachel and me together. I packed up all the clothes she had left behind and dropped them off at the Goodwill. I *wonder if Rob felt this liberated when he got rid of his wife's things.* I went to the mall afterwards and bought myself some new clothes and cologne. I guess I looked either like a man going through a midlife crisis or like I had just won the lottery. After my excursion to the mall, I returned home and tried on some of my new threads. I put on Tracy's demo and had to stop for a minute, because the girl actually sounded good. Her style was a little Joss Stone but mixed with Kaye-Ree's smooth soul sound. *I need to hook this girl up with a label.*

As I was checking myself out in the mirror, wondering if I still had it in me, I noticed the yellow sticky on the counter. I stared at it for a minute, and then I picked it up. "*It's time to start living.*" I dialed the number and waited. As the phone rang, I became nervous about what I would say. I was about to hang up when a sultry voice answered.

"Hello?"

"Alanya, hello, it's Sean. Sean Winslow," I said nervously.

"Hello, Sean. So did you make it home to your Cohibas?"

"As a matter of fact, I did." I laughed. "I didn't think you would remember me."

"Well, it's kind of hard to forget a tall, bald, handsome brother who loves Cohibas and Pyrat rum," she purred.

"It is nice to know you have excellent taste."

"The feeling is mutual. Actually I didn't think you would call me."

"Why is that?"

"A man like you, you probably are some kind of player in Washington, D.C. You probably are too busy trying to keep your game tight down there."

"Hardly. I am a recent divorcé, and I don't play games."

"Divorced? So what did you do?"

"No, it was the other way around."

"Are you sure it wasn't a case of who was caught first?"

"No, not at all. When I'm in a relationship, I am one hundred percent committed to that person."

"Ahh, a man with good taste and integrity. I'm impressed. So tell me, do you help old ladies across the street as well?"

"Hey, I even carry their groceries into the house for them."

We both laughed.

"So Mr. Winslow, when can I expect you back in New York for my Cohiba?"

"Well, right now I don't have any plans to come to New York. I was actually calling to find out your schedule."

"My schedule? Are you trying to fit me around your work, Mr. Winslow?"

"No, it's the opposite. I'm trying to fit into yours."

"I see. So what if I don't have any room?"

"Well, I'm pretty sure you could cancel some of your prior engagements for me."

"Oh my—confident, are we? I love confidence."

"It's one of the keys to success."

"And I take it you're used to being successful?"

"Let's just say failure is not an option for me."

"You know, you shouldn't be afraid of failure."

"I'm not afraid of failure. I'm afraid of not succeeding."

"I like that. So let's just say that I can free my schedule for this week up until Friday. When may I expect your arrival?"

As our conversation had progressed, so had my confidence—so much that my next statement came out before I even thought about it. "Not my arrival, but yours."

"My arrival?" she asked, puzzled.

"Yes, your arrival. I want to fly you down to D.C., tonight, if possible."

"Tonight?"

"Tonight."

The phone fell silent. I knew my invitation had caught her off guard. I could sense her contemplating her next move. I didn't want her insecurities about the unknown to outweigh her taking a chance on a little adventure.

"Alanya, are you still there?"

"Yes, I'm still here," she replied timidly.

"Look, I know this is coming out of the blue, but I find you very attractive and interesting. I just want to get to know you outside of your comfort zone, no hidden agendas."

"What if you are some kind of psycho—or I'm a psycho, for that matter?"

"I assure you I'm not, but if you need evidence, I'll give you the number to my office, and you can have my license and identification to give to a friend.'

"Why tonight? I mean, what's the rush?"

"There's no rush, but you have sparked my interest and I believe in no time like the present. Besides it's such a cool, crisp day in February, I figured we could warm this town up a little."

"I see. My, you are confident, aren't you?"

"Very. So is that a yes?"

"Let's just say I'm interested. How will I get there, and where would I stay?"

"Let me take care of the reservations. I will book you a flight around, say, eight o'clock tonight?"

"What about my living arrangements?"

"I will make reservations at a hotel in the city."

"Where will you stay?"

"I can either book a separate room for myself or go home. This is not a booty call. I want to get to know you and see what you're about."

"And what if I decide to come home with you?"

"Then that's your decision, Alanya. As you will see, I am a gentleman and at the very least you'll earn a good friend."

"You are a playa, but I am game though. We'll see if you show your colors."

"I'm not a player, and you will see that I'm just as I said: genuine."

"Very well then, Mr. Winslow."

"I'll make the plans and call you right back."

"I'm looking forward to it."

We exchanged good-byes, and I was set to make the plans. My heart was racing as though I were a seventeen-year-old boy going to the prom again. They had a plane landing in D.C. at 8:05 p.m., so I took it. I made hotel reservations at the Melrose in D.C. as well. I looked at my clock. It was 2:15. *I hope that gives her time to get situated,* I thought. I called her back with the information.

"Okay, so what are you planning to do with me when I arrive?" she asked in a seductive tone.

"Well, I was thinking dinner and maybe some sightseeing. Then we can chill out at a club or something."

"As long as the dinner is Italian. I'm not too sure about a club on Tuesday night, but hey, I'm game."

"Italian it is, and don't worry about the club scene: it will be cool."

"Okay, you're in charge. Just don't disappoint me."

"I don't plan on it. So you're sure you can stay out for a couple of days? I mean, I don't need a jealous boyfriend or husband chasing me down."

"I don't belong to anyone," she chimed. "And who said I would spend the entire time in D.C with you?"

"I don't know. I mean you might get caught up with my irresistible charm and want to stay."

"Is that so?"

"Very much. Seriously, though, thank you for agreeing to fit me into your schedule. I'm looking forward to meeting you again."

"Don't mention it. Well, Mr. Winslow…"

"Sean," I interjected.

"Sean, I guess I will see you in a couple of hours then."

"I am looking forward to it, Alanya. Until then."

"Until then."

We hung up the phone. "Yes!" I turned up the volume and danced down the hall. I called up a couple of business associates to set up the night. I wanted to make sure things went perfectly; after all, I hadn't been on a date in the past seven years. I wanted to make sure that this date would set Alanya off. If I couldn't spoil the woman I had been married to for six years, maybe finding someone worthy enough to spoil was just as good. Alanya was beautiful and the fact that she worked in an airport, unafraid to get her hands dirty let me know that she just didn't rely on her looks to get her places.

After I made the final arrangements for the night, I set off to get myself ready. I worked out at the gym and visited the barber to get my goatee edged up and my head shaved. Then I bought fresh flowers for Alanya and the house. Just in case I got lucky, I changed all the sheets and linens and cleaned up the bathroom. I then took a long bath and threw on a new pair of slacks and a sweater I had bought earlier. I left the house and drove to the airport a full hour before Alanya's arrival time.

Rachel

The night had seemed to drag on for an eternity, as I was unable to fall asleep. So many thoughts were racing through my mind. All the mistakes of my past; potentially losing the one man that I finally realized that I could honestly be happy with forever. I was furious at my mom for even telling Sean where I was, but deep down I knew that I had only myself to blame. He wouldn't take my calls, and the only message I had was one from Tony begging for forgiveness and then asking me if I missed his dick yet. The thought of having to see him at work sickened me. I needed to see Sean. Why did he still have his ring? Had he truly loved me through everything I had done and put him through? I needed to see him in person. I was ready to tell him everything that I had hidden from him. I wanted to give him my heart. If Sean didn't return any of my calls, it was time to take action. Show him that I can make plans for us, and show him that I truly wanted to work at our marriage again. As soon as daybreak came, I called my mom and explained the situation and what my plans were. I made my way over to my mom's house with Devin. As he went upstairs with my father, my mother ushered me into the living room.

"Rachel, are you sure you want to do this?"

"I am, Mom. I have to know how Sean feels about me."

"Well, how do you feel about him?"

"I love Sean. I've tried to tell you that before. I know my actions may have shown otherwise, and I know that I forced his hand to give me a divorce, but maybe it took me seeing his hurt and seeing my mistakes up close to make me realize that I do need him, and that I am ready to give my heart to him."

"I am glad that you feel this way, but I have to ask you, what if he has had enough?"

"That's a chance I am willing to take, but I know that if we can sit down and I show him that I do want to change and work for us for real this time, maybe I can win him back."

"Rachel, I don't want to see you hurt."

"I know you don't, but Sean told me before I left that he would always love me, and I believe he still does."

"Seeing you with that scum at Nick's may have hurt far too much, though."

"Again, Mom, that's a chance I have to take. I want my man back, and I want us to be a family again, and I have to believe that even through his hurt and anger Sean wants that as well."

"I am praying for you, and I hope you are able to get your family back. Whatever you need, Gerald and I are here for you."

"Thanks, Mom; it means a lot. You never left my corner through all the crap I put you through. I just want to say thank you."

"Rachel, you are my daughter, and somehow a part of me feels as if I let you down somewhere along the way," she said, tearing up. "I just want to make sure I never make that mistake with you again."

"Mom, you didn't make any mistake with me; it is I who let you down. Maybe if I had spoke up a little more, maybe if I had trusted in you, I would have seen the love you and Dad share and I would have wanted that type of connection instead of the one I sought from men."

We both started to cry and my mom gave me a hug. I felt renewed energy flow through my body, a sudden rush of excitement building in my heart. I needed to capitalize on my new understanding with my mother and show it to Sean.

"Okay, Mom. I gotta go. I'll call you as soon as I can."

"Okay, Rachel. Be safe and give Sean our love."

We said good-bye, and soon I was in the terminal awaiting my flight. Once we boarded, I couldn't help but reach into my purse and pull my house key out. I played different scenarios over and over in my head. How I would show Sean how sincere I was in wanting to be with him. How we would kiss and make passionate love, resealing our relationship. I imagined it all. This was going to be our new start.

As the taxi made its way up the drive to our house, I could tell Sean was not there. *All the better,* I thought to myself.

I wanted it this way. I wanted to surprise my man with something he had thought other men had coveted. I was going to show him how wrong he was and that tonight, that pedestal he had always desired was his amd only his. I was ready to be the freak in the sheets and the professor in the streets for one man. I paid the cabdriver, and for a brief moment I shuddered to think how crushed I would be if he had changed the locks. My confidence was restored when the knob turned and I found myself in the foyer looking up at the upstairs landing. I made it into the living room and noticed right away the absence of my pictures. With a frown I made it to the kitchen to retrieve a bottle of wine. Again my picture was gone. I knew Sean would be mad, but I hadn't thought he would get rid of my pictures so quickly. I took a long sip of wine and made my way upstairs. After observing the now empty walk-in closet that had been mine, I suddenly felt that maybe my plan B would definitely come into play.

I drew a hot bubble bath and soaked, not even realizing I was drinking an entire bottle of wine. I decided to put on my "ace in the hole" outfit. A sexy aqua blue see-through teddy with white thigh-high lace stockings. I pulled Sean's ring out of my pants pocket. Soon he would have all he needed and wanted from me. Now I was going to feed his desires until his brain and manhood were full.

"Come and get me, Sean!"

Alanya

We hung up the phone, and I let out a deep breath. Okay, girl, so here's your test. Can this man restore your faith in trust, love, passion, and romance with the opposite sex? If anyone could, I was sure it was this man. I hopped out of bed and took a shower. Then I went to my salon for my body pampering. I stopped at the mall and picked up a little lingerie from Fredrick's. Nothing wrong with Victoria's Secret, but I'm a more outspoken lady, and I wanted to make sure that if it did come to me and Sean being in that environment, he would not forget it. I also picked up several new bra and thong sets. I had things at home, but I didn't like to wear something I'd worn for someone else. Call it vanity but I wanted Sean to be the first to see me in it. That is, if he played his cards right.

The weather was cold but not cold enough to prevent me from getting out a pair of black, tight skinny-girl jeans that accentuated my curves. The nice black turtleneck I had bought at Brioni's the other week would definitely complement the black lace bra as well. I decided to wear my hair down. Black Alexander McQueen boots completed my outfit of seduction

I returned home and soaked in a warm milk-and-honey bath. While my body marinated in the love concoction, I fantasized about how the night would go. I just prayed that he could work it in the bedroom as well as he worked it in public. I arrived at the airport and waited for my flight. It always felt funny, waiting for a flight at the place I worked.

Sean had booked me a first-class seat to Reagan International Airport. I played scenarios over and over in my head of our pending date and time together. Soon I was going to be in the arms of my prince.

The flight was surprisingly full. An hour later we were landing, and at 7:58 p.m., we taxied into the gate. Although I departed the plane with the rest of the first-class passengers, I decided to let a couple of people pass me up. Not to make him sweat; I just didn't want to seem like the eager freak looking to get her ho on. We made it out into the terminal, and I spotted him first. He was turned around, looking at some children from the flight who were hugging what were probably grandparents. I too looked at the kids for a moment. I had always wondered what I would be like as a mother, having a family and visiting my parents for the holidays.

I had almost given up on those thoughts, but drawing my eyes back to Sean, I realized that maybe I could have those things one day. He must have felt my stare, and turned to face me. He seemed taller now that we were not separated by the counter. He really made a bald head look sexy. His size suggested he was in great shape. I almost melted when I saw the roses in his hand. *If this man is half this good in bed, then I'm in trouble.* I could tell by the way he studied me that he was equally impressed by my appearance. His look was hungry. We probably would have stood there all night staring at each other, but I needed more substance and wanted to feel his arms around me. I gave him a grin and walked over to him.

"Well, do I get a hug or not?"

"You surely do."

We hugged, and as we embraced, I cupped my arms under his, drawing his body closer to mine. No friendship hug would be felt tonight. Feeling the firmness of his chest and having to stand literally on my toes to grasp those broad shoulders, I felt safe in his arms. He smelled good, not overly powerful like some brothas who have no idea what "a splash" of cologne really means. He buried his face in my hair, and the longer we stood in our embrace, the more I wanted to feel every inch of him inside me. I could feel the moisture starting to build, but I also felt something rigid poking me in the stomach. I couldn't help but smile.

"Umm, I take it you approve," I whispered into his ear. "You and Sean Junior."

"Oh damn, my bad," he exclaimed, pulling away from me. I could see his embarrassment. "I'm sorry. I didn't mean for that to happen."

"Don't be sorry. You can't see my embarrassment."

"Is that so?"

"Yes. You are even more handsome than I remember, taller, and you smell good."

"Thank you. It's called Beyond Paradise, and you, my dear, are very beautiful and smell good enough to make a man insane."

"Well, thank you. The perfume is Angel...Beyond Paradise, huh? Well, take me to paradise first."

"It will be my pleasure. These are for you." He gave me the flowers—yellow roses. Very smooth on his part; you never want to give the color of love when you first meet. I closed my eyes and smelled them. There's something to be said about the effect flowers have on a woman. No matter what a man has done wrong, he can always start over by first giving flowers. Sean Winslow was batting a thousand so far.

I opened my eyes and looked at him as he was staring at me. I couldn't read his gaze. "What are you thinking about?"

"Nothing," he insisted. "I was just hoping that you like the roses."

"I do. Thank you very much."

I came closer and kissed him on the cheek. His strong jawbone was prominent, and I savored the smell of his cologne now on my lips. "So, Mr. Winslow, where shall we begin this little adventure of ours?"

"Well, I figured since we are in D.C., we could eat first and then take it from there."

"That sounds great. You know, with such short notice, a lady didn't have time to eat, and I'm starving."

"You're going to love this place."

"Is it Italian?"

"The best."

He carried my bag to his vehicle—a black Range Rover—and as a gentleman, he opened the door for me. I made it a point to have his door open before he made his way back around to the drivers side as well, a move I'm certain he took note of. Downtown D.C. was all bright lights as usual, and although the weather was nippy, people were out and about taking in the evening. We arrived at Café Milano's, which was packed. By the look of the crowd, I figured this place must have an awesome menu. The makeup of the patrons was reasonably mixed. You could tell from the wardrobes that there were some movers and shakers here.

As we walked through the restaurant and upstairs to the Wine Room, I couldn't help but feel a little proud to be with a man such as

Sean. I mean, he was older and thus far seemed to have all the qualities a woman looks for in a man. That in itself was a puzzle I still couldn't quite figure out. D.C. and Maryland have some of the most beautiful sistas in the world—women who have their own jobs and own money, but even still, they would be crazy not to try to hook up with someone like Sean. Why would a man waste time bringing me all the way down here? Was he looking for a notch to add to his belt, or was I something easy to conceal? I had always thought of myself as beautiful and a good catch, but I prided myself on not being arrogant. I also knew there were others just as beautiful and just as fine. All I had to do was think about Ava. She was beautiful, and she knew it. I had to leave my guard up. Mia always used to say that if it was too good to be true, then it probably was.

I tried to refocus on my date and politely smiled as the waiter finally showed us to our table. I removed my jacket, and Sean stood by as the waiter pulled out my chair. I looked up again at Sean. His stare now was an all too familiar guy stare—the kind where he just saw some ass he was thinking about tapping.

"Careful, Sean, you're close to being a pervert." I laughed.

"I'm sorry. I know you hear this a lot, but you, my dear, are fine as hell."

"Yes I do, and thank you. Not to sound conceited, but after a while it gets old."

"How so? I thought telling a woman how beautiful and attractive she is never got old."

"It loses its sincerity. Pretty soon guys are saying it just to see if it goes to your head. So they can get laid."

"I see," he said, amazed. "I never thought about it like that."

"That's okay. You're not a woman."

"That's true, and fortunately for you I'm not, because if I were, one of us would be coming out of the closet tonight."

I was caught off guard by his comment. If only he knew the truth—but then I felt myself get a little offended. Shit, if only he knew how great some same-sex relationships were. I kind of let out a halfhearted laugh just to let him know I was amused. *Okay, enough with the jokes, Mr. Winslow; I want to know how often you do this.* The waiter brought us bread and wine. I smiled and looked at Sean as he was looking at me. "So, do you fly ladies into town often, or do you just have them on standby at your destinations?"

"Hardly." He laughed. "This is a first for me. I've been divorced for seven months now, so I'm very new to the dating game, considering the fact that I was faithfully married for six years."

Married for six and divorced for only seven months? Why was I suddenly feeling like Annie Opportunity? "Well I certainly hope you're not using me as a rebound."

"Alanya, I would never do that to anyone. When I first saw you, I was genuinely struck by you and wanted to get to know you better. I am a "go-getter" and time is of the essence for me. There is no one else, and this is certainly no rebound date."

"So you say. And your disappointing trip to New York? Was that business or pleasure?"

That comment stumped Sean harder than his comment about lesbians had hit me. All of a sudden the brotha was a distant image of the confident man I had talked to on the phone. I didn't know what his trip was about, but obviously it was a source of his hurt. I felt a little guilty about my comment. After all, he had called me and then brought me to spend time with him. If I did stay the entire time here, I didn't want to spend it with this distance between us. I reached out and touched his hand. He looked up with his deep brown eyes.

"Sean, I'm sorry if I offended you. You don't have to share that with me if you don't want to. Actually, no one has ever flown me anywhere to meet them. I feel honored."

I smiled, and I guess he felt my sincerity, because his gaze seemed to lighten up and he smiled sweetly at me. He placed his hands on top of mine.

"I know you've heard it before, Alanya, but you are a very beautiful woman, that I am grateful to have the chance to get to know, and this is not a rebound affair. I hope you see my sincerity."

"I do," I said softly.

We sat and just held hands until the waiter came to take our order. We both decided on the Linguine Valentino. As we waited for our food, I got to know more about Sean. An only child from Atlanta, he was the proud son of a judge and a professor. I was impressed by his drive and ambition, having left an established company to strike out on his own. He was very vague about his marriage and divorce from his wife, Rachel. No woman likes to hear about a man's life with another woman, least of all one who had such a profound effect on him. I wasn't here to judge his past experiences, though. What I wanted to know was what his current situation looked like, and what his intentions were as far as me. Before I could even expound on any of his information, he flipped the script.

"So tell me about yourself, Alanya. Where are you from and what does your name mean?"

"Well, I'm originally from Turkey. I am part Turkish and part Egyptian. My father, who's Turkish, worked for the government in

Antalya, Turkey. My mother, who's Egyptian, was a nurse working at the American embassy. My name is from the place my parents met. It is a beautiful seaside resort in Turkey rivaled only by the French Riviera for beauty and scenery. As a child we would always go there for vacation. My father died when I was fourteen, and my mother met my stepdad when I was sixteen."

"Sorry to hear about your dad. I know how that affected me when I was twenty-five. I can only imagine what it must have been like for you at fourteen."

"It was very hard for me and my mother, but when my stepdad came into my mother's life, I felt better knowing she was not lonely anymore. He also welcomed me and loved me as if I were his flesh and blood daughter. I also got two stepbrothers out of the deal."

We both laughed.

"So no longer the only child, huh?"

"No, I'm not. My stepdad is a retired air force colonel."

"Oh, so he's American?"

"Yes. He's American, and he had two sons from a prior marriage. He was stationed in Izmir, Turkey. He met my mother when he came to Alanya for a vacation."

"Wow, so your parents met there and then your stepdad met your mom there as well. That must be one helluva vacation place," he said, laughing.

"Oh, it is. It is so beautiful and the people are so beautiful and the culture is beautiful. It's perfection. It's the perfect place to find love and romance. You should take a vacation there sometime."

"Only if you are m tour guide, Alanya."

"I'd love to go bac and see my home and show you where I grew up."

"Who knows, mayl the love bug will bite us there too," he said with a sexy look in his es.

"Anything is possil ," I responded with a sexy look of my own.

For minutes we jus tared at each other, not moving—just looking at each other and smil g. He gently caressed my hand.

"I'm sorry. Now, wl re were we?" I asked jokingly.

"We were planning trip to Alanya."

"Oh, is that where e were?"

"Yes, we were, but st I'd like to visit and explore the Alanya who has blessed me with h presence."

"Careful with that rip, Sean. Once you explore this Alanya, you won't want to leave."

"Trust me, the beau y Alanya is radiating right now I'm certain that I wouldn't leave."

"Is that right?"

"Yes." He was smoo h and suave. I could feel my body wanting to give him a magical tri o my love he would never forget.

"So your brothers do you see them?" he asked, changing the subject.

"I'm sorry."

"Do you see your stepbrothers?"

"Oh, yes," I stammered, regaining my composure. "As a matter of fact, we just recently had our family reunion. One of my brothers actually moved to the Netherlands where he works in the art industry, and my other brother is an emergency room doctor. He works in Boston. After we returned to the States, my folks moved to Connecticut. I left there five years ago when I got accepted into NYU."

"I'm impressed. So what are you majoring in?"

"I'm pursuing a career in journalism."

"Now, you would definitely give me a reason to watch the ten o'clock news."

We laughed.

"I always dreamed of being a broadcaster—you know reporting the news and being a face on television."

"So why NYU? I mean, why not attend UConn?"

"I don't know. I guess I just wanted to discover America, and New York was close to home but a good place to start, especially in journalism."

"I know your parents hated seeing their baby leaving."

"Well, I am still considered Daddy's little girl, and they offered to pay for my school, but I wanted to prove to them that I could make it on my own, so I'm doing this on my own—well, with the help of a partial scholarship, working part time at the airport, and some student loans that I'll be paying on until I'm a hundred." I laughed.

"Okay, so how old   e you?"

"How old do I lool "

"No way, baby girl.' Ie laughed. "I've been around long enough to decline that guessing g me. Either way my answer is not the right one."

"I'm twenty-four,"   said, smiling, and as I did, I could see Sean shift in his seat. It was   't an uncomfortable "*Oh-my-God-I'm-dating-my-daughter's friend*" shift,   ut it was an uneasy one nonetheless. I needed to deflect his thoughts gain.

"So, Sean, tell me a little more about you, any kids from your marriage?"

"I have a son, Devi ."

"How old is Devin:

"He's almost four.'

"No more kids? Ju Devin?"

"Just Devin. So are y u going to ask me?" he said with a grin of his own.

"Ask you what?"

"How old I am."

"Well, let's see," I s: d, pretending to really be concentrating, looking intently into his e s. "Hmm, well you graduated college, started and built your busine , marriage of six years, a child who's almost four, and a divorce...I say thirty-four."

"Wow, I'm impress 1," he said, stunned. "That's exactly right."

"Well, you know I have a pretty good feel for these things," I said confidently.

"I guess you do," he said, taking a sip of wine.

"Not to mention I got your birthday off your driver's license when you booked your ticket in New York."

Sean almost spit out his wine, he was laughing so hard. I cracked up right along with him.

"So that doesn't bother you?" he asked, wiping the wine from his lips.

"Not at all. I've never dated a guy in his thirties before, but you seem mature and not into playing mind games, and besides, you don't look your age."

"Thanks for the compliment, and don't worry, I don't play games. Just don't take out any big life-insurance policies on me just yet, okay?"

"So I guess you won't sign this, then, huh?" I said as I picked up a napkin and waved it at him as if it were an official document.

We laughed some more, and then our food arrived. As we ate, I couldn't help but notice Sean checking me out. Then again, I was checking him out as well. His table manners were top notch. I hate eating at a nice restaurant with a guy who has no table etiquette, especially when they have their elbows on the table and wolfing the food down as if they were tossing back French fries at McDonald's. From the way he ate you could tell he was used to dining in nice restaurants and had class. The meal was indeed the bomb. There is something to be said about a properly cooked lobster and linguine. I was stuffed, but a girl was taught to clean her plate. One of my personal rules is to never act like a light eater.

When we finished our main course, the waiter brought a dessert menu. Just looking at the pictures of so many sinful treats made me full. I shook my head, though. Besides, I was hoping to have my dessert later.

Sean looked at me. "No room for dessert? You have to try the L'Albicocca."

"No thanks, I'm stuffed."

"Okay, so how about we check out a club?'

"But it's a Tuesday night."

"Well, we won't have to worry about a big crowd, and besides, this club is only for two."

"Hey now, I haven't had that much wine," I teased, knowing full well I would have stripped for him right here if he had told me to.

"Woman, please," he said, smirking. "I told you I am a gentleman. Come on: live a little and check it out. You game?"

"I'm game."

"Cool. Let's do this."

Zara

The days had seemed to merge together ever since I had been awakened the previous week with the news of my father's death. Although I was trying my best to be there for my mom, I couldn't help myself. Every chance I got, I sneaked away and cried alone. Too afraid to add to her misery, her sorrow, I didn't know whom to turn to. For the first time in my life, I felt alone and helpless. Mikel tried to lend his ear and time, but it just didn't feel right. My mom and I almost became a bit hermit like, we didn't go out. My mom had lost her appetite, and I could tell she was weak. Most of our time was spent going through my father's effects, stopping to reminisce about certain events. Laughter would be followed by tears at the notion that he was gone. I knew I had to do something. I needed to feel myself mourn, feel myself loved by a man again.

I thought of Sean. We were sitting on my mother's bed looking at an old picture of our families together after Sean and I graduated. "Momma, have you talked to Mrs. Winslow?

"No, I haven't. I can't bring myself to call her."

"Why not, Momma? You two are like sisters."

"I don't know. She went through this with Todd. I know this will remind her of her own pain and loss."

"Momma, you can' —we can't—go through this alone. I think Mrs. Winslow would feel even worse if she knew you were going through this alone."

"I know you're right, Zara, but my mind can't begin to process how I'm going to tell her. There's still so much left to do."

"Don't worry about anything, Momma. I will take care of every-thing. In the meantime I need you to take care of yourself. Have you eaten anything yet?"

"No, baby, I'm fine," she said reassuringly. "I'm not hungry."

"You need your strength, Momma," I begged. "Please, at least eat some soup for me. Please?"

"Okay."

"Good. I'll be right back."

I went to the kitchen, warmed some soup, and added a slice of French bread and a cup of juice to a tray. By the time I made it back to her room, she had fallen asleep. I sat the tray down and went into the other bedroom, where I pulled out my cell phone. I was hoping to get Mrs. Winslow, but her voice mail said she was out of town on business.

"Mrs. Winslow, this is Zara," I said. "When you get this message, please call me or my mom back."

I didn't want to tell her via voice mail that my father had passed. I hoped she would call me back sooner rather than later. I scrolled my address list and came Sean's contact info. I put the number in and pressed Send. Before i started to dial, I heard my mother call out for me. I hung up the call and returned to her room.

"Is everything okay, Momma?"

"I saw him, Zara. I saw your father in my dreams. It was so real."

"What was he doing? Did he say anything?"

"No, he didn't say anything. I tried to call out to him, but all he did was stand and look at me and smile," she said in a quivering voice. "It was so real, I could feel him."

"He's looking down at you, Momma," I said, tears swelling in my eyes. "He sees you and he wants to let you know he's okay."

"I don't know if I'll ever be okay, Zara," she said, crying.

I went to her and we hugged.

"Momma, there's something I need to do."

"What's that, baby?"

"I need to tell Sean. I need to tell him face-to-face."

She looked at me and closed her eyes. She nodded. "You do what you have to. I will be fine."

"Momma, I am not leaving you until I know that things are taken care of and you are okay."

"I will be fine. If anything good can come from this, I hope it's your realizing just how precious life is."

Her words seemed to resonate in my mind for a minute. I was focused only on telling Sean about my loss and, I hoped, having a shoulder I badly needed to cry on. Now I saw what so many people had tried to force me to see so long ago. I had wasted ten years of my life without ever knowing if his love still existed or had been buried. I finally had the motivation I needed.

"Momma, I will take care of everything, and if it's okay, I'll go to Maryland on Thursday to see Sean."

"That's fine."

As soon as we had made our arrangements, the phone rang. It was Mrs. Winslow. "I'll call Sean as soon as we get off the phone and we'll be there for you," she said when I told her what had happened.

"No, Mrs. Winslow, please don't call Sean," I pleaded. "I need to see him in person."

"I understand," she said. "I'll return home tomorrow."

"That's great. I'll pick you up at the airport. My mom really could use the company."

"She will have that and more, Zara. Your family is my family, and you did so much for me when Todd passed away. The least I can do is be there for you in your time of mourning."

"I'll tell Mom the news. I can't wait to see you again."

"Same here, sweetheart. You take care of yourself."

Hanging up I felt a little relieved from the burden that had been placed on me, and yet I knew the biggest burden would not be lifted until I made peace with Sean.

Alanya

We left the restaurant and made our way to this place called Club Love. When Ava and I had come here to visit her friends, we went to Acropolis, and though Acropolis was nice, this club was decadent in every aspect: plush designer carpets, highly metropolitan contemporary huge oversized couches, and love seats were all around. Flat-panel screens at every turn. This was strictly a status club. We made our way through the club and Sean briefly introduced me to the owner, who had to have been a business partner or client of his. He wished us a good time, and we made our way to the elevator. I was having fantasies about kissing Sean in the elevator but decided to stay passive and allow him to continue leading the night. He was on point thus far. *No need to rock the boat,* I thought.

We made it to the VIP suite, and again I was in awe of the opulence. A huge flat-screen television complemented the art deco on the walls. A raging fireplace was warming the room, and a huge aquarium with exotic fish drew your attention to the lounge area. The window curtains were open, and there was a deck with what appeared to be another seating area outside. "With You" by Marsha Ambrosius was playing through the stereo. Sean took me by the hand and led me into the oversized lounge area. The lighting was seductively dimmed. There were vases filled with roses on the counter. A bucket holding a chilled bottle of Krug Brut was waiting to be poured, and a crystal bowl was filled with white and dark chocolate-covered strawberries. I was speechless.

"This is incredible," I sighed.

"Yes it is, and I don't know of anyone I'd rather be here with than you."

I looked at him and shook my head. "You are a player, but I'm not going to lie: your game is tight."

"I am not a player Alanya; I am just trying to share a beautiful night with a beautiful woman."

"And you mean to tell me that you don't have anyone else to share this with? If you're not a player, you must be a psycho or a wife beater."

"I'm none of the above," he said, laughing. "I am just a man who has had terrible luck with women."

"What do you make of your luck with me so far?"

"So far so good, but then, the night is still young."

"Yes it is, Mr. Winslow," I said as I poured us a glass of champagne.

I handed him the glass and then raised mine in a toast. "Here's to tonight."

"To tonight—oh, and please call me Sean. You make me feel old when you call me Mr. Winslow."

We toasted and I felt the tingling of the champagne bubbles dance around my tongue. I looked at Sean. I wanted to feel his tongue dancing with mine. All bets were off right at that moment. I needed him, I wanted him, and I was determined to show him just what I thought about him and his age. I came over to him and took his glass. I placed the glasses on the table and then I walked slowly back to where he was standing. I was so close, I could feel my nipples getting hard from the touch of his chest. The whole time I never took my eyes away from his gaze. He looked so damn fine. I wanted to feel those big hands all over my body and to hear him tell me how much he wanted me.

"You don't like it when I call you Mr. Winslow?" I asked seductively.

"Well, when you say it like that…," he said, looking down at my body. "When you say it like that, you can call me whatever you want."

"In that case," I said as I moved his face back into my eyes, "in that case, I'm calling you mine."

I leaned forward and stood on my tiptoes to kiss him. Sean wrapped his arms around me, and I could feel the strength this man had. He pulled my body strongly up into his. Our lips parted, and my tongue finally tasted the essence of a real man. The longer we kissed, the more I wanted him. Our tongues danced in a slow, passionate ritual. I could feel his lust, his desire; he wanted me just as badly as I wanted him. He dropped his arms from around my waist long enough to slide his hands down to my ass. They were so big, they made my ass feel small. He squeezed it and brought me closer into his body. I could feel my juices dripping down my legs. I felt his manhood pressing firmly on my stomach. It felt so good, all I could do was let out a moan. It had been so long since I had felt a real one that I wanted, and judging from the amount of space he was covering, I could tell he truly wanted to be deep inside me.

I couldn't help myself; the passion was building inside of me. All I wanted was to feel it. I dropped my arm down and pulled away just enough to place my hand on his stomach. Sean felt my intentions and relaxed his grip on me, and I slid my hand from his stomach and started to rub the outline of his dick. His breathing became heavier. I could tell he was enjoying my touch, but I was enjoying it a helluva lot more. His dick felt so good. He was blessed. All I could see was him inside me, working me the way I needed to be worked. I grabbed his dick and attempted to wrap my hand around it, which I couldn't, but my grip got to Sean, and he pulled away from me.

"I've never wanted anyone as badly as I do right now," he said, trying to catch his breath.

"And I've never wanted to feel someone inside me so badly."

"Alanya, I want you. I want to give all of myself to you.'

"I want all of you inside me," I said as he pulled me back into his arms.

"Your hotel is about ten minutes from here," he whispered in my ear as he gently kissed my neck, giving me goose bumps.

"No, not the hotel like I am just your date. I want to make love in your bed, like I'm your woman," I moaned, trying to resist creaming right there from his touch.

"I'd love to take you home. I want you to be my woman."

"Your woman just for tonight?"

"No, my woman forever, but are you sure you want this?"

Hearing him say these words took away any doubts about this being just a booty call. Not knowing if I would feel this way about a man again had been plaguing me and not knowing what I would do about Ava had been a huge cloud in my mind. Right now this handsome man was here in front of me, and for the first time in a long time, I knew what I wanted. There was something about the way he said things that just let me know he was sincere. I needed him. I once again found myself stroking his manhood.

"I've never been surer than I am right now."

We kissed again, and left the club. The ride back to his place seemed to take forever, but I wasn't complaining. There were no words spoken, just Will Downing playing on his radio. Sean looked at me constantly as he drove. We held hands, and I fantasized about being with him forever. Could every day be like this with him? Was this real love or lust? His smile and warm, strong hand seemed to reassure me that this was more than just lust for him. We made it to his house, and I was impressed by the size of his property. I guessed De Stijl was doing well. The front yard was huge, complete with a circular drive. He parked right out front and led me into a huge foyer with twin stairwells.

He took my hand and led me upstairs and down a wide hall to his bedroom. I was amazed by his neatness and decor. A huge wooden sleigh bed was in front of me. A fireplace was in the corner. Sean walked over and lit the fireplace. I was noting the big plasma television mounted on the wall when he turned me back to him. A simple gaze and once again his tongue was inside my mouth. His passion was even more intense than it had been at the club, and I could tell he didn't want to waste any time. *We can do a tour of the house tomorrow,* I thought. *Right now I wanted him to tour me.*

We were kissing in the middle of the room, and once again his hands found my ass and drew me into him. Unlike at the club, though, he bent just a little and hoisted me into the air. I wrapped my legs around his waist, completely submitting myself to his dominance. I wanted him to control me, use me tonight however he saw fit. Tonight I was his slave. I moaned; my clit was now swollen and pushing against the seam of my jeans. Sean moved us to the bed and gently laid me down. He ran his hands over my breasts, making my nipples hard. He then slid his hands under my sweater, and I felt the heat from his hands as they touched my bare skin. His touch felt good, and he seemed to relish the moment of being with me.

He cupped my breasts through my bra and lay on top of me. I felt his weight push me down into the bed as we kissed once again. It was getting hotter by the second, and the rest of my body needed Sean's attention. I broke away from our kiss and started to remove my sweater. Sean held my hair as my sweater went to the floor. Now my body felt the coolness of the air, and I felt the soft Egyptian sheets against my back as I lay down. Sean seemed in awe as he looked at my body, paying extra attention to my breasts. I guessed the black bra had been a good idea. His fingers traced one of my cups down to the pendant Ava had bought for me. He picked it up and looked at it, then back at me. He then started planting soft, gentle kisses down my neck and to my chest before making it to my navel. I felt his hands undo the button to my jeans, and my stomach erupted with butterflies. This was really happening. I mean, I knew this was what I wanted, but all of a sudden I became nervous about how my body and passion would react to our making love. He unzipped my jeans and I wiggled out of them. I was now just in my underwear, and he paused again in admiration. No man had been this close to me for quite a while.

"You have the body of a goddess," he said as he scanned me from head to toe. "I could worship this body forever."

His comments made my womanhood wet with desire. If there is anything to be said about feeding a woman's ego, it's that you can never underestimate it. I was set on fire again, and now there was only one way to find out just how well we would connect.

"And this goddess yearns for you to be inside her temple," I moaned.

With that Sean kissed my thighs and spread my legs. His breath and moist lips were driving me mad with desire. He then kissed my thong and placed his tongue right at the entrance to my womanhood. It took everything I had to not grab his head and use it as my own personal clit licker. I could tell my moans were getting louder, and my thong was soaked with my juices. I was moving my hips back and forward, allowing his tongue to part my lips slightly.

Sean could sense I was ready for more. He rose up and slid my thong down to my ankles and raised my legs to remove it. Before my legs touched the bed, he was back on top of me, kissing his way up to my chest. He removed the clasp on the front of my bra and let my breasts free. He chewed gently on my nipple and licked my entire breast, sending me once again closer to the edge. He looked at me lovingly as he kissed and sucked on my breast. His eyes were mesmerizing. I grabbed his arm and felt his muscles bulging. I closed my eyes, enjoying the sensations my body was feeling. Sean moved up to my neck and kissed it gently. He kissed my earlobe…

"I want to taste you. Can I taste you?" he begged.

"Yes." I sighed.

He kissed his way back down to my now overly sensitive pleasure box. He paused just for a second, causing me to look down at him to see what he was doing. Before I could say anything or even prepare myself, his tongue gently pushed back my curtains and entered my window to life. I closed my eyes and lay back down, breathing in deeply. I felt something similar to what I had felt when Ava had first gone down on me, but this was different. It felt stronger. I arched my back a little to tilt my pelvis. Sean's tongue seemed to know exactly what I was doing and exactly where to go. I put my hands on top of his head.

"Oh yes, that's perfect, Sean."

His touch was indeed perfect. Not that I had been with a lot of men, but the ones I had been with all had one flaw. They had no clue how to taste a woman. Either it was too hard and rough, like they were poking you with a finger, or it was too sloppy and most of their saliva would be on the bed instead of my juices. Not Sean. His touch was perfection. Not too hard and not too soft but with just the right amount of pressure to stimulate my desire. I could feel goose bumps rising on my arms, and tiny little electrical bolts started going off all over my body. Before I realized it, I was at a point where I had never been with a man. My lips now had a mind all their own, and the intensity of my pleasure bolts were growing. I squeezed his head. I knew I couldn't control this one. It had felt like this the very first time I had had an orgasm. I was losing control over my body, and I was afraid and excited at the same time.

I made a last feeble attempt to regain my composure. "Please stop. I want to feel you inside of me," I moaned.

My request fell on deaf ears, and I knew it was too late. Sean had sensed my weakness, and now he was really going to dominate my ass. He picked up on my moans and my reactions and knew I hadn't been at this point before, at least not with a man. All I could do was lie back and accept the fact that he had control over my body and my pleasure. My body reacted to his every lick, his every touch. His tongue was like a mind reader: every way I moved, he was there, building the pressure, building my satisfaction to the point where my body seemed to be in convulsions. He was there and so was my body. I knew I couldn't last any longer, and suddenly my mind was like a plane coming through the clouds. I could see the runway and I just needed Sean to keep it steady so I could come in for an earth-shattering landing.

"I can't control it, can't hold it any longer," I moaned. "Please don't stop. Right there. Yes, Sean, yes. I am going to…"

And that's all I got out before my body was rocked by wave after wave of unimaginable pleasure. Like being tickled by a thousand people, my body shook. I tried to get up, but Sean was intent on draining me of every last drop. He locked his arms around me, holding me down so I couldn't move. I tried to move his tongue, but he pinned my arms to my stomach and his licks continued, only faster and a little firmer. This just sent my body over the top. Even Ava hadn't brought me to the second level like this. My body shook, and I felt my juices squirt all over the bed.

Overcome by the rush of emotions and the feeling of euphoria, I couldn't help myself. I started to cry. Every part of me was sensitive to his touch. Even his breath sent me shivering. When Sean heard me crying, he stopped. I was too overcome to even let him know I was okay. I just lay there, trying to catch my breath. I felt Sean make his way up near my neck, and then I felt something like a hot piece of pipe near my womanhood. When I felt the circumference of his head push past my walls, I opened my eyes. Sean looked at me lovingly. I grasped his arms and braced myself as he slowly slipped his tongue into my mouth. I had only a moment to enjoy the taste of myself on his tongue before I felt pleasure once more erupt from my fortress as his knight slowly slipped inside of me.

I knew he was endowed, but the feeling was becoming too much to bear. He was teasing me, and it was too much for me, especially since I was still sensitive from his tasting session. I wanted to feel all of him at once. Not only because I wanted to feel him but because I wanted to take all of him in. I wanted to show him he wasn't the only one who could hold someone down. I wrapped my legs tightly around his waist and pushed his ass down, drawing his pride deeper inside me. I felt my womanhood gush from the sudden feeling of being stuffed.

If his oral skills were a prelude to him working his staff, I might cry all night, I thought. Once again our eyes met. His look of satisfaction was a welcomed sight. He felt so right inside me. I think we had both known our connection would be a good one, but never could I have imagined it would be this explosive so quickly. I was in heaven right then. A tear formed in my eye and slid down my face. I had my hands on his arms and he was stroking me slowly, working up a nice, slow pace. The deeper he went, the wetter I became. He was no novice. Sean could use what the Lord had blessed him with, and I was reaping the rewards. He paused for a second to pull his sweater over his head. I leaned up and marveled at his chiseled chest and a nice six-pack. He was cut. Looking at his body trapped me even more into his web. I kissed his chest and neck and pulled him down all the way into me and just held him there.

"Sean, you feel so good. This is yours for as long as you want it," I moaned.

Sean's reaction seemed to suggest he was going to take me up on my offer. He picked up his pace and became more forceful with his downward stroke. I tried to control him by squeezing him with my walls, but his stroke was too good. As soon as I tried to squeeze, my body was shaken by how deeply this brotha was inside me. Nervous butterflies danced in my stomach, overcome from the wave of pleasure flowing throughout my body. Again I gave up and just clung to Sean as he took us both through our paces. His stamina was incredible. After about twenty or so pun[ch]s, most guys were exploding all over the place. *If Corey could see this, he would truly know what I wanted.* Sean was defi-nitely a man's man. He was making love to my body and mind at the same time. Soon my moans became all-out screams as he was turning my body into his.

"Yes, Sean, it's yours. Tear it up, baby!" I screamed.

My body was once again an electron field. I could feel goose bumps on Sean as he picked up the pace at my request. He was tearing every wall of security down. He was at the bottom, he was at the top, he was everywhere. I prepared myself to cum when he did. I felt it would be at any moment. That moment wasn't to be—at least not then. Sean had maintained a pace at which most guys could get only a few strokes in before they either slowed the tempo or released themselves. My body and mind were in awe again. He looked at me with a look of conquest. He had turned me out and he knew it. I didn't care, though. My body was ready to explode once again. I dug my nails into his shoulders and arched my back as I climaxed. Again I squeezed Sean from inside, and again he would not let up.

Tears just started to flow. Sean slowed the pace and wiped my cheek. His look was passionate and loving. I looked at him, and at that moment I truly knew I could have everything I had ever wanted out of life and that I wanted to share my life with him—so much so that I was about to do something I had never let anyone dare do, even with protection.

"Sean, you are the best. Don't let me go. I want to feel you explode inside me."

Sean looked at me as if I had just given him the keys to the city. He slowed his pace even more and really stirred himself inside me. I felt his muscles start to tighten and knew he was coming closer to his climax. I could feel my own anticipation building. Knowing what was about to happen and that I was in control now fed my ego a little. I clutched him tightly. I kissed his neck and rubbed his back. His pumps became a little faster, and then I felt his manhood twitch inside of me. Suddenly I felt the warmth of his soul filling me, literally overflowing. He tried to get up, but I locked my legs around him and would not allow him to move. Feeling his eruptions caused my own body to respond by giving me another orgasm that was not nearly as strong as the first three, but just as gratifying.

For a brief moment I just held his body close to me, feeling the firmness subside. This was some kind of wonderful. I let my legs dangle on both sides, and Sean let out a long, deep breath and collapsed on me. I wiped his head, which was now covered with sweat, and kissed it tenderly, my heart taking in everything that had just happened between us.

"No one has ever made me feel the way you just did, Sean. Never have I felt something so strong, so wonderful, as I just felt with you."

He raised his head and looked into my eyes.

"Alanya, the feeling is mutual. You awakened something in me that I hadn't felt in a long time—something I thought was dead."

"Well, I hope that something is here to stay," I said, smiling.

"For as long as you want it."

"At this moment, I want it forever."

We smiled and kissed. I felt his nature stiffen inside me and moaned in approval. I wrapped my legs once more around his waist. Indeed, tonight was the first night of a new and wonderful life with Sean Winslow...

Rachel

Slowly I made my way back downstairs and sat on the couch. I looked down at my hands still trembling from shock. I couldn't believe what my own eyes had witnessed, and yet there he was, in the bed we used to share, in the house we lived in, making love to her. It had to be Zara. The way he made love to her was too passionate, too intense for a casual encounter. This woman was someone he cared about, someone who was so special, he had removed all of my things and the pictures of us together.

Only one woman could be all of that to him. How had they met up again? Had he reached out to her? I couldn't help but replay her screams of pleasure, the desire and satisfaction in her voice. *Hell no, this is* my *house!* I stood once more and took a step toward the stairs. I stopped short when I looked in the foyer mirror. I had literally forgotten I was wearing lingerie I had bought, waiting to pounce on him the minute he came through the door. Now I felt like a total idiot. Only hours earlier, I had arrived here to an empty house, looking for any sign that I even lived here. I knew he had been hurt in New York by Tony, and I was willing to accept that he would retaliate by throwing my stuff away or packing it up for me. I guess I never thought he might have been making room for her things. I returned to the couch and hastily put my clothes on. I had already been one-upped tonight. There was no need to further my humiliation at Zara's hands.

For what seemed l e hours I sat there and listened to their love-making. During it all I lever once felt angry enough to exact revenge or want to be with som one else. Instead I was filled with the notion of what I had been putti g Sean through. Unlike Sean, though, I didn't have to wonder if he w s as loving and passionate with other women as his soul had been torn nted by my indiscretions. No, this night I was given a front-row seat t just how good my man, my ex-man, really was. It was another revelati n for my spirit, my conscience, to feel the loss, the anger, and the hel essness he must have felt.

After it was quiet f a minute, I slipped out of the house and met a cab in the driveway. made it back to the airport, but there were no more flights leaving fo New York for the night. As I pondered my next move, I remembered e ring. I looked in my purse and my pockets, but it was gone. It m t have slipped out somewhere in the house. *Damn! Now he'll know I as here.* I made reservations at a local hotel and finally collapsed in a l ap on the bed. With no friends and no man, there was only one pe on I could talk to about my life.

"Hello, Mom?"

"Rachel, how are y u? Did you talk to Sean?"

"No, I didn't talk t Sean, Mom," I said, holding back tears.

"I see," she said, a paused. "Did he not want to see you?"

"I never saw him. I 's with her now. He's with Zara."

"You know that ho ?"

"I saw them togeth r. She's in the house."

"I'm sorry, Rachel.

"What? No 'I told you so, Rachel'? No 'serves you right'?"

"I love you, and after you told me what happened at Nick's, I honestly believe you are ready to face your demons, and..." She paused. "You're still my daughter."

"I love you, Momma."

"I love you too."

"So what do I do now?"

"Come home and we will visit Dr. Solomon together."

"Will you come with me?"

"I will."

"They didn't have a flight tonight, but I'll be in first thing tomorrow."

"I'll come get you from the airport, and I will make an appointment with Dr. Solomon in the afternoon."

"Thank you for being here for me mom. I feel like a fool for throwing my life away."

"Rachel you have not thrown your life away. You are still young, and you have so much more to live for. As much as I want you and Sean to reconcile, I want you to be happy and find peace within yourself."

"I want that as well, but right now I have to be honest and tell you that I miss Sean. For the first time in my life I honestly know how a man should love and treat me, and I want that love back with him."

"Then I will pray for you and hopefully you will find that love again with Sean. Now try to get some rest. I'm also looking forward to getting to know my daughter again."

"I'm looking forward to that as well mom." I said as I began to cry. "We have a lot of catching up to do."

We said our good-byes and for the rest of the night I lay in bed staring at the ceiling and thinking about my life and the changes I would vow to make. I also thought about Sean. Did he reach out to Zara to get back at me for Tony or was that where his love truly belonged? No way, he had come up to New York to win me back. If he had waited for me for seven months, then was still a chance that I could undo whatever spell Zara Rivers was trying to cast on his heart. *I'm not giving up so easily Zara, I will be back for my man.*

Alanya

I awoke the next morning with a smile on my face as big as Texas. Sean was asleep behind me, his arm around me. It felt natural to be here with him, as if we had been living together for years. The previous night had truly changed my life. We shared a connection; a positive bond had been formed between Sean and me that I welcomed.

I decided to get up and make my way to the kitchen. Any woman knows that when you have a good man, you keep him fed in and out of the bedroom. His arm felt like it weighed thirty pounds as I slid from underneath him. I didn't want to put anything of mine on just yet, and his walk-in closet was open. I entered and it was like walking into an upscale men's store. Cherrywood dressers and shelves lined the walls. A flat screen television angled down from the ceiling, and a glass-topped cabinet showcasing watches and jewelry centered the room. I looked through all of his suits and shoes. I pulled out a long-sleeved dress shirt and put it on. It fit me like a dress. I admired myself in the full-length mirror on the wall. I glanced back over my shoulders and went back through the clothes. I couldn't help but double check for any women's clothes, but I found none.

I left the closet and returned to the bedroom where Sean still lay sleeping. I took one last gaze at his fine ass and made my way down-stairs. His living room was immaculate: a warm, apricot-colored room adorned with dark mahogany-brown wooden furniture. The entire room was accentuated y trees and plants of different shapes and sizes. A nice-sized aquarium with exotic fish was encased in the far wall. A huge flat-screen was a bove the fireplace. He had expensive taste and style. Only pictures of his son and what appeared to be of his family were on the coffee tab es and the walls. Not one picture of him with the ex was around.

I turned the corn r and could have passed out in his kitchen. *Modern contemporary* ca me to mind. All the appliances were stainless steel. Even the refrigei tor boasted a mini flat-panel television screen. "The brotha loves his ESPN," I thought aloud. An island counter shaped like an L sat i the middle, with granite tops throughout. I found some pancake iix and eggs and bacon. I finally figured out how to work the home sound system, and soon Kaye-Ree was playing through the entire he se. After I started the coffee brewing, I once again found myself fee ng like I had belonged here all along. I started singing along when "D n't You Worry" started.

I was singing like newlywed and flipping pancakes when I felt Sean's strong arms arc und me. Feeling his arms and body heat made me smile. I turned arc nd and gave him a hug. Sean broke away and stepped back, staring me in his shirt. He had on some silk pajamas and looked like he h d just stepped off the cover of *Ebony Man*'s Unforgettable calend . His chest and stomach looked like rocks of perfection. How in th world had I gotten so lucky? I turned back and flipped the rema ing pancakes onto the plate and cut off the stove.

Sean let out a sigh Now, this is something I could get used to."

"Play your cards ri ht and you just might." I smiled. "I hope you don't mind the shirt."

"Oh no, please, th t shirt never looked so good," he said, gazing at me.

"I was thinking the same thing when I imagined you wearing it."

I stepped closer to him and rubbed his chest, marveling at how he flexed his pecs. His eyes were warm, and his smile invited me to his face. I placed my hand behind his head and kissed him. Our embrace was strong, and I felt my warrior rise to the occasion. The light from outside was bright, and the sunlight seemed to add to the warmth I was feeling for Sean. I just wanted to please him and feel him inside me once more. I stepped back and admired the bulge in his pants: all that dick for me, as if heaven were trying to bring me back up to speed. *Time to show my appreciation,* I thought. Slowly I began to unbutton my shirt. Sean's bulge stiffened.

"I see someone is a little hungry this morning."

"Well, I kind of worked up an appetite last night." He grinned.

"Yes, you did," I said softly, "and your work was so good last night, you may have your dessert before breakfast."

I reached the last button and allowed the shirt to fall from my shoulders, leaving me standing with nothing but a smile on. My nipples began to harden in the coolness. But hard nipples were not even on my mind. Looking at Sean, I only wanted to feel one thing hard. I walked over to him and placed my hands on his pajama strings. We looked at each other, and I knew he saw the yearning look in my eyes for him. I untied his strings and slid his pajamas down his hips until he was as bare as I was. For a minute he seemed unsure of just what he wanted to do. I didn't know if my boldness had been too much for him.

Sean just looked at my body. His manhood was still rigid, a most welcomed sign. Before I could even analyze anything else, he moved into me and, with the gracefulness of a cheetah and the strength of a lion, picked me up and set me on the island counter. My heartbeat began to increase as my prince positioned himself in front of me. I wrapped my legs around his waist, drawing him closer. Then I nibbled on his neck to show my approval.

"That's right, Daddy, give Momma what she needs," I moaned.

I lost track of how many times I climaxed. All I know is that it was more than I had ever had in my entire sexual life. Sean fed my ego and nurtured my body unlike any other man or woman before. We were like crazy-in-love newlyweds on our honeymoon. I desired him in every way. On me, in me, around me—in any way possible, I needed him. We ate breakfast on the kitchen floor and made love again. I would have been content to make love to him all day, but we ended up going upstairs for a bath.

After freshening up I met him back downstairs. I lay on his chest on the couch and we just enjoyed holding each other. Once again, my mind began to wonder about this fairy tale. How, after so much disappointment, could I find the man who had everything I desired? Why didn't Rachel fight for him? I caught the glimpse of a wedding band on the floor near the coffee table.

Sean

Relaxing on the sofa with Alanya felt like heaven. Almost overnight a home that had once been cold and empty was now filled with warmth, love, and life. In seven years never was I able to convince Rachel to do what Alanya and I just did in the kitchen. It was like my manhood had been reborn. Alanya fed my ego and she made me feel proud of who I was. She also had a genuine sense for adventure and not afraid to show her sexuality and desire. I fed off her energy, and her spontaneity. Alanya didn't need to be told she was beautiful, sexy, and a dyme, she knew it. *Damn, if the first night was like this, what would a lifetime be like?*

"I'm not trying to pry, Sean, but exactly how did your and Rachel's marriage end?"

"Well, it was more complicated than just your usual marriage; I've never discussed it with anyone."

"You can tell me, Sean. I want to know you and your life."

"My life—my life has been like Dr. Jekyll and Mr. Hyde. The business side is great; the personal side is a monster."

"You don't think your personal side is better now?"

"Don't get me wrong: I am on cloud nine right now. Fate has a way of playing with my emotions, though."

"There is no fate except for what you make. So are you going to open up and tell me or not?"

"It is going to take a while to tell you all of it."

"I'm not going anywhere," she replied, holding my hand.

I took in a deep breath and told Alanya everything from the beginning: about Zara, my dad dying, Rachel, and Tony. I told her about the baby and then the last affair Rachel had with Jason. After I finished, she just lay on top of me, taking it all in.

"I see. So through all of that, you still wanted to stay with her?"

"Yeah, I thought we had something worth fighting for. I guess I was the only one who saw it that way."

"And now? Do you feel like that now?"

"My marriage is over, and so are my feelings for Rachel," I said, thinking about her and Tony sharing pizza at Nick's in my mind. "It was made perfectly clear to me that I had to move on, and I couldn't be happier."

"I'm glad to hear that," she said, hugging me tightly.

"All right, beautiful, now it's your turn. What is your story? You know mine, so tell me, how can a young, beautiful woman like yourself be single in New York?"

"There's really no story to tell."

Drake Wilmore

"Well, don't tell me some bullshit about how no guys hit on you, because I know you'd be lying."

"I would not lie to you; yes I've had my share of guys trying to hit me up, but I've seen a lot of my girlfriends hurt in meaningless relationships, so I just stayed focused on going to school and working."

"So you're saying you have no time for fun? When was your last relationship?"

"You have to define *fun* for me. My last relationship was a little over a year ago with a guy who was twenty-eight."

"What happened?"

"What happened was that I really didn't want to join him in his ménage à trois, especially given the fact that they started without me, if you understand what I'm saying."

"Damn! Please tell me he was over to his house when you busted him."

"No, it was our apartment that we shared," she said, her anger building. "The bastard didn't even have the consideration to at least get a hotel room or go over to her house."

"I'm sorry, Alanya; believe me, I know how you feel."

"You know the thing that hurts the most was not him cheating, but that the girl was actually quite beautiful."

"Really?" I asked, puzzled. "How is that worse?"

"If she had been some ugly ass skank, I would have totally been content to let him know he had messed up a good thing with me. Since she was beautiful, he probably picked up with her, while I was left to sort my life out again.'

"She surely wasn't as beautiful as you, and he did mess up the best thing that will ever have happened in his pathetic life."

"Thanks, Sean. You are good for my ego."

"You're good for me. So have you seen him since?"

"No, I haven't. I didn't even slap the bitch. I just told them to both be gone by the time I got back, and that was that."

"I don't know how people can play with other people's hearts like that."

"I know, and then you feel so nervous and insecure in your next relationship. It's like a part of you never fully recovers."

"You hit the nail on the head. You become isolated from having fun and it's hard to get back into living life. So why did you approach me?"

"You're very handsome, and to be honest it's been a while since I was with a man. I was unsure how it would end up. I was genuinely attracted to you, though, and with your demeanor and charm, you came across as a very interesting and stimulating man to know."

"I felt almost the same when I saw you. Your beauty and your assertiveness turned me on. I was very flattered by that. I've never had a woman slide me her number before."

"No way. Never?"

"Never."

"Did you ever cheat on your wife, Sean?"

"Never. Not once did I even think about it."

"Even after everything she put you through?"

"As much as she put me through didn't matter. We both took vows, not just her, and just because she chose to violate those vows, that didn't give me the right to violate mine."

"That's very sweet. I respect you for maintaining your own self-respect and moral beliefs."

"That's all I've ever had in my life."

"Now you have something else."

"What's that?"

"Me," she said softly.

"Alanya, I know you prefer older men, but I've never done this, any of this before. Are you sure you want to give this old man with baggage, and no experience a try?"

"Just promise me you'll protect my heart, and I will do anything to make you happy."

"You have my word, Alanya."

"And you have my heart, Sean."

We shared a deep kiss and held each other for a minute. I felt so complete at that moment. It was like, for once everything in my life was in unison: my job, my family, and my love life. I felt like celebrating, and I knew just the place to go.

"Tell you what: let's go upstairs, get dressed, and take a little cruise on the Potomac."

"You have a boat?"

"Yes, I have a boat." I smiled. "Why do you ask like that?"

"No, it's nothing. You are too good to be true. I mean, you're handsome, successful, and awesome in bed. Why hasn't another lady stepped to you?"

"Well, it's like you said yourself: I didn't make myself available. I just focused on my business."

"I'm glad I got to you first."

"I'm glad you got to me as well. Now go upstairs and get ready. I'm going to check in at the office, and I'll be up in a second."

"Okay. Can I be your first mate or have you already christened your boat?"

"No, I've never christened my boat. We never did anything like that on the boat."

"Good, because when I get you on that boat, we'll see if we can make some waves."

"Deal."

"Don't be too long," she said, as she went up the stairs.

I smiled and picked up the phone. I had told Rob I would check in when I returned from New York. I decided not to tell him about Alanya just yet. As I was waiting for Carol to connect me to Robert's new office, I noticed something shiny on the carpet next to the coffee table. I had started to walk over to it when I heard Rob's voice on the phone.

"Good afternoon, Chief. How was New York?"

"New York was New York," I said evasively.

"I'm sure. So did you run into anyone in particular, I mean, perhaps someone whose last name used to be Winslow as well?"

"You know, Robert, I ran into so many people." I laughed. "It was actually hard to remember faces."

"Okay, you lost me on that one, but hey, as long as you break it down for me when you get back."

"I promise I will be in Friday morning."

"Friday morning. Hmm…Sounds like someone has some company," he said, laughing.

"Or had company," I mumbled while kneeling and picking my wedding ring up off the floor.

"I'm sorry, what was that, Sean?"

"Nothing, Rob. Look, keep up the good work and I'll see you on Friday," I said, rushing off the phone.

I sat down on the couch and studied my ring. The last time I had seen this ring was in Rachel's hand in New York. How or when had it gotten here? I remembered that I had never gotten the house key from Rachel when she'd left. had hoped she would one day use it again, but not this day. Did she know I was here with Alanya? I decided to call her. I was waiting for the call to connect when I looked up and my jaw dropped at the sight of Alanya. he was in the hallway wearing black stockings, heels, and lingerie, complete with the garters. Her body was flawless.

"I hope you don't mind, but this is what I'm wearing on the boat."

"Not at all," I said hanging up the phone and placing the ring inside my pocket. "It's little cold outside, though." I smiled.

"Don't worry. I noticed you have a certain long cashmere coat that will keep me warm until we get to the boat. Once we're on the boat, it's your job to keep me warm."

"Now, that's a job I will take very seriously."

"Is everything okay at work? You looked a little stressed when I first came down."

"It's nothing," I said, going over to her and placing my hands on her waist. "Nothing that will keep me from enjoying every moment with you."

"You don't ever have to worry anymore, Sean. I'll be here for you whenever and wherever you need me."

"That means a lot to me, Alanya."

"Then let's get you upstairs, so I can have some fun undressing you."

She led me upstairs, where she indeed had fun undressing me. After an impromptu striptease, we made it to the boat and proceeded on our trip. Although my mind sometimes wondered about the ring, for the most part it stayed on Alanya. Her laughter and enjoying all the beauty and openness of being on the water was exactly what I needed to see. Finally I had someone with whom I could enjoy my success, someone who appreciated me and would love me. Alanya would allow me to be the one to feed her ego, her affections, and her desires. No other man would have her heart. We hugged and enjoyed going up to Annapolis and passing the pier.

I knew she was good for me, but I also knew we needed to be strong to make this work. As I kept looking at her and marveling at her beauty, part of me felt guilty because I knew how much of life I had lived and experienced. I mean, I was divorced and had a child, not to mention the fact that I was turning thirty-five in a few months. She was barely in her twenties. Although she had been in other relationships with older men, I didn't want to cheat her out of living a healthy single life. Add to that Rachel and the ring, and I knew I had to make sure all doors to my past were closed.

After our boat trip and the immaculate christening ceremony Alanya gave me on board, we made our way back to my house. By the time we arrived, I had actually forgotten about the ring. We shared another magical night together, and our lovemaking was even stronger than the night before.

The next morning, the drive to the airport showed just how good we were together. We had a lot in common. Our tastes in music, food, and even sports were mirrored. She loved basketball, and the Knicks were her favorite team. She talked more trash than some of the guys at work. I was very impressed with her knowledge of the game. We pulled into the parking garage, and our conversation became subtle. Alanya stared out the window; her mind seemed a million miles away.

"Hey, are you okay?"

"I'm fine. It's just that it feels like being on the best roller coaster ride of your life, and now it's ending and you have to get off."

"Hey, don't forget you have an unlimited pass."

"I hope so, because I don't want this ride to end, Sean."

"It won't, trust me.

"So when will I get a chance to see you again?"

"That depends on your schedule. I'm somewhat flexible."

"Well, I have class tomorrow, and I work this weekend. Maybe sometime next week, say, Tuesday or Wednesday?"

"That sounds good. I'll keep my schedule clear. Unless an emergency pops up, I should be okay."

"I hope so."

"Are you ready?"

'No, but I guess it is unavoidable."

We made it inside the terminal and checked Alanya in. She waited inside the terminal with me until they called her flight for preboarding.

"Well, that's my flight."

"Yes, it is. Call me when you land."

"Of course. I'll be thinking of you, Sean."

"I'll be thinking about you, Alanya."

"I'm falling for you, Sean."

"I'm falling for you, Alanya."

We embraced and shared a soft, short kiss. We pulled away, and I looked into Alanya's deep brown eyes to see them glossy with tears.

"Alanya, don't do me like this. I'm not supposed to cry in front of you so soon."

She smiled. "I'm sorry, Sean, but this feels so right, and I don't want to leave you."

"I feel in my heart that this relationship is the start of something very special. Trust me, Alanya, one day soon I know you'll never have to leave my side."

My words seemed to reassure Alanya of my feelings. She gave me another kiss and walked to the gate. She turned and smiled. I returned her smile. I stayed until her plane left. All of a sudden I felt lonely and sad. *Alanya is definitely looking like my future,* but how could I be sure, though? How could I make sure my mistakes from my past didn't come back to haunt me? I wanted to trust her totally, and I wanted to spoil her madly.

I turned and started walking out of the airport, thinking about Alanya. Then I heard a woman's voice call my name. I turned to look, but I didn't see where it had come from. I heard it again, and looked to see the hand of a beautiful woman waving frantically at me. She was making her way to me, and I moved toward her. As we approached, the eyes and smile became familiar; the walk and the body became more apparent. *What the hell kind of game is this? Why here and why now?*

Zara

I didn't imagine I would meet Sean right at the airport. Was this fate or some kind of tragic bad luck? *Is he coming or going? He doesn't have any bags. Oh God! He's here to pick up someone. What if it's his wife? I can't do this now. Not in front of her!* My body began to stiffen as I walked toward him. Sean stood there with a perplexed look on his face, but I couldn't blame him. We hadn't seen each other in a long time. The closer I got, the more a part of me wanted to run into his arms. I felt myself wanting to tear up. I fought back my emotions, and in one swift moment I put a smile on my face.

"Hello, Sean."

"Hello, Zara."

Wow. No emotion, just a businesslike hello. I suddenly began to feel like this had not been the best idea.

"Are you just getting in from somewhere?"

"No. I just dropped someone off," he answered cautiously.

"Oh, well, you look good, Sean."

"You look good as well, Zara."

The awkwardness of the moment was getting to me, and I could feel the tears trying to make their way up to the surface. I really needed to just feel him again, be near his heart.

"Well, can a sista get a hug?" I asked nervously.

We embraced, and I hugged him as if he had just returned home from battle. I could have held on to him forever, but I sensed the absence of emotion in his body. There was no strength in his hold. It was as if he hugged me only so he wouldn't be disrespectful. I sensed his coldness and stepped back, looking into his eyes. For a moment my pain and sorrow was replaced by hurt and rejection. I didn't need this right now, not from someone who I at least had thought would give me the benefit of the doubt and at least still be a friend.

"I see your feelings for me haven't changed."

"What did you expect, Zara?" he replied coldly.

"I don't know: a fresh start, the chance to say I'm sorry, and the chance to explain."

"You got a fresh start, Zara. You got your business, and you got your success. There's nothing to apologize for. There's nothing to explain."

"Sean, please don't treat me like this," I said, my eyes beginning to tear up. "I really need you."

"I needed you too, Zara. Ten years ago, I needed you and you rolled out on me, on us. So save those tears for someone who gives a fuck."

And with that, the one man who could comfort me and console me turned and began to walk away. I wanted to walk to him and grab his arm and give him a piece of my mind, but I was suddenly overcome with a weight unlike any other I had ever felt. My throat filled with tears. I could only blurt out a sentence.

"He's dead, Sean!" I shouted.

"Who's dead?" Sean asked, turning around.

"My father—he's dead."

Saying those words seemed to take my knees right out from under me. Sean quickly made his way back to me, and as soon as he reached out to touch me, I collapsed in his arms and cried. He held my body tightly, close to his this time. It felt like the first night we made love. Sean Winslow right at that moment held me with all the love and strength that a husband uses to hold his wife. It was as if his body was trying to let me know I was going to be okay. He held me right there in front of the airport for what seemed like an eternity. Some passersby looked at us, unsure whether this was a joyous reunion or a tearful good-bye. I regained my composure and broke away from his embrace.

"Zara, I'm sorry, I'm so sorry. Does my mother know?"

"No, she doesn't. It happened so suddenly. He and my mom were on vacation in Jamaica. He had a heart attack."

"God, I'm so sorry. How's your mother holding up?"

"Not well. She won't speak, and she hasn't eaten in days. I don't know what to do." I began to cry again. "I needed to get away for a bit. All I could think about was you and needing to feel someone who cared about me."

"Oh Zara—damn, girl, I'm sorry for acting the way I just did." Sean spoke with regret building in his voice. "Come on. Let's get out of here."

He grabbed my suitcase and we headed to his house. I told him my dad had died the previous Thursday in Jamaica and that I had flown from Frankfurt and met my mother at the hospital in Miami the next day. Seeing my mother's grief and how she wasn't even able to call anyone, and having my own sorrow and grief to deal with, had become too much for me to bear. I had needed to feel someone that I was close to, someone who knew me, and that was why I had sought him out. I had just arrived an hour before I had seen him.

We arrived at Sean's house, and he asked me what I wanted to drink. With the whirlwind of emotions I was feeling, I needed something nice and strong, and although I hadn't seen Sean in a long time, the one thing I did know was he always stocked the good stuff. So I asked for a double shot of Inchgower Scotch whiskey straight. That raised his eyebrow, but given the stress he knew I must be under, he understood. While I sat in the living room, Sean called his mom and explained the situation. Ms. Joyce kept her promise and didn't let on that she knew what was going on, and told him she would be strong enough to help my mother until we got there. I guess she also made him promise to take care of me, because I heard him say, "I promise I will, Momma. Once she's okay, we'll fly down."

I went to the bar and poured myself a second double shot. Sean hung up the phone and rejoined me in the living room. He noticed my second drink. "Slow down, baby girl. That's a Persian rug, and I don't feel like cleaning it tonight."

"Don't worry. I can handle my whiskey," I said proudly.

"Judging by the way you're taking those double shots straight, I believe you. I can just get you a bigger glass if you prefer." He laughed "Sorry just trying to make you smile. Seriously, though, are you okay?"

"He was my daddy," I said, my eyes tearing up once again at the mention of my father. "I miss my daddy."

"I know, Zara, I know." He sat down and placed his arm around me. "He was a great man."

"Yes, he was. I love him so much."

"He knew that too you know that, Zara? He knew how much you loved him."

"What will I do without him? What will Momma do without him?"

"You will continue to live your life to the fullest; that's what he would want. You and Mrs. Rivers will celebrate his life and live yours."

"Oh, Sean, I don't know if I can."

"Nonsense, Zara. You can and you will. He is counting on you."

"He is?"

"Damn right he is. He knows your mother needs you now more than ever. Together you two will build an even stronger bond. Remembering all the love and devotion your father had for you. Embracing life and allowing your mother to know that within you both Mr. Rivers is still alive."

"I didn't think about it like that."

Sean poured himself a double shot and raised his glass in a toast.

"Here's to Todd Winslow and Kevin Rivers, two of the greatest men in the world."

"To Todd and Kevin."

We drank the shots, and I thought of a toast I wanted to say, so I fixed two more shots. "I have a toast. To the two greatest fathers in the world: to Kevin and Todd."

"Kevin and Todd," he toasted.

The whiskey had lost its sting, and I was feeling its effect. Suddenly my mind took me back years ago to the day in the hospital with Mrs. Joyce and Mr. Winslow.

"I dreaded this day for so long."

"Why? You didn't see this coming?" Sean asked.

"When your dad died, I became afraid for my own dad. I just knew he was next."

"Is that why my father's death shook you so badly? You did feel like you had lost your dad, didn't you?"

"I was just so scared, Sean," I said, crying. "Seeing your mother grieve and knowing what you must have felt like on the inside. Dealing with everything else you and I had been going through."

"I never said thank you."

"Thank you for what?" I asked, puzzled.

"Thank you for being there for my mother. She really needed someone, and that person was you. So I want to say thank you."

"Sean, Ms. Joyce is like my second mother. I wouldn't have been anywhere else. No thank-you is needed."

"Well, I'm saying t ank you anyway," he said, pouring us another drink.

"Another toast?"

"Yes. This one is to amily."

"To family."

"Family."

We drank our sho , and I could feel my buzz starting to kick in. I felt warm, and then looked at Sean. He was staring right at me. A different look was now n his eyes, one that was much warmer than the one at the airport. I co ld feel him studying my body, and for whatever reason, I actually appr ciated his look of admiration. Even under the circumstances I knew had never gotten completely over Sean. I just never knew if he had e er gotten completely over me.

"Did you ever thin of me, Sean?"

"You're joking rigl ? Zara, there were days I couldn't sleep or eat because of you."

"I felt the same wa I wanted to find you, but you moved away to New York, and by the ne I found you, your dad was sick and I didn't want to add to your gr f."

"I didn't know tha I just assumed you were too busy in Germany and had chalked me u as a loss."

"Sean, there was n way I could just chalk you up as a loss. I loved you."

"You have a funny way of showing it," he said in a harsher tone.

"I tried to explain, Sean, but you ignored me. You made me feel as if you wanted nothing to do with me, and it wasn't until your dad became ill that you even came back home."

"How was I supposed to feel, Zara? You left me and didn't have the consideration to tell me the truth of why you actually had to go, and then I see you in Germany working with Karl on my project, my ideas, I was through with you when I left Germany. You could have explained yourself while you were playing daughter to my mom."

"That's not fair, and you know it. That was neither the time nor the place to bring up what we were going through when you and Ms. Joyce were dealing with your dad dying. After he passed away, you didn't stick around long enough to let me explain myself, and you wouldn't take my calls, Sean. I felt so bad for putting you through that on top of everything else, I didn't know what to do."

"I was so angry with you, and then having to deal with my dad dying, I just felt like my world was ending."

"You may not believe me but my world was also ending. Then to add insult to injury, your mother called to tell me you were engaged to be married and that if I still loved you, I should speak up then."

"Wait—my mother told you that?" Sean asked in astonishment.

"Yes, she did. She knew I still loved you, and she just wanted to help us out."

"I suspected that she was still holding out for us, I guess Rachel was right."

"She loves you so much. Don't be upset with her."

"I wish she hadn't done that, though. I was really trying to move on, and Rachel and I really needed her support and not for her to undermine our relationship."

"She wasn't undermining your relationship, Sean. She didn't do anything but try to give me the courage to do what my heart wanted me to do— what I should have done."

"And what was that?"

"Get my man back but I guess I was too late, huh?"

"Nearly two years went by, Zara, and I thought you were overseas enjoying your new life with Karl. I was in New York trying to put my life back together; I thought you had moved on, I couldn't wait."

"Is that why you didn't respond to my request?"

"What request?"

"I mailed you a letter before you got married. Did you ever get it?"

"Letter, oh yes, I remember the letter now. So much was going on during that time. Rachel had just lost a baby and we were dealing with some major trust issues. Not to mention we were in the process of also moving to Maryland in an effort to save our marriage. I'm sorry, Zara, but I never opened that letter."

Right then the buzz I had been feeling was gone. I sat up, my excitement and anger all rolled into one. All this time, and it could possibly have been avoided? *No, it couldn't be happening like this.*

"Sean Winslow, do you have any idea what was in that envelope?" I asked excitedly. "And you threw it away!"

"No, I didn't," he replied nervously.

"Well, where is it?"

Sean disappeared upstairs and seemed to be gone for an eternity. I stood up and paced the floor back and forth, replaying the letter I had written and the incentive I had placed inside for Sean. I couldn't stop thinking about the fact that he had never opened it. Did I mean that little to him? Or had Rachel hidden it until later? Sean returned downstairs and gave me the letter. I studied the envelope and saw no sign it had even been peeled back. I closed my eyes. Ten damn long years, so many lonely nights, and a cold bedroom. Tears streamed down my face. Sean rubbed my shoulder. I opened my eyes and our eyes met. A look of confusion was on his face. To him it was just a letter.

"You never knew," I said.

"Knew what, Zara?"

"Open it and see for yourself."

I handed him the letter and walked over to the bar to fix myself another drink. Sean looked at me and then opened the envelope. He pulled out a card, and as he opened it, a check fell out. He picked up the check, and as he read it, he paused in disbelief. My heart froze.

"Pay to the order of Sean Winslow, two million five hundred thousand dollars! What the—Zara, what's this about?"

"Read the card," I said as I drank my drink, trying to find a warm feeling for my heart again. Sean opened the card once more and began to read aloud.

"Dear Sean,

"Words can't express how much I've missed you and how sorry I am for what I did to you, to us. I've tried to talk to you, I've tried to reach out to you, but you've rejected all of my attempts. I figured this would be my last chance to get your attention.

"The check is real, and it is all yours. I know I stepped over you to take Karl Schumacher's offer, but I knew you were making a mistake by waiting for Coke. I loved to give you a chance at running your own company, for us. This was never about me or me and Karl, it was all about giving you the opportunity you deserved. I became so wrapped up in making this work that I forgot about what mattered most to me, and that was you Sean.

"After your father died, I had a heart-to-heart with your mother and told her what I had done. I made her promise not to tell you. She knows how much I love you, and it's because of that love that I am reaching out to you now. I know you are engaged, and though you may love her, I know that you still love me. I know this because I never stopped loving you, and deep down I can still feel your love for me.

"Sean, please give me a chance to talk to you. Give me a chance to see you. I know you would see my sincerity and my love. We belong together, Sean. Before you say 'I do' to her, give me one night—one night to show you just how much I need you and what we could be. My number is listed below. I will await your call. Yours forever, Zara."

Sean sat in silence staring at the card and the check. I went and made another drink for myself and one for Sean. I passed him his drink, and he downed it so fast, I don't think he even tasted the burn or the moistness as it hit the back of his throat. He looked at me in amazement. Many emotions must have been going through him right then, but my buzz was going so great, I didn't care. I remembered all of a sudden that this wasn't just Sean's house, and I didn't give a damn.

"So where's the lady of the house?"

"We're divorced going on about eight months now," he replied softly, his eyes now glued to the card.

"I'm sorry to hear that," I lied

"Do you mean that?" He said as his gaze returned to me.

"Did you truly love her?"

"Yes I did."

"Then I meant it," I lied again.

"Zara, I don't know what to say."

"There's nothing to say, Sean. I broke your heart and you broke mine. We're even."

"Zara, it wasn't supposed to be this way."

"But it is, and now I've lost the two most important men in my life." The combination of drinks and emotions finally took their toll on my composure, and instead of a few tears streaming, I began to all-out cry.

"Zara, I'm sorry. I don't know what to say except I'm sorry."

Sean raised my face and wiped my tear-soaked cheek. I looked into his eyes and stroked the side of his face, and in the blink of an eye, there he was…the Sean I knew, the Sean I loved. We looked at each other for what seemed like minutes. Then I leaned into him, and he felt compelled to lean into me. Our lips touched slowly, softly, briefly. Tasting his full, rum-stained lips tasted good. We pulled back and looked at each other. Once more we leaned into each other, into a zone that was old to us but at the same time new. More passion sprang from our mouths as we became wrapped in an intense embrace. My yearning to have Sean was mounting with every touch. Everything seemed right, but something was preventing him from taking me right then...

"Zara, I can't do this," he said, pulling away.

"No, Sean, please don't do this to me. I need you badly. It's been so long. Please, Sean," I moaned.

"I can't. It's not right."

"I still love you, Sean. Make love to me, please."

"Zara, I can't. I belong to someone."

"I thought you were divorced," I said, rubbing his chest.

"I am, but I've met someone," he stammered.

"Sean, please don't do this to me," I moaned even louder as I kissed his neck and stroked his manhood. "After all that we've been through, don't do this to me again."

"Zara, please don't make me do this."

I stood up over Sean and removed my sweater and dress to reveal what I had kept sacred from any man for a long time. My purple-colored bra and thong set Sean's eyes raging with desire.

"Sean, I have waited so long to bring this body back to you, praying that you would come back to me. Don't turn me away again. Please,

I'm not asking you for forever, just tonight. Right here, right now, please just make love to me, let me feel loved again Sean."

Sean could not maintain himself any longer. Looking at my body, and reliving the past ten years of our lives coupled with my plea, his conscience lost to the emotions he still felt for me. Sean grabbed me and pulled me down onto the floor. We made love right there for the entire night. A passion filled session that knew no limits. We ravished each others bodies like we had been held captive for years and now our souls and bodies were free to be together again. As if the angels from heaven were singing to us, our emotions overflowed. I cried, he cried, we cried. I fell asleep in his arms. I was back in Sean Winslow's heart again, at least for the night.

Alanya

"No way, Lani!" Mia shouted in my ear. "No way! Wow!"

"I know, Mia. I am, like, on cloud nine right now."

"This sounds like a romance novel. I mean, seriously, you meet by chance at the airport, and then you're whisked into his arms and a week long passion-filled retreat."

"He is like a storybook lover. His love, his life—I mean, I am still waiting to wake up."

"You are so awake, Lani, and you are so lucky. I am so happy for you. Still…"

"Still what?"

"What are you going to tell Ava?"

My heart stopped. In all my jubilance I had forgotten about my pending talk with Ava. "I need to tell her the truth."

"Will you tell her about Sean, about everything?"

"That's the plan."

"You know, I know we talked about this before, but now I'm worried about you and Ava, telling her you need to be free is one thing, but telling her after you have stepped out on her is another."

"I know, but I can't lie. I have to be truthful. She'll be here any moment, and now I'm a nervous wreck."

"Just be honest about your feelings and ideally it won't be too hard."

"I will. Hey, I want to talk to Sean before I talk to Ava, so I'll call you later, okay?"

"Okay, Lani. Good luck, and again, I'm so happy for you. I hope you and Sean can grow this connection into something wonderful and lasting."

"Thanks, Mia. I know we will."

We exchanged good-byes and I tried dialing Sean. It went to his voice mail, and I found myself sitting on the couch reliving every moment I had spent in his arms. My daydream was cut short when the doorbell rang. I opened the door and Ava gave me a big hug. "Hey, Lani, how's my girl?"

"Hey, Ava," I said, smiling. "I'm fine. How was your trip?"

"It was wonderful, but it would have been better if you had been there. I could have just seen you on the beach."

I smiled. "Maui would have been nice indeed."

"I know it's getting late, but I really had to see you, after hearing your voice."

"Me too," I said, walking around to the couch and sitting down.

Ava followed me around and sat down beside me. She stroked my knee with her hand. "Hey, what's wrong? You haven't been acting yourself lately, you seem bothered by something."

"Ava, I don't know where to begin."

"Okay, you're scaring me now," she said, a look of uncertainty on her face.

"I'm not trying to scare you, but I have to be honest with you about everything for both of us."

"Lani, what's going on?"

"Ava, this has been a whirlwind relationship we have built. From the first moment I met you, you have been nothing but wonderful: a breath of fresh air, a rock, a source of inspiration for me."

"I feel the same way about you, Lani."

"Still, I have always felt that something was missing," I said, standing. "You know I went to my family reunion a couple of weeks ago, and it became evident that I need to be a part of a family, a mother."

"Lani, are you saying you want children?"

"No...no. I mean, I do, but not now...That's not what I'm trying to say."

"What are you saying?"

I let out a deep sigh. "I'm saying I met someone, Ava. I met a man."

"A man?" she said in disbelief. "You met a man?"

"Yes, we met by chance while I was at work last week."

"Have you seen him since?"

"Yes, we spent the week together."

"You spent the week together!" she replied with shock and anger now building in her tone. "Alanya, what are you saying?"

Her hurt overshadowed her words, and I knew that this was in no way going to be amicable or easy.

"Ava, I never sought to hurt you. You do know that, right? I mean, for seven months now, we've—"

"We've been in a relationship!" she interrupted. "For seven months now we have been in a monogamous relationship and now you're telling me you spent the week with a man. Were you two intimate?"

"Yes."

Ava stood and looked dead at me, tears burning her eyes red. "Alanya, how could you do this to me?"

"Ava, please believe me. I didn't intend for this to happen."

"Wow. Now you are the one who sounds just like a guy." She laughed sarcastically. "What happened? Did you trip over his dick?"

"I know you are hurt, but I…"

"Hurt? I moved my entire life for you; I gave my all to you, I trusted you. This goes much further than hurt."

"Ava, please let me try to make you understand."

"There's no need to, Alanya. You have shown me that just like your age, you are still immature. I thought you were different. All the talks we had about men and their infidelity, their weaknesses, about how you were hurt by Corey, and you said to me you had sworn off men. Yet here you are, just like a man, expecting me to accept that you can't keep your panties up because things just happened!"

She was hurting, but her anger and her words were scaring me. Like a jilted wife, I was suddenly made aware that this night of resolution and admission could go in the wrong direction.

"Ava, I am not a man, and I am not trying to lie or hide things from you. I want to be honest about my feelings and what happened."

"Really? Well why couldn't you tell me last week, last month, about your feelings of needing a family, to be a mother? Why wait until after you stepped out?"

"You're right. I should have, but I honestly didn't know how to say it, I felt guilty for the way that I was feeling, knowing how much you have done for me, the time we have spent together, but even you felt the uneasiness that has been building between us."

Ava just shook her head and stared up at the ceiling. Suddenly an eerie grin spread across face. "You're pathetic."

"Excuse me?"

"I said you are fucking pathetic. Now I see why men take advantage of women. Sometimes we can be so gullible."

"Ava, please, can we discuss this rationally?"

"Oh, this discussion is over," Ava said as she made it to the door. She stopped and faced me, her eyes glaring with hate. "Karma is a bitch, Alanya. Just like you found yourself happening to fuck someone while in a committed relationship, so to shall it happen to you. Let's see how you deal with it. I never want to see you again."

With that she slammed the door.

Sean

Midnight! Shit! I said to myself, looking at my watch.

Zara had her head on my chest, sleeping peacefully. *Probably the first sound sleep she's had in a while, considering all she's endured recently.* I rubbed her head and stroked her hair. So much had passed since the last time we had been together like this. I slowly slid from underneath her. I took her upstairs to my bedroom, where I tucked her into bed. Zara barely stirred. Looking at her as I stood over her in my bed sent chills down my spine. She was so beautiful, so perfect, *so wrong*! I made my way back downstairs and checked my phone messages. I had four from Alanya, and the other two were blocked. I didn't know what I would say to Alanya, but I knew I had to call her. I picked up the phone and hit the Call Back button.

"Hello, Sean."

"Hello, Alanya. Did you make it in okay?"

"Yes, the flight was fine, but I'm missing you." She sounded really down.

"I miss you too," I said, my voice quivering with guilt.

"Are you okay, Sean? You sound different."

"You sound different too. Is everything okay?"

"Hey, I asked you first."

"Alanya, I have to tell you something, but I don't know how."

"Sean, you can tell me anything. I made you a promise. I'm here for you."

"It's a little complicated."

"Life is complicated, Sean. It's okay. Tell me."

"It's about Zara."

"Zara?"

"Yes, Zara."

"What about her?"

"It's her father; he's dead."

"Oh no, I'm sorry to hear that. Is she okay?"

"She and her mother are taking it pretty hard."

"So you've talked to her?"

"Yes, I have. If by fate I met her at the airport right after I said goodbye to you. She didn't have anyone else to turn too. She and her mother have been dealing with this all by themselves. Alanya, I have to go to Georgia and be there for her and her family."

"I understand, Sean."

"You do, I mean th   is not a test or anything. You can tell me how you feel."

"Sean, she was the   for you and your family in a time of grieving, and regardless of what   feel or think, I know they need you."

"Alanya, I'm sorry   out this. The timing of this sucks"

"It's not your fault.   ean. Do what you have to do."

"I'm glad you und stand."

"Is there anything   can do?"

"You're doing it n   , Alanya. A prayer wouldn't hurt either."

"In that case I'll sa   two."

"You are wonderfu —you do know that."

"Only as wonderfu   s you, Sean. Besides, I want to be there for you in any way I can."

"It means a lot to   ."

"So when are you l   ving?"

"As soon as she is   ady, possibly within a few days."

"Well, be safe, anc give my condolences. If you need to call me, Sean, no matter the ti   e, just call, okay?"

"I will, Alanya, I pr mise."

"I'm thinking abo   you, Mr. Winslow."

"And I'm thinking of you, Ms. Gellar."

We exchanged good-byes and I was left to ponder my actions alone on the patio. The crisp night air felt good against the heat of my sins. I felt guilty for allowing my emotions for Zara to override my commitment and feelings for Alanya. Did that mean my feelings for Alanya were not real? Would I have made love to Zara if we hadn't been overcome with the sudden rush of emotions over her father and the letter? Hell, would I even have stayed devoted to Rachel if I had known about the letter and money? One thing was for certain: I needed another drink.

I went back inside and fixed myself a drink. As I was taking a sip, I heard Zara scream from upstairs. I dropped the glass and ran upstairs to my bedroom. Zara was sitting up in bed screaming and crying. "No, Daddy! Please don't go, Daddy!"

"It's okay, Zara, it's okay."

"My daddy, Sean, my daddy!"

"I know, baby, I know. It's going to be okay, baby girl—it's okay."

I held Zara until she calmed down and went back to sleep. I was drained as well, but I couldn't bring myself to lie in the bed beside her. Instead I stretched out in the lounge chair beside the bed. I knew that all the questions tormenting my mind would have to be blocked out for now. Zara needed me.

The next morning I called Carol and Robert to explain the situation with Zara and nothing more. Zara surprised me by asking to rejoin her mother in Georgia as soon as possible, so I booked the next available flight to Atlanta. We barely said two words to each other on the flight or on the way down to her father's hometown of Macon. I didn't know if it was gu t from our night together or if perhaps she was preparing herself to b strong in front of her mother.

We made it to her grandparents' house, where I was relieved to see my mother's silve BMW parked out front. The front door was open, so we went rig t in. A couple of relatives and friends were in the living room wa hing TV. There were flowers and gifts everywhere. I spotted my m m in the kitchen with Mrs. Rivers. Mrs. Rivers looked very solemn b t at peace. My mother saw us moving toward them.

"Hey, Momma."

"Sean, Zara, you m de it in!"

"Hello, Ms. Joyce; hi, Momma," Zara said as she gave the two women hugs.

"Sean, it's been so ng since I last saw you. Boy, have you grown."

"Yes ma'am, it has een a long time."

"Still the polite ge leman as well."

"I try, Mrs. Rivers."

"Joyce, he looks ju like his father."

"I know. Todd cou never deny this one."

"Ladies, you're m king Sean blush," Zara said, coming to my rescue.

"Oh, baby, we were ust giving Todd and Sean compliments."

"Thank you, Mrs. Rivers. It's an honor to be compared to my father."

"Anytime, baby. Well, I know you kids are tired, but Momma Rivers is in her room and I know she's eager to see you, Zara."

"I know I'm eager to see her. Sean, if you want to leave and get some rest, that's fine."

"I'm fine, Zara. I'll stay here and relax."

"Are you sure?"

"There's no place I'd rather be, Zara."

"Ahh, sounds like love to me." My mother sighed.

"Momma," I said sternly.

"You said it, Sean, I didn't."

Mrs. Rivers chuckled, and I looked at Zara, who was now blushing herself. They went down the hall to her grandmother's room. Big Momma Rivers was eighty-nine and had outlived her husband and all but two of her five children. She was up there in age, but she still had her wits about her. While they said hello, my mother walked out to the backyard where I followed, hot on her heels.

"You know you were wrong for that, Momma."

"Oh, Sean, I was just teasing."

"You have a way with teasing, Momma."

"And you have a way of denying the truth."

"Okay, change of subject: How's Mrs. Rivers holding up?"

My mother gave me the contemptuous look she would always use to let me know she didn't appreciate my tone or abruptness. She closed her eyes and then turned, walking farther into the yard. "Pat is holding up fine. She has made peace and come to terms with knowing Kevin is with God now. What about Zara?"

"She's really hurting, but I think she will be okay. It was her idea to get back here early."

"You didn't argue with or upset that girl, did you?" she asked sternly.

"No. Why would you ask such a thing?"

"Because I know you hold grudges."

"I do not hold grudges."

"Uh huh—like the time you wouldn't speak to Michael Young for a year because he dunked on you in front of Brandy Davis."

"How do you remember this stuff!" I gasped. "And for the record, he didn't dunk on me. I slipped and fell under the basket. I was upset with him because he came down on my hand."

"You got dunked on, Sean. That's why you're a businessman and not in the NBA."

"Momma!" I pleaded.

"That's okay, baby. Momma didn't want you around all those sweaty, obnoxious men and those floozy cheerleaders anyway."

"You win, Momma. I'm sorry for being abrupt."

"Momma always wins. Now give me another hug."

I couldn't help but laugh. I gave my mom a bear hug and kissed her cheek. That woman could always tear me down and build me right back up before I had a chance to be mad at her. Still, though, she had some explaining to do. "Zara told me something, Momma—something that you've known for a long time."

"Oh my! Did I leave those greens on?" she said, trying to make a hasty exit. "I better go check on them." She turned and began to walk back toward the house.

"Not so fast, Professor Winslow."

"That's Mother to you," she said, turning around. "Watch your tone."

"I'm sorry, Momma, but why didn't you tell me she told you what happened between us?"

"I didn't want to interfere in your life."

"Momma," I said sarcastically.

"Okay. She made me promise not to tell you, and I gave her my word."

"But I'm your son. How could you hold that from me; do you know how much hurt could have been avoided?"

"I withheld it the same way you held it from Todd and me."

I stopped in my tracks when I heard my dad's name.

"That's right, Sean. You moved to New York for two months and never told us why, or what happened between you and Zara. Then when Todd became ill it was Zara who was there and not you. Only after he passed did she tell me what really happened. I am very disappointed in you even to his day."

"Me?"

"Yes, you, mister. Is she the reason you didn't come when you first heard your father was ll? Is she the reason you couldn't stay behind and help me out after e died? Your father did so much for you and I needed you, but all yo could think about was your own damn pride."

Those words felt like a knife penetrating my gut. I had known that one day I would have to answer for my actions. I had just figured that after time passed, the anger and hurt might too, but I had been wrong. My whole life I had struggled to succeed and not let my parents down, yet in the blink of an eye it became apparent that I had done just that. I felt like my world was ending, hearing the hurt and anger in my mother's voice. There was no building me back up after this. Nothing that Rachel, Zara, or even Michael dunking on me could make me feel like I felt at this moment.

"Momma, I don't know what to say."

"You don't have to say anything to me, Sean; I wasn't the one who needed you at my bedside."

"Don't do this to me, Momma. Not now."

"He asked for you, Sean. Right up until he lapsed into a coma, he called for you." Her eyes filled with tears.

"No, please don't cry, Momma," I said, my own voice now trembling with hurt.

"How do you think I felt, Sean? I didn't know what to think about why you were not there."

"Momma, it wasn't all because of Zara."

"Then what was it, Sean? What was it that kept you from your father's side?"

I couldn't answer her question.

"You are just like your father except he never let his pride get in the way of doing what was right."

"Momma, I don't know—"

"I have to check on those greens," she interrupted.

She turned and walked back into the house, leaving me once again alone and with more guilt. I stood there and reflected upon every choice I had made in my life and why. The more I thought, the more obvious it appeared. Indeed my pride had clouded a great deal of my judgment. I knew what I had to do, but I didn't know how. I was so deep in thought, I didn't hear Zara until she tugged my arm.

Zara

"Sean, are you okay?"

"Yeah, I'm fine," he replied, but his tone told me otherwise.

"Your mom seems upset about something."

"She has every right to be."

"You sure you're okay?" I said, rubbing his shoulder.

"I'm fine, Zara. Besides, I'm the one who's supposed to be asking you that."

"It still hurts, but Big Momma made me feel better."

"I'm glad. Big Momma Rivers has still got it going on, you know."

"Yes, she is something else," I laughed, "to be eighty-nine and have been through what she's been through and still be perfectly sane. Meanwhile, I'm thirty-four and I'm losing my mind."

"Well, you know I'm already steering that ship. All aboard the cuckoo clock express!"

We both laughed, and I gave him a kiss on his cheek.

"Well, hell, I can get crazier if I can get more of that," he joked.

"Whatever, silly. Seriously, though, thank you, Sean, for being here for me."

"Don't start on that, Zara. You're family, and I wanted to be here."

The words melted my heart. I wanted to jump into his arms right then. "Family huh?"

"Always have been, always will be."

"Sean, look, about yesterday, last night, I…"

"Yes, Zara?"

As I was searching for the right words, my mother appeared at the door. "Hey, you two, dinner is ready. Come on in and set the table."

"Yes, Momma."

"We better get in there before we wind up having to eat takeout," Sean joked.

"Yeah, we should."

"You can tell me later, Zara."

"Okay, Sean."

We turned and walked back to the house. Sean held the door as I walked into the house. I rubbed his chest and smiled innocently at him. The aroma of dinner sent hunger pains to my stomach. It was a shame that my first down-South meal in ages came at the expense of losing someone dear. Real collard greens, deep southern fried chicken, black-eyed peas with country bacon, and made-from-scratch corn bread were all on the menu. It seemed like the masses had smelled the food, because there were more people in the house than had been present when we had arrived. They all paid their respects to Dad, though. With each story my mother's mood seemed to lift, as did mine.

After dinner Sean excused himself and made his way to the backyard. After I helped Momma put away the dishes, I decided to get outside to continue my earlier conversation with him. I had a smile on my face, imagining the joy I would feel after we had decided to rekindle our love and our relationship. My smile quickly dissipated as I peered from the back door and watched Sean on his cell. The smile on his face indicated he was definitely talking to another woman. Suddenly I felt like a fool for even thinking I could ever get Sean Wilson back. He had fought to not make love to me and yet I had enticed him. Had he made love to me out of sympathy?

He finished up his telephone conversation and was headed back toward the house. He stopped when he looked up and saw me exiting the door. He put his phone back in his pocket. "Was that business or personal?" I asked.

"It was personal," he quietly replied.

"Oh. Was it your ex?"

"No. It was Alanya."

"Alanya. That's a beautiful name. Is she a beautiful girl?"

"What?" he asked, puzzled.

"Is she beautiful, Sean? It's okay. You're not being disrespectful to me by answering that question." Even though I felt myself dying inside, I managed to put up a good smile.

"Yes, she is beautiful."

"Is she more beautiful than I am?"

"Okay, hold on now, Zara."

"All right, Sean, but you know we women have to ask."

"Yes, but I just never imagined we'd be discussing details of my love life."

The comment shook me. *Love life.* Wow, how much more of this could I take? "So you do love her?"

"We are off to a great start and I am really feeling her."

"How long have you guys known each other?"

"We've known each other since Monday."

"When, this past Monday?"

"Yes." Sean laughed.

"Damn, Sean. You don't waste any time, do you?"

"It's not like that. We have a connection."

I stood frozen with dismay at the words that had spouted from his mouth. Never in a million years had I imagined him saying that phrase. What about *our* connection? Years we spent together and our connection was not enough for him to see past his anger for me? Not even to open the letter? I suddenly felt Sean didn't love me at all.

"That must be some connection, Mr. Love at First Sight."

"Love has no limit when it comes to finding the one that makes you happy."

"You sound like a true romantic. Okay, so how did you two lovers meet?"

"You're kidding, right? I can't tell you."

"Why not?"

"Why not? It feels weird just having this conversation now. I just don't feel comfortable talking to you about this."

"Oh come on, Sean we used to share everything..."

The statement caught us both off guard. So much guilt and emotions could now be felt on both sides. We looked at each other.

"I'm sorry, Sean. I shouldn't have said that."

"It's okay, Zara. You're right: we did share everything. I'm sorry for not showing consideration for our relationship and the connection we shared."

"Now this situation seems awkward."

"Yes it does, but then I guess we knew that yesterday."

"I guess so."

"Speaking of which, what did you have to tell me?"

"Tell you what?"

"You were going to tell me something about yesterday."

"Oh yes, I remember," I said, and paused. Trying to search for new words to say, I turned away from Sean. There was no way in hell I was going to tell him I loved him and wanted him back. Not when the writing was on the wall. Sean had moved on, and his new love, Alanya, was all he could think about. I wondered if he had told her about me and that I had spent the night with him the previous night.

"Do you want to tell me now, or wait until later?"

"No. Now is fine."

I paced around for a moment. The sun was setting in the distance and the sky was burnt orange. I looked at Sean as he looked at me. There was no sign of romance or love written on his face. To him it was as if the previous night had never happened. I knew what I had to do, and it was not going to be easy.

"Sean, I can't explain my actions for what happened between us yesterday. I was overcome with so many different emotions; I allowed my feelings to override my judgment. I took advantage of your kindness and compassion, and for that I am sorry."

"Zara, you were not the only one who allowed their feelings to take control over their actions. I'm just as guilty as you."

"Tell me, why did it feel so right yesterday yet it feels so wrong today?"

"I don't know, Zara. Maybe because our lives are so different now and we couldn't see that clearly last night."

"So much pain, Se 1, so many years of guilt."

"So many what-ifs. ara, I feel like such an idiot."

"Why?"

"For letting my pri e ruin my life."

"What do you mea ?"

"It was my pride t at wouldn't allow me to say anything to you when I came to Germ 1y It was my pride that kept me away from my father's side while he v s dying, and it was my damn pride that allowed a marriage to continu down a doomed path for six years, a marriage that the bride never r lly wanted."

Sean's words sent nfusion throughout my mind. Here I was trying to let him go and y he was throwing all this at me now, at the end?

"Sean, I think you : being too hard on yourself."

"Am I, Zara?"

"Yes you are. No ne is perfect, Sean. We all make mistakes. Everyone has to make hoices. Some are good and some are bad. You know they say everythi g happens for a reason."

"So what was the r son for us ending?"

"Maybe we were n meant to be together like that."

"Come again?"

"I don't know, Sea Maybe we just happened at the wrong time."

"So was last night the right time?"

"I'm not saying that."

"Then what *are* you saying?"

"I don't know, Sean, I don't know," I stammered, turning away from him. "I'm just trying to make sense of everything that's happened myself. I don't know why."

"I'm sorry for my tone, Zara," he said, massaging my shoulders.

"It's okay, Sean."

"We were good together."

"Yes, we were. Those were some great times," I said, smiling. "You were my first."

"You were mine."

"Liar!" I shouted playfully, turning around to face him.

"You were, Zara; you were my first true love."

Hearing him say *love* melted my heart. Sean would always be a part of me, and right now I was feeling selfish for even wanting to keep him from happiness with Alanya. Maybe that was the reason why we were together; maybe we had been meant to be friends and not lovers.

"Okay, I'll give you that one. You were my first true love as well, Sean Winslow. God, that was a long time ago, and deep down I think we know what that means now."

"You don't think that we can go back?"

"You said it yourse : our lives are different now, and we would be fooling ourselves by tr ng to re-create the past."

"There is also a lot c hurt tied to that past, and everything that we just found out adds more h t. I'm killing myself thinking about what I would have done differently. W uld I have married Rachel or would I have gone to you. The unknown is to painful to even try to mend, and now my heart is yearning to be with som ne else. Someone I can honestly see myself with."

"You deserve to be ppy, Sean, and if that happiness is with Alanya, then you should give it chance."

"You deserve happ ess and someone who will love you as much as you love them. I also w nt to let you know I forgive you, and I am sorry for ever doubting you.

"Do you mean it, S an?"

"Yes, I do. So muc time has been wasted with hate and anger— feelings that never sho ld have had the chance to grow and infect our lives so negatively. I on hope you can forgive me, for the way I acted."

"I've never been m d at you."

"Then it's official."

"I guess this is the osure we never got for our relationship."

"I guess so. So can keep the check?" he asked, smiling.

"Not that you nee it by how well De Stijl is obviously doing, but the money was always urs." I smiled back.

"Good, because I l ow two wonderful men I want to start a scholarship in honor of."

"Oh Sean, that's a great idea," I said, tearing up.

"I think we have a foundation to start, Ms. Rivers."

"You are still a wonderful man, Sean Winslow."

"You are still a beautiful and wonderful lady, Zara Rivers."

"You know, we always talked about starting a company together."

"Yes we did, so are we partners?"

"I want to be more than a partner, Sean. I want to be a friend if you'll let me."

"I never thought that I would be asking you to be that friend either."

"Well I've never had a close male BFF."

"Sounds like another first for us."

"I guess so." I laughed.

"Friends?"

"Friends."

We hugged for a moment. It felt good to have Sean back in my life. It was as if a lost part of my soul had been restored. I guess I was right. Maybe we had not been meant to be lovers. Maybe our lives had split for this reason: so we could reach a new plateau of maturity and understanding and forgiveness. I didn't even mind hearing about his new love. If she was truly about Sean, she was about to be one lucky lady. I released my embrace and kissed him on the cheek.

"Good. Now, tell me how you met this Alanya, and don't leave out any details."

"Damn, we're just going to start this relationship off with a bang, huh?" he joked.

"Hey, you tell me what I want to know and I'll do the same."

"Okay, sexy. I've been dying to know some juicy insider secrets to your company."

"Hey now."

"Just kidding."

"Okay, so spill it."

Sean and I stayed up until the early hours of the morning catching up on our lives apart. He filled me in on Rachel; his son, Devin; his company; and the troubles with his marriage. When he broke it down and told me about the divorce, his trip to New York, and how he met Alanya, I was shocked at everything he had been through since his father's funeral.

I filled him in on my career in Europe, my business ventures, and how I had submerged myself to make the company successful. I couldn't tell him it was because of my unresolved feelings for him that I had gone so long without a suitor but somehow I sensed he knew. The more we talked, the easier it became to open up to him. We talked about the foundation we would start in our fathers' honor, and just family.

We went to bed early that Saturday morning. I did manage to get up and talk to Big Momma before the wake. My mom asked if Sean and I were okay, and I told her we were better than ever and left it at that. The rest of Saturday was spent running errands for Momma.

Sean and I picked up relatives from the airport, went grocery shopping, and picked up flowers. His secretary, Carol, had sent a beautiful floral arrangement from his company.

Sean excused himself for a while, probably to call Alanya. He met my family and me at the funeral home for the wake. Sean couldn't bring himself to stay, though. With so many people coming by to pay their respects, I thought he was reminiscing about his dad dying. He left and went back home and went to sleep.

Rachel

"Where would you like to begin, Rachel?"

"How long is the session?" I joked.

"It will be as long as you want it to be."

"Well, I have a flight to catch, so I won't be too long."

"A flight to catch?"

"Yes," my mom chimed in. "She's going to Georgia to console him, and she wants to get answers to her questions."

"I see," Dr. Solomon replied. "Why is he in Georgia?"

"He's there because his mother died, and I need to be there for him before she takes control of him."

"*She* as in this Zara person? Rachel, how long have you been divorced now?"

Her question sent a sudden rush of anger to my eyes, and I reflected it in my stare at her. "We've been divorced for almost eight months now."

"Do you think that that was enough time for them to rekindle a relationship?"

"Maybe so, but the last I remember is that she lives in Germany, and Sean has always been consumed by his work and his company. They would have had to have some type of connection to go from nothing in almost ten years to making love in a house that we used to share."

"You seem very passionate about Sean now. Why do you suppose that is?"

"Because I've finally realized just how much I love him, and how much he loves me. How much of a fool I have been. I sacrificed my life and my son's need for a family, all for my own selfish desires."

"Do you honestly feel that way, Rachel?"

"That's the only real explanation I can think of. I blamed everyone else for my past. I always knew or thought I knew that I was the victim, and my actions were only because of what had happened to me. When Sean came to New York to ask me to be his wife again and then to have Tony humiliate me, I finally saw the woman I was. I don't like that woman. I finally know that I am not that woman."

"Let's back up, shall we? Tell me again, where would you like to start?"

"Dr. Solomon, look, I really appreciate your seeing me again so quickly after our intial visit, but I really don't think now is the right time to start at the beginning. I need to see him. I need to see him and be there for him."

"Why, Rachel?"

"Because I love him, because I am afraid that with every day that passes their chemistry grows stronger. I knew I should have opened that letter."

"What letter?"

"There was a letter years ago that came to him from her. I waited to see if he would open it or tell me about it. Instead he hid it. I guess he must have opened it up after our divorce and when he saw me with Tony she must have been there to console him, and steal him back."

"Rachel, you are mad and upset right now. I think you need to—"

"Yes, I am angry and upset. A woman who did so much hurt and pain to this man is now back in his life, in our house, as if she had been there all along. Now she is there comforting him, and I need to be there."

"Rachel, don't you think that you have done just as much hurt and pain to Sean as Zara?"

Hearing Dr. Solomon remind me of my own indiscretions caused me to really put myself once again in front of my self-mirror. How would I be able to convince Sean to choose me and my betrayals over Zara and their past? The only thing I had in my corner right now was the fact that he had come back to me once, he never went after Zara. Now it was my time to come to him.

"Do you think it's wise to see them together in Georgia? What will you do?" Dr. Solomon asked, interrupting my thoughts.

"Trust me I know may be irritated now, but I too am well educated. I'm not going down there to cause a scene especially at a funeral. I will remind Sean that his love for me bought him up to New York to ask for my love again. That I was a fool for ever rejecting him and not treating him like my husband, and that I am no longer the woman he was married to—that am better. That I don't need his money, and that I found my passion for teaching again. I will show him that I have

227

tact and class. I will show Sean that I am here for him. He's already lost his father, and now to lose his mother must be devastating for him."

"What if he's made his choice and it's Zara?"

"I will accept that as well, but only after I at least have a chance to explain myself to him. I will never be at peace if I don't."

"I want you to call me and keep me posted. I don't care what time it is,"

"I will, Dr. Solomon."

My mother and I left the office, and soon I found myself yet again on a plane to somewhere, chasing Sean. This time I would not allow myself to leave without seeing him. Although I had contempt for his mother, her passing saddened me. No one should have to lose a loved one. I shuddered at the thought of losing my own mother. As much as she had put up with me and still loving me and being there for me now, all I wanted to do was make the rest of my life more meaningful. I arrived in Atlanta and went to Sean's mother's home. I had expected to see a line of cars out front, but surprisingly there were none.

Strange, I thought. *Seems very empty.*

I walked across the street to the neighbors to ask if they knew anything. Their stunned looks when I asked about funeral arrangements caught me off guard.

"Oh no. Mrs. Winslow didn't die. I think it was another family member. She said she would be in Macon with her daughter and family."

Hearing *her daughter* sent a chill down my spine. I knew who that daughter was, and suddenly I got the feeling that Sean was not the one needing support. Rather, his lover did. There was only one way to find out…

Alanya

"You have to give her some space. Some time to heal from this."

"I know, but I can tell you, her tone and the way she looked at me scared me."

"You were her love, I guess she was definitely in love with you and that her feelings for you were stronger than your feelings for her. Put yourself in her shoes, if she had stepped out on you and you found out afterwards, how would you feel?"

"I know, I know.It's all my fault. Why did I allow myself to fall for her, Mia especially knowing or not knowing if all my feelings for men were gone?"

"It's not your fault Lani," Mia said reassuringly. "You connected at a time when you both needed to. Remember, you didn't go out looking for love— hell you had never even been with another woman before, not to mention she wasn't with anyone at the time. You guys just found each other."

"I suppose, but it doesn't take this guilty feeling away."

"Only time and you building a meaningful relationship with Sean will tell you whether this was meant to be."

"Right now I want that more than anything else in the world." I smiled.

"Wow. One mention of his name and I can feel you cheese up through this phone as if you were in a Colgate commercial."

I laughed. "Mia, you have to meet Sean Winslow. He is too good to be true. He's fine, sexy, strong, and a real romantic. I feel like my destiny is finally being fulfilled."

"Well, don't leap off the Empire State Building just yet," Mia cautioned. "I mean, I am very happy for you, but feel this one out a little more. You said he's in Georgia right now with an ex-girlfriend?"

Mia's words reminded me of Sean's description of his and Zara's relationship, but it also reminded me of Ava's last statement to me before she stormed out...*Karma is a bitch.*

"I'm not going to jump off the building yet, but I would climb a hundred flights of stairs with him to the top."

"Damn, Lani! You are sprung. Does he have a sister?" She laughed.

"No, he doesn't. Besides, that would take a helluva lot of explaining to Jazz."

"You know I'm joking. No way would I ever leave my own Sean Winslow. So when are you guys seeing each other again?"

"Well, the funeral is tomorrow, and as soon as he gets back in, I am planning to fly down to surprise him—cheer up his spirits."

"And you are sure he is over his ex-wife and his ex-girlfriend?"

"I don't think he'll ever feel love for his ex-girlfriend, and as for his ex-wife, Rachel, I know they will only be parents. He doesn't even have a picture of her in the house. That chapter of his life is closed."

"When a man removes all images of you, the writing is on the wall," she said softly.

"Mia, are you okay?"

"Oh yeah, I'm fine. I'm so happy for you, Lani. Listen, I gotta go, sweetie. Maybe when you come down, we can all go to dinner or something."

"That sounds like a great idea. I can't wait to introduce you two."

"Okay. Take care of yourself, and good luck."

"You too, Mia."

I hung up the phone with Mia and sat and smiled to myself, thinking about Sean. I really needed to hear his voice, so I decided to check and see how he was holding up. I was glad when he picked up after only the second ring.

"Hey, princess, how are you?"

"Well, hello, my prince. I am fine, how are you?"

"Better now that I've heard your voice."

"You know just what to say. Sure you don't have a script?" I teased.

"My only script is the love affair my heart is having with you."

I felt my heart skip a beat. "When will you and your heart return for another recital?"

"The funeral is tomorrow, and as soon as I can get my mom back home, I'll be on my way. I'll fly up to New York no later than Tuesday."

"Seems so far away, but I can be patient."

"I know it feels like an eternity, Alanya, but I made a promise to you and I hope very soon we won't be separated for too long ever again."

"I needed that reassurance. How's Zara holding up?"

"So many people knew her father, and I think they are at peace with his homecoming. It even made me reflect on my own dad's passing and how I should have done things differently."

"Sean, I wish I had been there for you, but I am here for you now."

"Alanya, do you believe in love at first sight?"

"Yes I do. Why?"

"I love you, Alanya."

"I love you too, Sean." *God, please speed this time up until I am in his arms again, and then you can let it stand still.* "You just make sure you bring that love back to me, okay?"

"I will, Alanya. I promise."

"Good night, Mr. Winslow."

"Good night, Ms. Gellar."

We hung up and I masturbated myself to sleep, imagining my prince was taking care of me as only he could.

Sean

You would have thought the president had died if you had seen how packed Ebenezer Baptist Church was that Sunday morning. So many townspeople had known Kevin Rivers in some form or fashion. Loyal customers or people to whom he had been generous came out to grieve. Although the mood was somber, Zara looked breathtaking in an all-black Dolce & Gabbana dress. Mrs. Rivers and my mother decided on Liz Claiborne attire. The hardest part of the funeral for Zara was when the procession made it into the church and we filed past the coffin. I felt Zara shake as we walked past, and I placed an arm around her and led her to her seat.

Once the service began, my mind drifted in and out of the pastors' and guest speakers' speeches to my own father's funeral. I could see him lying there instead of Mr. Rivers, and I became so overcome with guilt and remorse, I lost it. I couldn't stop the tears from flowing. Zara held my hand, and I squeezed it tightly. Indeed, that day we were burying both our fathers for the final time. The service wrapped up with a beautiful solo from a childhood friend of Mr. Rivers's.

We made it to his final resting place, and as we were taking our seats, I noticed a woman in an all-black pants suit standing behind the rest of the mourners. The long ponytail on her shoulder and dark glasses resembled Rachel's. The pastor asked us to bow our heads in prayer, and when we raised them again, she was gone.

After the funeral my mother and I accompanied Zara and Mrs. Rivers back to Atlanta. We left them to sort through Mr. Rivers's belongings while we returned to my mother's home. I knew the whole ordeal had been very draining for my mother. I wanted to wait until she had time to relax, but I had to talk to her right away. She went into the living room and lay down on the couch. I joined her and removed her shoes and massaged her feet. "That feels good, son."

"Momma, there's something I need to say to you."

"What is it, Sean?"

"My whole life, all I wanted to do was make you and Dad proud of me. I spent my entire life trying to be successful and wealthy, but along the way I forgot what really made a man wealthy and successful. Something Dad had with you."

"What was that, Sean?"

"Love, Momma—an unbreakable, undying love for each other; no amount of money or materialistic wealth ever compared to it. You were right about my pride, Momma. I should have been there for you. I should have been there for Dad. I let my fear of failing, of losing, keep me away from the only two people who had that same undying love for me. I'm sorry, Momma, for letting you and Dad down. I promise you, I will never let you down again."

"Oh, Sean," my mother said, breaking down. "Your father is looking down at you, and I know he feels the same way I do right now. We are so proud of you, son. Don't you ever think otherwise."

"I love you, Momma."

"I love you, Sean."

We cried and hugged each other. Hearing my mother say that made me feel better about my actions. I felt a little weight off my chest, but I needed to ask one other person for forgiveness.

"I have to go, Momma. There's one more person I need to apologize to."

"I understand, Sean. Be careful. I know he's already forgiven you."

I stopped by a grocery store and picked up some flowers. Then I took them to my father's grave, where I placed them and had a heart-to-heart with my dad. I felt a presence around me as I stood over his grave, almost as if something were surrounding my body, wrapping me with warmth unlike anything I had ever felt before. I knew he was listening, and by the time I said good-bye, I knew he had forgiven me.

I stopped by Zara's house to say good-bye. "Thank you so much for everything, Sean," she said.

"I didn't do anything that you wouldn't have or have done for me Zara. Are you and your mom going to be okay?"

"It's hard, but I think we'll manage. I think it's time we had more mother/daughter time, you know?"

"I understand."

"Something tells me you are here to say good-bye."

"I'm leaving for D.C. tonight."

"Tonight? What's the rush?"

"I have to get back and face a lot of demons, you know."

"I don't know what to say. Be careful, Sean, and take it slowly—one step at a time, okay?"

"I will. Call me if you need anything."

"I will, and you do the same."

"I'll be in touch about the foundation."

"Definitely. Take care of yourself, Sean."

"Give your mother my regards."

"Okay."

We hugged, and I returned to my mother's house. I said good-bye and made it to the airport, arriving back in Maryland at 11:47 p.m. It felt good to be home. I tried to call Alanya, but her answering service picked up. I left her a message letting her know I was back and that I would try to reach her when I made it into the office in the morning. I then stretched out on the couch and watched ESPN, trying to catch up on some of the NBA games I had missed. I drifted off to sleep, thinking about my dad.

Sean

"Good morning, Mr. Winslow, and welcome back."

"Good morning, Carol. It feels good to be back. I trust you have my agenda ready?"

"It's already on your desk, along with your coffee and all the reports from last week."

"You're the best. Carol, and thank you for the floral arrangement. It was beautiful."

"Not a problem, Mr. Winslow. I knew you would be busy doing other things for the family. It was the least we could do."

"Well, Zara and Mrs. Rivers were very pleased."

"I'm glad."

"When Robert comes in, would you send him to my office?"

"He's already in your office waiting for you," she said, smiling.

"Well, I guess I'm late."

I turned to walk into my office, and as I turned, I could have sworn Carol's eyes went straight to my ass. I turned to look at her, and she quickly looked away. I smiled and entered my office.

Robert stood and greeted me. "Hello, Sean, how are you feeling?"

"I'm feeling a lot better now that I'm back at home."

"Sounds like you had one hell of a week."

"You don't know the half of it."

"Let me sit down for this."

"You better call your secretary to clear your morning schedule," I joked.

"I'll order some pizza and beer also." He laughed.

"Brotha, if you had been with me last week, you could've popped a bag of popcorn and watched my reality TV show."

"Well, break it down for me, boss man."

"All right, well, first…"

Robert sat down and I began to tell him all the details of the previous week. I filled him in on every detail, right down to the ring on my floor and meeting Alanya. As with our first conversation, Robert was struck speechless for a moment. Then I dropped the bombshell on him. I showed him the letter and check from Zara. He jumped up from his seat.

"Damn, Sean!" he exclaimed, studying the check.

"I know, I know."

"No, you don't know. Man, you could write a book about this shit."

"I hardly think this s Pulitzer Prize material." I laughed aloud.

"So all this time Zara was thinking you had washed your hands of her because you were hurt and all this time you thought she had left you for Karl and the money, and the both of you were just too proud to reach out to each other?"

"That's about it in nutshell."

"And this Alanya. She's the one?"

"Oh yes, she is definitely the one."

"And how old is she again?"

"Twenty-four. Why"

"She's single, twenty-four, beautiful, and in New York? Normally those are your psychos or bookworms."

"Yeah, well, if she is then I'm a psycho- bookworm–loving man." I laughed.

"Yeah, you're right. We're all a little crazy." Robert laughed. "Anyway, back to the ring."

"I don't know what o make of that."

"Are you sure you st saw it in Rachel's hand?"

"I'm positive. I threw it at her and she picked it up. We never touched each other after that. What do you think?"

"I think she was at the house, and—oh shit!"

"What, Rob?"

"It just hit me. I stopped by to ask Carol if everything was okay with you, and she was getting off the phone with Rachel. She told her you were in Georgia dealing with a family emergency."

All of a sudden I felt an eeriness creep inside me. I remembered the woman at the burial site in the distance. It had to have been Rachel. What was she up to, and why hadn't she called?

"Hey, Sean, you okay? Sean," Robert said, trying to snap me out of my thoughts.

"Oh—sorry about that yeah I'm okay. I'm just trying to piece this all together."

"You need to call her up."

"Who?"

"Rachel, that's who. Ask her point-blank what was the deal, and no matter what, make sure you change the door locks."

"You're right. So how should I tell Alanya what happened?"

"That's a touchy one, Sean. You never want to start a relationship off with dirt like that, but then again, if you and Zara are history and that night gave you the closure you needed, Alanya might understand. There's no easy way to do that. Just make sure you're prepared to accept any reaction, and tell her everything. Any left-out details always come back to haunt you."

"I can't believe all this shit happened to me."

"You'll do what's right and things will work out."

"I hope so. Even though we haven't known each other long, Alanya is incredible, and I don't want to lose her."

"So you and Zara are closed?"

"Officially closed."

"And there are no regrets?"

"I can't say that. I mean a part of me still loves her and finding out the truth really had me rethinking the choices I have made these past ten years. Would I have married Rachel, went back to Zara everything. We talked about it and we both knew that we couldn't go back, and with everything happening with her dad dying and me reminiscing about my own dad, I think of her more as a family member than a lover."

"Write a book, Sean. Oh and yeah just for the record regarding Alanya, you didn't rob the cradle but sounds like you kidnapped straight out of the dormitory"

"Whatever." I laughed.

As we were going back and forth with jokes, Carol buzzed the intercom.

"Mr. Winslow, I'm sorry to disturb you, but there is a Ms. Gellar here to see you. Shall I send her in?"

"No, Carol, I'll come to her."

"Looks like I'll get to see Ms. Too Fine for myself." Rob grinned.

"You hold her hand for more than five seconds and you're fired," I joked.

"I'll just nod and check out the booty." He laughed.

"Come on."

"I'm right behind you, chief."

We exited my office and made it to Carol's desk and the reception area. I could tell from Carol's stare at Alanya that she was trying to figure out the nature of her visit. Alanya looked gorgeous. She was dressed in a blue form-fitting pants suit. Her long black hair was down, and her makeup was flawless. I knew from Rob's sigh that he was impressed. Alanya smiled as we embraced, and gave me a light, seductive kiss on the lips. Carol's eyebrow rose, and she let out a light gasp.

"Welcome back, Mr. Winslow."

"I'm glad to be back." I smiled. "So when did you…"

"I got your message last night, and I booked the first flight I could. I hope you don't mind."

"No, not at all. I'm honored."

"Excuse me," Rob said as he cleared his throat.

"I'm sorry. Alanya, this is Robert. He's a good friend of mine. He's also the senior director of marketing. You've already met my wonderful secretary, Carol. Carol, Robert, this is Alanya Gellar."

"Nice to meet you," Carol and Robert said in unison.

"Nice to meet you as well."

"Carol, will you hold my calls for me ?"

"Not a problem, Mr. Winslow."

"Rob, we'll pick up later?"

"Sure thing, Sean. Well, Ms. Gellar, it's been a pleasure," Rob said as he took her hand and held on to it purposely longer than usual.

"Five!" I shouted.

"I'm sorry, Sean, what was that?" Rob quipped.

"Oh, nothing. I just remembered the number of new junior marketing interns I'm interviewing today."

Rob and I laughed. Carol and Alanya looked puzzled. I escorted Alanya into my office while Carol and Rob stood to observe us. No sooner had the door shut than we heard a loud *Damn!* from outside. I turned and looked at the door and let out a chuckle. I turned back to Alanya, and she rushed into my arms and kissed me deeply.

"That's what I wanted to give you when I first saw you," she purred after our tongues separated.

"Well, better late than never." I smirked.

"How are you feeling?"

"Better now since you are in my arms."

"I missed you, Sean. You know it's not right to come into someone's life and then pull a disappearing act."

"I know, Alanya, and I'm so sorry I—"

243

"Sean, I was joking," she interrupted, laughing. "You couldn't help what happened, and I understand. I would've done the same thing."

"You had me going, you know."

"Well, it's nice to hear you apologize even for something you had no control over. That's very considerate of you."

"It is I who should applaud your consideration. I mean, for being so patient and understanding of my situation, and being so supportive when we barely have built any trust in each other. I really appreciate that."

"We barely know each other, Sean, but that doesn't change or diminish how I feel about you."

"I told you I was coming back to you."

"Yes you did, and now that you're back, I can't wait to resume where we left off."

"Yes, but there's something I do need to tell you."

"Okay. You sound serious, like you did on the phone."

"It is serious, Alanya, and there is no easy way to tell you."

"Sean, I'm scared."

"Alanya, I'm scared too," I said, holding her hand and kneeling in front of her as she sat down. "I'm scared because I don't want to lose you over this."

"Sean, don't say that. Please don't say that."

"Just promise me that you will hear me out, please?"

"I will, I promise."

I told Alanya about how I had met Zara at the airport, and our night together. I told her about our revelation about our past mistakes and how we viewed that night as the closure to that part of our lives. I showed her the check and card. It felt like I said "sorry" a million times. Alanya had tears in her eyes as she read the card. She read it over and over again. After what seemed like an eternity, she stood and walked to my window and looked down on the bustling traffic of Connecticut Avenue. I stood behind her and waited for a sign.

"You made love to her only once?"

"Just that night."

"Did you sleep with her?"

"No. I slept in the lounge chair."

"Nothing happened in Georgia?"

"No."

"Is she beautiful?"

"Yes."

She turned around, her eyes searching mine for the truth.

"Give me one reason why I should forgive you."

"I'll give you three —I am still the man you fell in love with. I've fallen for you, Alanya, and I want to build a life with you."

"You have a funny way of showing it."

"I'm sorry, Alanya, and I wish to God I could change things. I've never been in a situation like this before, and trust me I swear I had no intentions of sleeping with Zara. I do love you, and my heart belongs to you."

"I gave you my heart, Sean. I trusted you."

"Please give me a chance to regain that trust. Alanya I am standing in front of you now admitting the second worst mistake of my life. Unlike what I did to my folks, I'm not trying to hide anything from you. I want to be honest about everything that has happened in my life."

"I don't know if I can, Sean. Maybe this happened for a reason: to show me that we rushed into this too fast."

"Alanya, remember when we were at the restaurant and I held your hand and asked if you could see my sincerity? Search your feelings and look at me. You can see my sincerity. This didn't happen too fast. This was a connection, our connection. Please don't walk out on me."

"This is too much for me right now, Sean," she said, turning to leave.

"Alanya, wait. Don't go."

"I need some fresh air and some time to think. Please, I have to go."

"Alanya."

Alanya pushed past me and left my office. I turned back to my window and looked down at the street.

Carol came into my office. "Is everything okay, Mr. Winslow?"

"I don't know, Carol, I don't know."

"She seems like a very nice lady—a bit young but nice. Besides, I haven't seen a smile on your face like the one you had when you first saw her in years. You're in love, aren't you?"

"I am, Carol, but I think I ruined it before it really had a chance to grow into what I knew it could."

"If she loves you like the way I think you love her, then things will work out."

"You think so? I mean, a part of me wants to go after her right now."

"Just give her some time, Mr. Winslow. Let her heart search out the answer."

"Thank you, Carol

"For what?"

"For this, for your words and support."

"They're not my words, Mr. Winslow. I only told you what you're feeling."

"Are you sure you're my secretary and not my guardian angel?"

"I appreciate that notion, but I'm your secretary, and this secretary will be out of the office this afternoon being a Hell's Angel to my dentist. Erica will be here to cover for me."

"You know that won't be necessary. Tell Erica to stay home. Would you cancel my afternoon schedule? I need to take a breather today."

"That won't be a problem, Mr. Winslow. Hang in there. Things will work out."

"Thanks again, Carol. I'll see you tomorrow."

"You're welcome, Mr. Winslow. Have a good day."

The afternoon came and went without a call from Alanya. I broke down and called her cell phone, leaving several messages before finally giving up on that course of action. Pretty soon it was four thirty and quitting time for the office. Once again I found myself staring out the window, wondering where Alanya was. I was so immersed in my thoughts, I didn't hear my door open or close. I did, however, feel the softness of her hands as they rubbed my chest when her body pressed up against me from behind. I felt a sense of relief. She had come back to me. I turned with a smile bigger than Texas, but as I stared at her, my smile quickly became shock.

Rachel

"I'm sorry, Sean; I know I'm not the one you were expecting."

"What the hell are you doing here?" he asked, puzzled.

"I wanted to see you, to tell you how much of a fool I've been."

"Rachel, it's a little too late for that."

"Sean, please let me finish."

"No, hang on before you begin," he interrupted. "I need to ask you something."

"I know, Sean,"

"You do?"

"Yes I do, and the answers to your questions are all yes."

"Why, Rachel?"

"Can I talk, Sean?"

"By all means," he said, waving his hands and giving me the floor.

"The night you came to New York has never left my mind. Seeing you and knowing you still loved me made me realize just how much I had screwed up. The most painful thing for me at that time was having you toss your ring at me. To know you still held to your vows and commitment to me touched me. It made me realize just how much I had thrown away. I wanted to talk to you, but no words could come out. I couldn't sleep or work the next day, so I took a flight later that night to Maryland. I couldn't reach you, so I took a cab ride home."

"You mean to my house," he said sarcastically.

"It used to be our house, Sean."

"Used to."

His look of contempt could have cut through a wall of steel. I ignored the comment. What I needed to say I was going to say. "So I took a cab to *your house*, and since I still had a key to *your house*, I went in and decided to wait for you."

"Rachel, you had no right."

"You never took back the key, and deep down you wanted me to use it again."

Sean stopped for a moment, and I could see him trying to gather his emotions. I knew that night had changed our lives, but it didn't take away what had happened to us before, either.

"I did, but after seeing you with Tony, you knew I was over you that night."

"Is that why you brought her home, to prove to yourself that you were over me?"

"I don't have to pr— e any—wait hold up, so you were there when I came home?" His look vas now more startled and dismayed.

"I had gone upstai to freshen up. I noticed you had cleaned out all my things, and I wa hurt by that. Then I heard you come in. I hid in the bathroom, and ictually I felt like going ahead with plan B of my plan to win you ba , so I removed my clothes to surprise you with some new lingerie I ha bought for you."

"I don't think Ton would have liked that." He smirked.

"I ended it with To y the night you left."

"I'm flattered."

"I deserve your sai asm and anger, Sean, but I did end it because of you."

"So why didn't you ome out of the bathroom?"

"When I realized ou were not alone, I just froze. I sneaked out when you laid h on the bed, and then I watched from the hallway."

"You watched us?"

"That took the pla e of you tossing your ring at me, and became the most painful thing ever for me concerning you. I didn't want to, and at first I was so cr shed that you had brought someone into our home and into our be but then the guilt set in and I felt compelled to see what I had take advantage of. I accepted my punishment, and saw what you could on imagine that I had done to you."

"I guess you now k ow how hurt and pain feels, huh?"

"You don't have to be so cold, but yes, I was hurt, Sean—seeing you make love to her, hearing how she felt and remembering how good it was with you. I've never been hurt like that before. I took my clothes downstairs and changed. I waited until you were asleep, and then I left."

"I found my ring downstairs."

"It wasn't until I was back at the airport that I missed the ring. It must have fallen out of my pocket while I was getting dressed."

"Did you come to Georgia for the funeral?"

"I left Maryland thinking the woman you had brought home was Zara. I went back to New York hurt and ashamed of my actions and all they had cost me. When I built up enough courage to call you and tell you what I knew, and to try once more to win you back before you sealed your new life with Zara, Carol told me about a family emergency. I thought it was your mother and immediately flew down to be by your side. When I found out it was actually Zara's family emergency, I became angry and had a mind to confront you both in Georgia."

"Why the hell would you think about doing something like that?"

"Again, I thought it was Zara you had brought back to our house and made love to in a bed you and I used to share. I knew you still loved her, and I guess I felt that maybe you had not been as faithful as you always had claimed to be, but when I made it to the funeral and made Zara's full physical features out I knew she was not the woman you had been with."

"Well, I'm glad you looked before you ruined an already sad day."

"Me too, and again I felt ashamed of my actions and what I was capable of doing. So I left."

"Okay, Rachel, you've told me everything, and hey it's okay, there are no hard feelings, but that part of my life is over, and I'm really in the middle of something right now."

"Wow so it's that easy for you now to just walk away and wash your hands of me?"

"Forgive me for being stupid, but isn't that what you did to me seven months ago?"

"And I was wrong, Sean. I was not thinking, and look at what it has cost me with you and my family."

"I said I forgive you Rachel. What more is there to say?"

"Sean, I didn't come here to ask you for forgiveness and to move on."

"So what did you come here for?"

"I came to ask for my husband back."

"Your what!" He laughed.

"Sean, I've been a fool. I know I put you through a lot. I took advantage of your love and devotion. Seeing you make love to that woman and seeing you comfort Zara made me realize everything you truly meant to me. I want us to be a family again. I want to be your wife."

"Rachel, I'm sorry but I can't. You broke me. When I saw how happy you looked with Tony in Nicks, and finding out that you were still seeing him while we were married destroyed any feelings for you that I had held on to."

"Do you remember the night before I left here?"

"Yes I do."

"You told me you would always love me."

Sean paused once more. I knew he was thinking long and hard about what he had said that night. He was a man of his word, and I saw him having no way out of such a comment. I really wanted to show him my new side, and each moment that went by fed my courage.

"Rachel, I told you that with the belief that you were being one hundred percent honest about your feelings for me, and you needing to get your life together. You destroyed that part of my love for you. Now I love you in a different way now."

"Well, then, in what way?"

"You are the mother of my child, and I will always love and care about you."

"Is that all you have left for me, Sean?"

"That's all that my heart will allow."

"Sean, listen to me. I can change. I'm trying to. I've started seeing a therapist for my problem, and I really need your support to help me get through this."

"You have?" He seemed surprised and amazed at my willingness to admit I had a problem.

"Yes, you see my parents were right about me and my personality. It took me seeing the hurt I had caused you and the hurt you caused me by moving on, did I realize I needed help. Sean the woman you were married to is not the woman who wants you now. I'm not saying

I'm cured. It's a slow process, but I'm starting to open up to her about things I've never been able to speak about, and to be honest I am scared of all the demons I need to face, and the one man I know I need in my corner is you. My husband."

"That's great, Rachel. I really want to be there for you, and in some ways I will always be there for you, but I can't go back to us. My heart belongs to someone else."

I knew from that comment that Zara and I both were too late. Sean was clearly moving on and the thought of losing his love after all this time hit me like a truck. I felt my heart beat faster.

"Please, Sean," I begged. "Please give me another chance. I'm even working on my insecurities, Sean. I'll do anything for you, anything…"

Suddenly plan B took effect. I stepped back and dropped my coat to reveal the aqua ice-blue lace bra and matching thong set I had bought for him earlier. It was his favorite color on me. Sean took a long gaze at my body in the daylight, and for a minute he was stunned.

"You see, Sean, it's daylight, and I don't care. I'm ready to give all of myself to you."

"Rachel, I can't," he stammered, trying to look away, but something kept his eyes fixed on me. I knew there was still something in his heart for me.

"Sean, I need you. Please, let me show you the pedestal I want to put you on."

"Rachel, if you have an ounce of sincerity as you say you do, then you'll put on your coat and leave."

"No, Sean. If you want me to leave, then you are going to have to put on my coat and tell me you don't want me."

I came closer to Sean, wrapped my arms around his neck, and slowly pushed my body into his. I rubbed my breasts on the lower part of his chest. His breathing became heavier. I was smiling at the thought of teasing my man, my one and only man, for the first time in daylight. I frowned, though, when I stroked his manhood to find it just as flaccid as it had been when I got there. His desire had not risen as it would have in the past.

"Rachel, I don't want you in that way anymore. Now it's time for you to leave."

I knew at that moment the disastrous effects of every indiscretion I had done to Sean. The one man who never resisted me, who was always in my corner and had fought for so long to keep me, was gone. Despite my pleas and my propositions, Sean had managed to stay devoted to this mystery woman. I should have known that, and in my mind I did feel good, knowing that if he was like this with me for her, then he must have been as equally devoted to me and our marriage.

Sean grabbed me by the arm, snatching me back into the reality that he was in fact kicking me out. I couldn't bring myself to put up a fight—at least not right here—but maybe he would think about us after I was gone. Surely seven years of us knowing each other had to count for something.

He picked up my coat and led me to the door without even giving me a chance to put it back on. Sean reached for the door handle, but the door swung open and a beautiful woman stood in the doorway and smiled when she saw Sean. Then she saw me standing there in my underwear. The bitch in me—which every woman has, I might add—got the best of me, and I flashed a mischievous smile as if I had just finished fucking her man. Her smiled quickly disappeared, and I could see hurt building in her eyes. Her hurt turned to anger as her gaze returned to Sean.

Alanya

I couldn't believe my eyes. How could I have been such a fool to believe that it was just an emotional mistake they made? Here I was, walking down the street thinking Ava's premonition had come true and I wouldn't know how to react to karma. Finally deciding to fight for my chance at love and not allow Ava's premonition to come true. Now Zara is giving him sex in his office only hours after I had left? *I guess that's his deal; he loves a rebounds fast.* I guess I was no different. Unlike the last time a man had broken my heart, I was not going to go as peacefully this time.

"Alanya, before you say anything, I can explain."

"You bastard!" I screamed as I slapped his face. "To think I was here to tell you how much I loved you and how I could forgive you if you could forgive me for walking out on you."

"When did you walk out on him?" she asked, puzzled.

"That's none of your business, tramp. It was bad enough you had to fuck my man before your father's funeral. What, now you're back for seconds?"

"Alanya, wait, she's not Zara," Sean said, half dazed from my slap.

257

If that's not Zara, then who the hell is she? Damn. I was really a fool. Before I could reach out and slap his sorry ass again, she stepped in.

"So you did sleep with Zara!" she exclaimed as she slapped his ass. "I knew it, you lying son of a bitch!"

There is something to be said about a woman scorned even if she is the mistress. Never cross a woman and break her heart. Yet who was this jilted lover?

"What the hell did I lie to you about, Rachel?" Sean shouted.

Oh, so this was some classic Jerry Springer shit now. Not the cheating ex-wife, Rachel? Guess she was still a wife with benefits. *What the hell did you get me involved in, Sean Winslow?*

"Rachel? As in your ex-wife Rachel?" I gasped.

"Alanya, please let me explain this. It's not what you think."

"Oh really? And I suppose the next thing you're going to do is ask me to join the two of you in a ménage à trois as well, huh?"

"Alanya, please. Rachel was trying to—"

"I don't want to hear it," I interrupted. My stomach was turning and I felt like the walls were coming down around me. "You're nothing but a dog. I told you when we first met that your true colors would show in the end. It's over."

I turned to leave. I needed to get away as fast as I could. I didn't want them to see my tears, and unlike with Corey, I felt more anger building this time. Had I put too much trust into something so new, so fast? Then Sean did something I wasn't expecting. He reached and grabbed me by my arm, as if he was running shit here and I was going

to stay whether I liked   or not. Unfortunately for Sean I had made my
rounds to the gym wit   Ava, and no sooner had he grabbed me than
I used the force he wa   pulling me back around with. I turned with a
swift swing of my free   rm, landing a shot dead in his balls. The shot
was so wicked, it sent h   n sprawling to the floor gasping for air and an
ice pack. I watched as   e lay on the floor.

Rachel was standin   over him still in her underwear. She was beautiful, just as exotic lool   ng as I was, and the thought of having another
beautiful woman fuck   ig my man without getting a little retaliation
fed my anger. I steppe   over Sean and faced Rachel. A look of uncertainty was on her face   et she tried to be brave. "A year ago I walked
out before I finished s   ne business just like this bullshit."

"What business is t   at, bitch?" She smirked.

This heffa had ju   given me the green light. "This right here,
bitch," I said as I coc   ed back and slapped Rachel, rendering her
speechless with shock.   he stumbled back, and if the wall hadn't been
there, she would have   allen. She knew better than to jump back up
and try to defend her   lf. I was the mightier woman scorned in this
scenario.

"You can have him   bitch, and as for you," I said, turning back to
Sean as he looked up f   m the floor like a wounded dog, "stay the fuck
out of my life, Sean W   slow."

I stepped back ove   him and left the office. I couldn't bring myself
to turn and see their   pressions. I got to the lobby and didn't even
take a cab. Instead I co   tinued down Connecticut Avenue toward D.C.
It was 5:45 p.m., and r   h hour was still in effect.

Sean

As Alanya stepped back over me and left the office. I couldn't bring myself to call out to her again, and I damn sure learned that I wouldn't reach for her again. Rachel looked at me with a look of contempt.

"So how many more crazy bitches are you fucking?"

"Rachel, just put on your coat and get the fuck out."

"Oh, believe me, I'm leaving, Sean. I hope she broke your dick."

"It was already broken from fucking you," I retaliated, trying to stand.

"Well, your precious Zara won't like this. So how long have you two been seeing each other?"

"That's none of your damn business."

"You're such a liar, Sean, and a hypocrite. I knew you were fucking her while we were together. You made me feel like shit when you're no better than me."

"You know what? Right now I wish that I had fucked Zara while we were together, because maybe all this shit would not be happening to me right now. I hate you, Rachel; I fucking hate you."

Rachel stood in silence. Once again I was able to strike a blow with my words and not my actions. No matter what we had been through, I had never said that to her, not once. I still knelt, now speechless. There was nothing I could say at this point to take the sting off. I just wished the pain would leave my balls so I could stand.

Rachel put her coat on and buttoned it up. "Almost seven years and you never said those words to me."

"Rachel, please just go," I said, struggling to my knees.

"I left my purse on your desk."

"Get it and leave."

Rachel walked back to my desk to retrieve her purse. I was so busy trying to regain feeling in my manhood and stand that I didn't turn to notice her picking the card and check up off my desk.

"Sean, before I go can I ask you a question?" she asked, reading the card.

"Rachel, there's nothing more for us to say."

"Please, Sean, I just want to know. Did you ever cheat on me while we were married?"

"Never."

"Never?"

"That's what I said didn't I? I took vows to cherish, honor, and love. Didn't you get the same ones?"

"Sean, are you seeing Zara now? I mean, are you guys intimate?"

"If you must know, the answer is no, Rachel. Zara is a part of my family and also a close friend. Nothing more. We got caught up in our emotions and made a mistake, but we know we were not meant to be together on an intimate level. That chapter of our lives is closed."

"And this lady Alanya, do you love her?"

"Yes I do. No more questions."

"Just one more."

"Rachel."

"Do you really hate me, Sean?"

"Look, Rachel, I'm upset right now and my balls are still in my stomach. I didn't mean to say that. I'm sorry if I hurt your feelings."

"Sean Winslow, you are something else."

"What do you mean by that?"

"I'm in your office practically naked, I'm the reason you and Zara didn't get back together, and I'm the reason why you and Alanya are not kissing and making up right now. Yet you still care enough about me to not want to hurt my feelings, even in your anger."

"Rachel, a week ago I would have asked you to be my wife again. And in that span of time I lost you forever, I gained a friend I never imagined I would call that, and I met a woman I can see myself building an incredible life with, only to lose it all before eight p.m. the following Monday. Please tell me I'm not crazy."

"No, you're not cr y, Sean. Life is not always slow. Sometimes it's so fast, we miss living i '

"Is that so?" I aske finally able to stand and face her.

"Yes it is. Sean, righ now I'm realizing that I missed out on love, your love, and it's a life I kno now that I can't get back." She waved the card.

"Someone told me verything happens for a reason, Rachel, but so far I'm failing to see a t of reason in my personal life."

"I can't explain th t one, Sean. All I know is that I'm sorry for bringing a lot of pain i to your life. I was so stupid. I let my pride control me when I needed help. It cost me you."

"You're not the or one who let their pride ruin our marriage. I made the same mistak and in ways helped to destroy our marriage, but hey remember ou conversation seven months ago? It wasn't all bad. There are plenty fond memories we have to hold on to. Not to mention we do have D vin."

"You're right, and s long as he's fine, then I guess we will always have some sort of bon "

"You will always h e a place in my heart, Rachel—much more than a bond."

"I told you, Sean, u deserve to be happy, and I meant it. I hope things work out for yo "

"Thank you, Rach I hope you find happiness as well."

"I think the first st for me is finding happiness in myself for real this time. Then I can t nk about sharing that with someone else."

"You'll find it, and I will be there for you." I said, limping gingerly back to my desk.

"Sean, one more question?"

"I haven't been able to stop you yet, have I?" I smiled feebly.

"No, you haven't." She grinned.

"Well, ask away."

"This letter and check from Zara: I assume you didn't know about it because of when it's dated. Or did you hide it from me?"

"I found out about the contents of the letter and check this past Thursday, but I must admit I had it in my possession when we were married. I never opened it."

"That's funny."

"Why is that funny?"

"I remember when we were married and I lost the baby. You were at work and I checked the mail. I remember this letter from Zara came, and I wanted to open it. I remembered thinking I would test you to see if you would tell me what it said. So I left the mail alone and allowed you to find it. When you didn't say anything, I figured you were hiding your feelings for her from me."

"Actually I didn't open it because I was done with Zara and at the time wanted to focus on us. I didn't throw the letter away simply to keep it as a reminder of the betrayal I had thought she had committed. Why didn't you question me?"

"I don't know. At th time we were not on the best of terms, and with everything going on— ny, the baby, and the move—I guess I pushed it out of my mind, I was raid that you would choose her over me"

"Yeah, we went thr ugh a lot. I guess it made us stronger in some ways."

"Still I have to ask ou now, if you had known then what you know now, would you have k pt me as your wife?"

"Now, that's funny, I said, laughing.

"Why?"

"When I found o t about the letter and the money, I asked myself that same dam question. I didn't have the answer then, but now I do."

"You do?" she said n a softer voice, her eyes staring down at the floor…

"Yes. I would still h ve been your husband."

"You're not just say ng that, are you?"

"No, I'm not. It to k me a while to stop thinking about the negatives and look at all th positive ways you affected my life. You drove me to strike out on m own and be my own boss. You also gave me a beautiful son, whom I ve with my life. I could feel your love for me as well. I guess in a way y u loved me as best you could."

"That's the nicest t ing you've said to me in a while, Sean. Is there any room in your boat or another friend?"

"Hey, only if you agree to help me row from time to time."

"I think I can do that."

"Well, welcome aboard, friend."

We shook hands, and then we hugged. Again a peace fell over me. It was as if I could feel my dad looking down on me nodding with approval. Finally there were no more lies, no more feelings to suppress. I told Rachel about my week and how I had met Alanya. She told me what had happened between her and Tony, and her talk with Dr. Solomon. Afterward I drove her back to her hotel to pick up her bags and change into something suitable for her flight. I then dropped her off at the airport.

"I hope everything works out for you, Sean."

"Me too, and thanks again, Rachel. Let me know how things are going at your sessions, and let me know if you need anything."

"I will."

"Give my man a hug and tell him I'll see him this weekend."

"I will. I know he'll like that."

"Have a safe flight."

"Yeah, thanks, and you get some rest and take care of your...well, you know, your dick." She smiled.

"I'm still sore, but I'll be fine once I get home and sit in the Jacuzzi."

"Good-bye, Sean."

"Good-bye, Rachel."

Zara

I was relaxing inside my ld bedroom looking through an old photo album of Sean and me. Althou h I felt a new bond between us and was glad that we were back on speaki g terms, I couldn't help but reminisce about our night in Maryland. He s l had it in him, and I still loved having him in me. It had been so long sin e I had felt that chemistry. Could I maintain my distance and just be a f end now, or would I want to try to win him back with kindness? My thou its were stifled by the buzz from my cell phone.

"Hello, Mikel."

"Hello, princess. H w are you holding up?"

"Everything is oka Thanks again for flying down for the funeral."

"Hey, that's what f ends are for. Besides, I had another reason to be there for you."

"And what was tha "

"That was to make   re you had someone there in case Mr. Fantastic didn't show up."

I laughed. "Well,   r. Fantastic was there for me when I needed him."

"Hmm, I'll say. He was holding on to you like you were Mrs. Winslow."

"Mikel, please." I laughed, but relished the very idea of being Mrs. Sean Winslow.

"Hey, I'm just saying I can see why you held out so long. You two looked great together. Have you spoken to him about rekindling that relationship?"

"Yes we did look good together, and yes we talked, but we both decided that our relationship is not in that realm anymore."

"What?"

"We are friends—family, even. Our paths have both taken dramatic turns, and right now Sean and I are finding ourselves going steadily into a new, unique relationship."

"Okay, you have got to stop watching Dr. Phil," Mikel joked. "Zara, you don't believe that any more than I do. What happened?"

"I can't believe I'm sharing this with you, but Sean and I slept together two days before the funeral."

"Shut the hell up!"

"No, we did. I flew into Maryland, and he just happened to be at the airport. After a rather cold introduction I told him about my dad, and we went to his house. Once there I found out why he never responded to my letter or the money I sent years ago."

"It was the wife, right?"

"No. He never opened it."

"What, did she hid it?"

"I guess he and R hel were going through some difficult times, and he was trying to s y focused on their marriage. He still had it in his possession, so I ma e him open it."

"Stay focused on hi mistake of a marriage, I bet he felt like an ass." Mikel laughed.

"You are so wrong bout that, but it did hit him, and I guess after that, our emotions and he scotch got the best of us and we made love."

"I bet the sparks fl v off you guys like the Fourth of July."

"It was so emotion and so right, but it can't be."

"Okay you lost me ight there. So let me get this straight, he was there for you at the f eral, he knows you tried to reach out to him, and you did not steal h ideas, you offered him millions, and you made passionate love. Why w n't it work?"

"Sean is in love wit someone."

"What—someone her than you or his ex?"

"Apparently so."

"Damn. Well, who e hell is this mystery woman?"

"I really don't kno , but her name is Alanya and she is ten years his junior."

"Ten years younge Oh, Zara, that chick sounds like a gold digger."

"I don't know. Sea seems to think the world of her."

"Not enough to keep his dick away from you."

"Hey, that doesn't make me sound too good either, you know."

"No, Zara, you know what I mean. Obviously Sean is trying to do the right 'thing' and not make the right 'choice.'"

"Mikel, you are too kind, but really I understand where Sean's mind and heart is. We…I waited too long to try to get him back. I have only myself to blame and myself to love."

"Zara, don't give up yet. Something tells me Sean might be feeling his age and that once the newness wears off his young puppy love, he will see that the two of you are meant to be together."

"Maybe so, Mikel, but I think I'm ready to live life now. My father's death made me realize I can't put my life on hold any longer waiting for Sean's love. I have to move on."

"I don't disagree with that, but I know deep down you're going to keep a candle for Sean."

"I never say never." I laughed.

"Okay, well, get some rest and I'll see you when you return home."

"I will, Mikel. Give Lauren my love."

"Will do."

We said our good-byes and I lay down, thinking about Sean and his newfound love. *Maybe this Alanya is just a gold digger. What if I need to be that guardian angel for Sean? Either way, maybe I will try our new friendship and pay him a visit next week. Just to see how things are going…*

Rachel

Watching Sean drive off, headed back to a house that I used to call home, sent a weird shiver down my spine. I had never imagined this night ending with me alone in the airport. I had been visualizing Sean and me together again, him being my rock, the one constant I always had. Instead, both his heart and his love lay in the future with someone else; someone that, at this very moment, could be long gone out of his life.

Then, right there, as if I had just been shown hidden testimony from the trial of my life, I thought about my own indiscretions, and looked at what it cost me: Tony, Jason, the baby, Sean—and *hell, let's not forget about your soul, Rachel.* Knowing everything he had gone through in one short week really put all of my shit into perspective. I finally felt free from some of my demons. Although it had cost me my family with Sean, it gave me my own sense of self-worth and independence.

I was glad the baggage handler ushered me out of my thoughts and into the airport terminal. All I could think about was getting back home and to my son. I had to do this not only for me but for him as well. By the time I had finished checking in and made it through security, I found myself hoping that Sean and Alanya would forgive each other. After all the heartache he had suffered, I wanted him to get the love he deserved for once.

I was scanning for a place to sit at the gate when I spotted her and froze. Alanya's back was to me. She was standing alone, looking out the window at the plane. My first instinct was to behave like the old school Bronx Rachel, and I sincerely thought about sneaking up to her and knocking her ass out. Then I observed her stance and her posture, and I knew my answer to the question of whether she really loved him. She turned, and her gaze was a thousand miles away. She didn't even notice me.

Every woman knows that gaze. We've seen it on the faces of our girlfriends whose hearts have been broken by men they fell head over heels for. It was like the ending of a fairy tale gone terribly wrong. I was no longer filled with contempt that she had my former husband's heart. I wasn't even angry that she had stolen a shot in on me. For whatever reason, I felt compelled to look at her as a friend who desperately needed a shoulder to cry on right now. More important, though, she needed a caring voice to let her know not to give up.

Alanya finally broke away from her thoughts as she finally made me out. I began to walk toward her, and the somber look she wore was replaced by a defensive posture. She braced herself against the wall, ready to protect her back and strike. "What the fuck are you doing here?" she hissed.

"Take it easy. Please, I'm not trying to cause a scene," I tried to reason with her.

"You didn't answer my question."

I'm leaving D.C. I live in New York too, you know. I guess I must be on the same flight as you.

"Oh, so you're leaving? Did I put a damper on you and that dog's sexcapade?"

"Alanya, listen, it's ot like that at all."

"Just what kind of ol do you take me for?"

"Alanya, please ke p your voice down," I said as some uneasy glances toward us beca ne all-out stares.

"Keep my voice do n?" She scowled. "You know, that's nerve coming from you. I can't l lieve the two of you. You two were meant for each other."

"As much as I woul love to agree with you and make that possible, it won't happen. Sean ves you."

"If that's what he c ls love, then you can damn sure keep him."

"Alanya, nothing h ppened. Look, it was all my fault."

"Nothing happened That's not what I saw. I distinctly recall opening the door and seeing you sta ling there in your underwear in my man's office."

The heat of an awl ard situation shot up the back of my neck, and now the stares became wks. I rubbed the back of my neck, trying to cool my emotions. I wanted turn and walk away and save what little gracefulness I had left, but I kn v deep down that this was really my first real test to exorcise some of tho demons for good. I took in a deep breath.

"First off, that ma used to be my husband, and yes, I was in my underwear, but what y u didn't see was Sean reaching for the door to kick me out of his offi ."

"And why would h do that?"

"Because I had co e there to try to win him back and I was going to do it at any cost, eve to the point of seducing him."

Alanya's eyes went back to a thousand-mile gaze, trying to search for some kind of rationality to what she was hearing. Her eyes snapped back to reality, begging me to continue.

"Alanya, it didn't work. I had no idea you had been there earlier and that he had confessed to you what he had done with Zara. I had just gotten in from New York for the second time to beg for his heart."

"The second time?"

"Yes. You see, I was at the house the night you and Sean were there."

A look of astonishment came onto Alanya's face, and I even heard a couple more gasps from the onlookers. I knew what she was thinking.

"Relax; Sean didn't know I was there. He never changed the locks and I still had a key. When the two of you arrived, I was upstairs, thinking it was just him. When I realized he wasn't alone, I hid in the closet. For a brief moment I thought you were his ex-girlfriend Zara. I was crushed, so I went downstairs, waited until the coast was clear and then just left."

"Why are you telling me all of this?" Alanya asked uneasily. "I mean, if anything, why not try to get him back now that I'm gone?"

"You're not gone, Alanya, at least not yet. You are still here in D.C., and if you get on this plane you will be losing out on the best love that will ever come into your life. You still have Sean's heart—something that I didn't take care of."

"What makes you think I believe any of this bullshit, much less want anything else to do with Sean Winslow?"

"Alanya, look at me. I'm in the middle of an airport confessing to you with an audience; you know it's the truth. Judging from the way you were looking when I first saw you here, Sean apparently still has your heart as well. You can try to hide it, but it's all over your face—both the hurt and the love. It's the kind of love Sean deserves. I tried everything to sway him back and he would not break."

"Hmm. He should have shown that resistance with Zara."

I never had the chance to fully digest the scenario Alanya reminded me of. Her comment brought me back once again to the fact that Zara and Sean had made love once more. I knew Sean may be really over her, but how was Zara? Was she really over him? Besides, under the circumstances, who could blame either of them for holding a future on. *Damn, Dr. Solo. You are great.*

"Alanya, what happened between Sean and Zara is something that I think you and I both have a hard time understanding, but under the circumstances, can you really blame them? Did you see the letter and check?"

She nodded and looked to the ground, searching for reason.

"You know, the stress they were dealing with and maybe that situation was also partly my fault. He didn't hide it from you, though. He told you in person, and that has to mean something. No one is perfect, and I'm sure you have some skeletons in your closet as well."

Alanya really seemed to take that comment to heart. Her defensive posture was suddenly gone as we stood in the middle of the terminal, sorting through our differences with our own little studio audience.

"I'm right, aren't I? You do have some skeletons too, huh? Just be honest and tell me if you really love Sean."

"I do," she replied without hesitation. "Yes, I have skeletons, and I know I'm not perfect, but when I was with Sean, I felt like I was. I felt safe and like I was the most important woman in the world."

"I believe you, Alanya. I know that feeling. You *were* safe, and in his eyes you *are* the most important, most beautiful woman in the world. Sean doesn't give his heart to just anyone."

"So what do I do now?"

"Well, I know a certain someone who's probably home resting in the Jacuzzi, trying to take the sting out of his balls."

Alanya frowned. "I did hit him kinda hard, didn't I?"

"Yes, you did." I laughed. "He's a big boy, literally, and I think he'll be fine—with some of your TLC, of course."

We laughed aloud together, and the moment felt weird and right at the same time. Alanya's eyes went back to the floor, and I looked around at some of the passengers who were smiling now too. Right at that moment, Alanya and I were no longer enemy combatants. We were friends now, sistas with a common bond, wanting to do something right for a man we both loved.

She looked at me once more. "I really jumped the gun, huh?"

"No, it was instinct. I would have thought and reacted the same way."

"I guess so, but now how do I get Sean back? How do I even begin to apologize for my actions?"

"Oh, I don't think you'll have to do anything to get him back. All you need to do is show him that in fact you never left."

"Well, I guess I better do that now. He's at home. Should I call him first?"

"No. I think you need to get the hell out of this airport and go to him." I smiled.

"Rachel, thanks for everything you just did for me. You didn't have to."

"I know I didn't have to, but Sean and I are still parents, and if it's okay with you, I'd much rather be his friend as well and not his or your enemy."

"That's cool with me as long as you keep your clothes on." She smiled.

"I promise. Just make sure you take care of him and give him what he truly deserves…real love, Alanya. Real love."

"I will," she said as she turned to leave.

"Alanya, wait."

Alanya turned back around and I walked toward her as I fumbled in my purse. She seemed a little uneasy, but when I held up the house key, she smiled. I placed it in her hand. "I don't need this anymore." I smiled back. "Besides, I think it would be nice if you surprised him in the Jacuzzi." I winked.

Alanya laughed. "I will."

"There's just one more thing," I said, smiling.

"What's that?" she asked, puzzled.

"This right here, bitch," and with that I slapped her. Some of the passengers again let out a gasp. Alanya's look was just like the one I'd had in the office, but as she rubbed her face, she saw my smile and smiled herself. "Now we're even. Now go and get your man."

For an already confused audience what happened next made everyone smile. Alanya reached out to me, and we hugged each other.

"Thanks again for everything, Rachel. You know, I hope we can become friends as well."

"I'd like that," I said, fighting back tears. "I don't have any close girlfriends, and it would be nice to start out with you."

"Deal."

"Okay, girl, take care of yourself."

"You too. Have a safe flight."

We exchanged another hug, and as Alanya walked off, several people could not contain themselves and started to clap. I looked around and smiled. I found a seat and prayed the plane would board soon. My prayers were answered, and soon I was safely on board in my first-class seat, preparing for takeoff. After we took off, I closed my eyes, trying to soak in everything that had happened in just one short week. My thoughts were interrupted by the flight attendant when she brought me a glass of champagne.

"I'm sorry. I didn't order this," I said politely.

"I know, ma'am. This is compliments of the gentleman sitting in 3A. Seat 3B is empty if you would like to join him," she said, smiling.

"How does he look?" I asked nervously.

She simply winked and walked away. My heart was racing. I knew it was too early to say how I would feel or react to attention from another man, but something reassured me that my feelings and desires would be okay. I gathered my emotions and my glass of champagne and made my way up two rows to 3B. My heart stopped as I gazed down on a sexy fudge-colored brother, his thin goatee perfectly silhouetting full, thick lips. The dimples in his cheeks almost made me drop my glass.

"Excuse me, but is this seat taken?" I asked shyly.

"It is now," his deep, rich voice responded. "Please join me." He helped me into my seat. "My name is Howard."

"I'm Rachel. Nice to meet you, Howard," I said, shaking his hand.

"Rachel, you are very beautiful," he said as his large hand cupped mine, making me feel invisible in his hold. "I couldn't help but notice your form."

"I'm sorry?"

"Your form—as you were swinging on your friend in the airport." He smiled.

"Oh, that." I laughed.

"I didn't see the beginning, but obviously you two patched things up."

"Yes we did." I smiled. "We're good friends."

"Good friends are nice to have and even more rare to find."

"You can say that again."

"So, Rachel, will your final stop be New York?"

"Yes it is. Is it yours as well, Howard?"

"That it is," he replied.

"Do you live in New York?"

"As a matter of fact I am in the process of relocating there now."

"Wow. Where are you moving from?"

"Denver."

"Denver? That's quite a relocation," I said, amazed. "May I ask why the move?"

"I'm a professor. I teach psychology and just took an assignment at Columbia."

I laughed. Howard's smile and suaveness disappeared for a split second. Then a smile appeared on his face. "Okay, what's so funny? You don't like teachers?"

"No, that's not it at all," I said, still smiling. "I lecture foreign language at Columbia."

"No you don't." He smiled.

"Yes I do."

We laughed.

"Wow. Talk about a small world made even smaller by fate he smiled. Well, Rachel, in that case, we have a lot to talk about."

"That we do," I said smiling…

Sean

I left the airport and made my way home. There were no messages from Alanya. I tried to eat, but my appetite was gone. I tried to watch television, but I couldn't stay interested in it. Never mind the fact that the Wizards were putting a hurt on LeBron and the Cavs. I called Alanya, but again there was no answer. With each passing minute my heart sank deeper into the pit of sorrow. I knew right then that you could not put a timetable on when you should be in love or when you could say you were in love with someone. You just know it when you feel it. I decided I'd wait until morning before flying to New York, because I was not going to let my love die, or my pride let her go.

I poured myself a glass of rum and then got undressed and made my way to the sunroom. I grabbed a cigar and sank into the Jacuzzi. The warm water and gentle jets helped relax me and teased the soreness between my legs. I felt myself drifting off in the middle of my session when an angelic voice stirred me.

"I never did get my Cohiba."

"No, you didn't," I said, looking up in bewilderment.

"May I join you?"

"Please, by all means."

I watched her as she slowly undressed and stood before me, naked and glorious. She slowly stepped down into the Jacuzzi and straddled me. Although sore, my nature began to stiffen when I felt her womanhood rest on top of me. I gave her the cigar and she took a nice, slow, deep drag. Her eyes closed as she slowly exhaled the sweetness of the cigar in a long puff. She opened her eyes and smiled and then placed her arms around my neck.

"Perfect."

"I'm glad you like it. So should I even ask how or why?"

"The funniest thing happened to me at the airport."

"Oh really."

"You see, I ran into this lady named Rachel, and at first I was going to just leave and take another flight, but she wouldn't let me go."

"She wouldn't?"

"No, she wouldn't. She asked me woman to woman if I truly loved you, and I told her yes. She then told me what happened in your office and what happened here last Tuesday."

"She did?"

"Yes, she did. She then told me that if I got on that plane, I'd be missing out on the best love that would ever come into my life."

"I'm speechless."

"I was too until she slapped the shit out of me and told me we were even. Then she gave me a key and told me to use it."

"No she didn't!" I gasped. "Rachel?"

"Rachel."

"She told me one (her thing."

"What was that?"

"She told me to ta : care of you because you deserve to be happy and she would be look 1g out for you."

"Oh my God! So w at did you say?"

"I can't tell you."

"You can't tell me?

"I can't tell you be 1use I haven't apologized yet and you haven't accepted it."

"Alanya, you don't ave to apologize for anything."

"Yes I do. I'm sorr 'or acting like a ghetto queen and for hurting you."

"No apology need(!. Besides, that was a good shot."

"Girl radar."

"You should sell th t to the Air Force. We'd never miss a target." I laughed.

"I'll think about i she said, smiling. "So can we start over, Mr. Winslow?"

"I'd love that, but] ease call me Sean. You make me feel old when you call me Mr. Winsl(."

"You don't like it when I call you Mr. Winslow?" she asked seductively as she rose and knelt over me, allowing my manhood to stand fully erect in the warm water before she straddled me again, this time sliding slowly down my shaft.

"Well, when you say it like that…," I said as I let out a deep moan. "When you say it like that, you can call me whatever you want."

"In that case," she said, looking into my eyes with a smile of pleasure on her face, "in that case, I'm calling you mine."